CHARMING YOUR DAD

SARAH BLUE

SPOTIFY PLAYLIST

i hope ur miserable until your dead – Nessa Barrett
Step Mom – Catie Turner
Breakfast – Dove Cameron
I Did Something Bad – Taylor Swift
Bad Girls – M.I.A.
Rhiannon – Fleetwood Mac
Look What You Made Me Do – Taylor Swift
Bad Child – Tones And I
Dark Horse – Katy Perry, Juicy J
Voodoo – Godsmack
Smack a Bitch – Rico Nasty
Guys My Age – Hey Violet
Blood In The Cut – K.Flay
W.I.T.C.H - Devon Cole
Problem – Natalia Kills
Enemy – Imagine Dragons, JID, Arcane, League of Legends
G Walkin' on Yo Coffin – Lil Boodang

Magic – Coldplay
Bad Things – Jace Everett
What's New – Megan Thee Stallion
Hotter Than Hell – Dua Lipa

DEDICATION

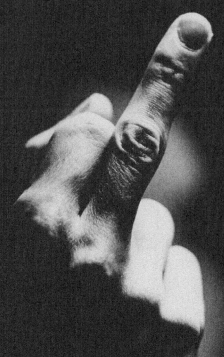

FOR MY PETTY BITCHES

P.S. RYAN, I'M GLAD WE NEVER FUCKED. YOU MADE A CRUDE SONG ABOUT MY NAME, SO I NAMED A VILLAIN AFTER YOU *MIDDLE FINGER EMOJI*

CONTENT WARNING

Please be advised that this book is darker than my other works.
For a full list of kinks/tropes/triggers please visit my website at
authorsarahblue.com/content-warnings/

CONTENT WARNING

Please be advised that this book is darker than my other works.
For a full list of kinks/tropes/triggers please visit my website at
authorsarahblue.com/content-warnings/

CONTENTS

CHAPTER ONE

BLAIR

My cousin Stevie opens the lid to the cocktail shaker as she mixes the latest drink she wants to add to the menu. She pours the liquid into a martini glass and slides it over the obsidian bar top and I clasp the stem of the glass between two fingers.

"What's this one called?"

"Love potion number 9," she says with a giggle. I roll my eyes and take a sip. It tastes like shit.

I sputter a little as I try to figure out what she put in the cocktail. It's a pinkish-reddish color and I hold it up to the light. "What the Hell did you put in this?"

"Pomegranate juice, peach vodka, grenadine, and orange juice."

"Swap out the pomegranate juice for something else," I say, and she groans but goes back to the drawing board.

"You're in a mood... well, in more of a mood than usual," Stevie says.

Stevie is everything I'm not. She loves coven life and gets along with everyone. Her outfits are always full of color, she wears long flowing skirts and weird clips in her hair. She's pretty much the quintessential witch, and well, I'm me. If she weren't my cousin, I would probably think she's being fake, but I know her better than anyone and I'd hex any soul who tried to hurt her.

"It's Ryan." I sigh. Feeling like one of those girls who doodles a boy's name in a journal. I'm not that girl. If anything, I'm writing your name in a journal to keep track of the people who need a good poisoning or impotence curse.

"I don't get it, Blair. Why are you still dating him?"

"His magic," I say with a sigh.

"You mean his magical signature. You and I both know he's an *exsul*." I know she's right. I've done multiple spells to figure out what he is. Sadly, he's just human with dormant magic in his blood. Likely, he has a magical parent, but for Ryan, his magic is latent, making him completely ordinary. I can't tell him I'm a witch if he isn't part of the supernatural community.

"It's like I can feel his magic wanting to connect with mine. Like every time we fuck, it's just bubbling up to the surface, but it can't come out."

Stevie grimaces. "That isn't an image I needed in my head this early in the morning."

"Want a worse image? Something I thought I would never say. I'm so tired of topping him all the time."

Stevie spits out her drink and can't stop herself from uncontrollably laughing. "Blair, you have got to break up with him. You don't really like him and you keep pretending to be someone you're not around him. I gotta say, Cousin, it's pretty pathetic trying to watch you play little miss nice girl around him."

My mouth gapes open. "Stevie, you're lucky I love you or I would charm your clothes to shrink so you thought you were gaining weight."

"That's just evil." I would never hurt Stevie; she knows she's my soft spot. Stevie is my person, and must be protected at all costs.

She slides over the new cocktail, and I take a sip. "This is much better. Add it to the menu. Is Heather printing the new menus for tonight?"

"Yes, she said she would be back around three."

"Good, I'm meeting Ryan for lunch, but I'll be back well before the dinner crowd."

"Don't forget about the meeting at midnight, full moon and all."

I groan and sit back on the stool. "Do I really have to go?"

"You've missed the last two, and you're on probation. You can't risk it. They're our coven. You know we need to do our rituals to keep the coven's strength up." The council governs all witches around the globe. Their job is to make sure we don't have another Salem situation on our hands. Fucking around with humans is the biggest way to get yourself in trouble. So far I've really just had some slaps on the wrists. Not being able to use certain magic, but if I get in more trouble with them they could potentially imprison me, restrict my magic even further or attempt to take it away completely. I would never let that happen, though. They would need to kill me first.

"You mean those cunts want to pull from my power to keep the coven strong? Why should I do that, Stevie?"

"You know it's not that simple. Aunt Josie will lose her shit if you don't come," she says, giving me big blue pleading eyes.

"Fuck my mom. I might not come just to spite her." I pick at my long dark matte nails. If my mom wants me to come to the full moon circle jerk, I'm going to need to be incentivized. It wouldn't be so bad if they didn't treat me like I was a pariah.

"Blair, you're so stubborn. Please, just come. For me?"

"Fine, but only for you, Stevie. If my mom says one thing about how I'm using my magic, I'm out."

Stevie gives me a huge, beaming smile. She's the only person in our coven that I actually care about. The rest of them are a bunch of tree hugging lunatics who run too closely on the side of happy-go-lucky. We have magic, we're magical beings. Witches shouldn't be wasting our power on dance circles around a fire and growing strawberry plants. We should use it to the benefit of our species, and well, our own personal benefit.

I'm the only witch in our coven who has a steady income. Between my restaurant, Hex, and a series of fortuitous investments, I'm the only one keeping the coven afloat. They all want to live out in the woods making moon water and shit, while I live out here in the real world making our lives possible. That's fine. The least they could do is stop scoffing at my methods.

Did I fuck and bewitch multiple finance guys to get where I am today? Sure. Did they deserve to lose their own stocks and bonds in the process? Undoubtedly. I wouldn't choose a human man who didn't deserve it.

"I'll make sure everything is perfect. Go to lunch, break up with the loser and come back so we can cheer to being single together again."

Single.

The word tastes thick on my tongue. It's not that I need to be in a relationship. I just need someone.

Stevie is pretty much my only friend, and it's nice to have someone who likes spending time with me. My entire coven loathes me. Everyone at my restaurant thinks I'm a bitch. It's just nice to have someone who actually enjoys spending time with me, or at least the version of me I'm presenting him with.

I grab my bag off the bar top and give Stevie a tight smile.

Ryan is a realtor and has multiple showings today, so I get to the cafe first and wait for him. I can do this, right? There's no future here, he's completely human with dormant magic, and well, I'm me.

"Hey, beautiful," I hear behind me and see Ryan dressed in a navy suit, looking handsome as ever. He has dark hair, blue eyes and deep dimples that I've licked on quite a few occasions.

"Hey, yourself."

"How's everything at Hex?"

"Good. Stevie is making a bunch of new cocktails as we get closer to Halloween. I've been her taste tester." I grimace.

"God, you have the cutest nose." He leans over and kisses my nose before he takes his seat next to me. I feel like a schoolgirl when it comes to Ryan. It's even more pathetic because he's four years younger than me. It doesn't make sense, I've never been this brainless over a guy before.

"How did your open houses go?"

"Great, I should have an offer by the end of the week." He pulls out his phone and looks at something before he looks back at me and gives me his charming smile. I swear I don't know how he's an *exsul*. Surely, he should be a siren of some sort.

I blush, and I hate myself for it. I hate not really being myself around him. Well, except in the bedroom. Ryan likes to be dominated, but doesn't like to return the favor. Doesn't help that I can't use any magic in the bedroom, either.

"That's great, so um, I was thinking..."

"Oh, before you mention anything. My dad just moved to town and dinners with him are awkward at best. Would you mind coming with me tomorrow night?"

He wants me to meet his dad? I've never met a partner's family before. Does he actually like me that much?

"Of course. I'd love to meet your dad."

"You say that now, but he's kind of a prick."

"You mentioned he wasn't around much."

"He would always send money and birthday gifts and shit, but it always seemed like I was a disappointment to him. I'm not sure how a child could be a disappointment, but that's how it always felt. At least my mom and my stepdad are great."

"They live out in Arizona?"

"Yeah, so I don't see them much." He grabs my hand and holds it across the table. The touch is so domesticated and sweet, I can't break up with him. We can keep this going a little longer. What's the worst that could happen?

"What's your dad's name?"

"Dax. I'm not even sure where he was living before, but he said he would be staying in town for a few months and wanted to see me."

"Do you want to get to know him?"

"Maybe. I mean, I don't see us becoming best friends, but I think I'll give him a chance." I smile at him, and he smiles back. He leans across the table and places a gentle kiss on my lips.

"What was your news, Blair?"

I clear my throat. "Just was wondering if you heard about the town's Halloween party."

"Yeah, it looks like fun. It's an entire month away, though."

"Sure, just wanted to see if you were planning on going."

"Probably, would be a great time to hand out business cards and see who wants to list their house." I nod my head and the waitress brings our sandwiches and drinks.

"Do you need anything else?" she asks, only looking at Ryan. She touches his shoulder before she turns around, and I can't help myself when I whisper *iter.*

The waitress trips over thin air, and I gasp in mock surprise. Her tray of waters clang to the ground with her.

"Are you okay?" Ryan asks her, being far too fucking nice.

She dusts herself off and looks at the ground, wondering what she tripped over. Her brows furrow, and she walks away, leaving the ice waters on the floor.

"Poor thing," Ryan says, and I hold back my eye roll. He looks down at his watch and groans. "Honey, I need to keep this short. I've got a closing I need to get to." I hate when he calls me honey. I'm not sweet. But I haven't really shown him that side of me, have I? He places two twenties on the table and kisses the side of my head as he takes his food to go. "I'll call you tonight with the details for dinner with my dad."

"Sounds good," I say as he walks away. I take a sip of my coffee as the waitress comes back out and starts cleaning up her mess from earlier.

"I'm so sorry about this," she says, and I roll my eyes.

"Sorry for touching my boyfriend or sorry for making a mess of yourself?" I ask, and she gapes at me with wide eyes. I place another twenty on the table, because you should always tip your server no matter what. "Be careful next time." I tell her as I put my black sunglasses on and walk to my car.

As I'm walking down the cobblestone path, a rumbling of an engine distracts me. I watch as a large figure rides a motorcycle down the willow lined streets. It must be hints of Ryan's signature clinging to me from just being around him, but I swear it's like I just got splashed in the face with cold water with the magical notes I'm picking up. I shake my head and continue my walk to my car.

CHAPTER TWO

DAX

This is Hell... literally. Meetings in Hell are monotonous and tend to drag on for what feels like eternity. You would think we were at a Hilton conference room and not the fiery depths of despair. The walls are off white, there's a long obsidian table in the middle of the room with multiple leather wingback chairs for guests to sit. Lilith sits in the corner, her blonde hair in a high pony as she takes notes. Does Lucifer really need meeting notes? Milcom is also in attendance, his enforcer of sorts. I wonder why he's here and not on Earth searching for the demon.

Lucifer sits at the head of the table. He nods his head in greeting to both of us and starts the meeting. You would probably think of Satan as a big red evil being, but you would be wrong. He's actually quite handsome and charming. As far as bosses go, you could do worse. Life in Hell isn't terrible, but living freely among the mortals is so much more fun. But demons need rules, or else there would be complete chaos. My job is to make sure that these rules are followed.

I look across the table at Asmodeus. He's such a pompous prick. He's in his human form, as am I. We were both blessed by Satan himself to have corporeal, unaging mortal forms. It's nice not needing to possess some poor fucker when we're land side. While he looks like a college douchebag frat bro, my meat suit is one that demands respect. I'm so caught up in my thoughts about having a partner for this mission, I didn't even hear the question Lucifer just asked.

"Yes, my lord, I have been out there spreading my seed far and wide, I plan to give you many magically inclined demons," Asmodeus coos at the Devil. *Kiss ass.* And totally full of shit. I'm not sure where Lucifer got it in his mind that we needed to try and create halfling demons. But as far as I know, it's never been done successfully. They're all sadly human with no magic to sustain them.

"And you, Daxaddon?" I hate my full name, but when Satan calls you by it, you answer.

"My progeny hasn't proven to have any abilities," I say.

"That's a shame. Either way, as your offspring, I'm sure he will join us in Hell one way or another. Do you plan on attempting again, or are your missions keeping you too busy?"

"Whatever you command, my lord," I reply and bow my head like the obedient little demon I am.

"Very well. With the increased demon population on Earth, it's important that we maintain a level of decorum. The last thing I need is more problems with the angels or witches again," Lucifer grumbles. His status as a fallen angel has always been a sore spot for him. "What are we doing about the asinine amount of possessions?" Lucifer asks.

"We're working on capturing the demons who are destroying the mortals' minds during their possessions."

"Yes, we will return them to you, my Lord," Asmodeus says, with an overabundance of confidence. We still haven't been able to find the demon that is body hopping and melting the brains of each mortal they possess.

"We need the precedent set that possessions are sanctioned, but only in the proper manner. Possess, use, erase," Lucifer says. Milcom chiming a grunt of agreement is the only noise he makes the entire meeting. Why is he here?

"Yes, my Lord," Asmodeus and I say in sync.

"We have intelligence that the demon we are looking for might be in Hallowsdeep," Asmodeus says.

I glare at him because he didn't share this information with me prior to the meeting. He knows what's in Hallowsdeep, what I haven't been able to face. My guilty conscience, something I didn't even know that I had, has been weighing on me lately.

"Very well. If you don't succeed in this mission, consider yourselves both back on breeding duty."

Asmodeus smiles, clearly not the right thing to threaten him with. Just what earth needs, a bunch of demon's spawn running around that look just like this smug fuck.

Lucifer nods his head and leaves the meeting space along with a perky Lilith and a mopey Milcom.

I steeple my fingers on the table. Now that the boss has left the room, I can drop the act. "Why the fuck didn't you tell me about the intel in Hallowsdeep?"

"What's wrong, Dax? Worried about running into your dud of a spawn?"

"You know that place is inundated with supernaturals. We can't just roll up there undetected."

"Like that has been a problem before," he scoffs, picking at his nails. His blonde hair sparks with tendrils of smoke, his inner shadow demon wanting to surface.

"We have to play this smart. I know you don't care about knocking up a bunch of mortals, but I would rather not."

"Such a conservative demon, Dax. Whatever will we do with you?"

"Hopefully, after this mission, leave me the fuck alone so I don't have to look at your ugly face again."

"Oh, Dax, stop pretending like we aren't half way to braiding each other's hair and making friendship bracelets." Asmodeus laughs as he portals out of Hell with no word of where he's going.

I groan and scratch my beard. *Here goes nothing.*

Hallowsdeep is just as I left the small sleepy coastal town. What looks like a perfect vacation destination is actually the hub for every supernatural being you can imagine. Witches, werewolves, vampires, golems, demons, angels. Whatever fucked up non-mortal thing you can think of, it lives here. It has me on edge as I ride my motorcycle through the single laned streets.

I've 'rented' a small bungalow to stay in while I'm in town. By rented, I mean demanded free room and board from the renters or else their souls would be bound to mine for eternity. Stupid fucks didn't even realize I wasn't a crossroads demon.

It's a two bedroom, two blocks from the beach. I wanted two bedrooms in case Asmodeus decides to actually help in this case. I can almost guarantee that he will leave me to do all the work as he fucks around, *literally*, likely impregnating anything that will let him between their legs.

I conjure my human mobile device that I use rarely and decide to face this head on. Being a complete asshole, I go the route of texting.

> **Me:** Ryan, it's Dax. I'm in town. Would you like to meet up for dinner?

> **Ryan:** Uh, sure. I'll bring my girlfriend.

A girlfriend is good, a third party barrier to the uncomfortable nature of dinner will be best. I would rather he not bring Janet, his mother. Though, I still think the woman got the deal of a lifetime. I couldn't just impregnate a mortal woman and leave her with my heir. I had to make a deal for one, and that's exactly what I did with Janet. She knew going into our arrangement that her son might be half demon. But Janet couldn't have children and wasn't married. If she gave me a child, I promised her, she could raise him and would find the love of her life within a year. Which she did, from me making a secondary deal with another gentleman who was desperate for love. Still doesn't mean I want anything to do with her, nevertheless.

It's taken me years to realize that taking out my disappointment on a child was wrong. Dealing with this whole having a conscience thing is new, and I don't really fucking like it. But I would like to make things right with Ryan. The way I have treated him as though he's less than isn't okay, even if he is a weak human. It's also why I don't want to be a part of creating more abandoned demon offspring. How can we continue creating creatures who are so breakable and with lifespans that last the blink of an eye. If I could go back I would have never sired a child. I won't make the mistake again. I should probably stop calling Ryan a mistake in my head.

Me: Great, tomorrow sounds good?

Ryan: Sure. I'll text you the place.

Me: Okay.

I put the mobile phone down and pull out my files on the demon who has been eluding me for months. What they're doing is fucked up, even by demon standards. This is something that borders on complete cruelty. They possess a new human around every three to four weeks. The possessions seem standard, the mortal's mind is shut down and in the background. Sometimes they have some idea what's going on with their body, but usually they're more so in a stasis.

Possessions can go a few ways: smoothly, when the demon moves on and the mortal has no recollection of what time has passed or horribly, usually when a demon abuses the mortal's body so badly that once they exit the mortal's form, the human immediately dies. Or what this demon is doing, which is complete destruction. They're jumbling the possessed mind so much that when the demon moves on, the vessel is in a constant state of fear and madness.

Of the seven possessions, one of them murdered their whole family, another killed themselves, two of them are in an asylum for the criminally insane and the other three have been missing since possession. More than likely they're deceased.

We have a few suspects, known demons wandering the realm, but other than that, no real leads. The biggest question being: why do they keep moving forms? If they find a mortal vessel they can thrive in, why keep possessing repeatedly?

There's a cracking noise and I know it immediately to be Asmodeus' portal. He doesn't even knock on the door, he just walks in.

"Please tell me you aren't hovering over that file again. It's time to have fun. We spent too long in Hell. Let's go have some mortal delicacies."

I groan, but agree. I could use a break. It has been a while since I've enjoyed the pleasures this dimension has to offer.

"I know the perfect place, and we might even be able to get some intel," he says, and I arch an eyebrow at him. It's been years since I've been back in this town, but not much has changed.

The establishment is called Hex, and I automatically know a witch owns the bar. Which is surprising.

Most of the witches I have come across are fucking weird. They like to stay in their groups in the forest worshiping their goddesses. For the most part, I don't pay them any attention. They stick to themselves and stay far away from demons.

Half of the place is set up like a tavern or bar. With magical memorabilia lining the walls. The bar top is sleek and black. It reminds me of Satan's meeting table. The back of the bar is designed to look like an alchemy lab with different liquors disguised as potions. The rest of the restaurant is set up with wooden tables and chairs. The ambience meant to make you feel like you're in a witch's home.

An over excited woman pops up from the bar. Clearly a witch, she looks joyous and like she hugs trees in her free time. Long red hair down with butterfly clips.

"What can I get you, gentlemen?" she asks, giving Asmodeus a once over.

"Well, love. What do you recommend?" he asks.

Her voice is cheery. *Too cheery.* Why are these witches always so fucking happy? "Well, I'm the mixologist here. What kind of cocktails do you like?"

"Tart, I like them with a little bite."

"Oh, well, you should try the love potion number 9. I just created it this morning."

"Sounds lovely, Dax?" He nudges me.

The witch looks at me, and her eyes widen. She looks at a door behind her and then cools her face, looking back at me. Can she perceive what we are? Usually witches have some sense of other magic, but not specifically demons.

I look over the menu. "I'll have an eye of newt."

"Great choice, be right back," she squeaks as she turns to make our drinks.

Asmodeus stares at her ass and rubs his bottom lip. "What do you think the success rate is for a magical offspring if both parents have their own magic?"

"Shut the fuck up, Asmo."

"I'm just saying, it has to up the chances of creating something."

"This whole breeding program bullshit is disgusting."

"Says the sad little demon with the non-magical child."

"You don't have any magical children, either, asshole."

"Not yet," he replies. I roll my eyes as the garden witch slides us our cocktails.

"Thank you," I tell her and Asmodeus tries to engage her in conversation.

"I'll be right back," she says, as she ducks under the bar. I follow her with my gaze as she approaches the most stunning creature I have ever seen.

I can't sense her powers from here, but there's no doubt in my mind that she's a witch. She has pale skin, black hair that is slightly out of control around her face, large doe eyes and a pouty heart shaped mouth. She's wearing a black plaid skirt that shows off her black and gray tattoos on her thighs. Her top is also black and tight around her breasts. I can see another tattoo poking out from the sleeve of her shirt.

Both of the witches look at me wide eyed before they go to the back room.

"What the fuck?" Asmodeus says. "Do you think they know what we are?"

"Maybe, but the witch behind the bar seemed pretty friendly with you."

He smiles. "She did, didn't she?"

I take a sip of my drink. Other patrons are standing by the bar, lingering for drinks and waiting impatiently.

"What the fuck? Where's Stevie? I've been waiting for ten fucking minutes."

"Blair, what kind of bullshit is this?" Another one groans.

Suddenly, both of the women bend under the bar post and behind the bar. The one with the dark hair is fiery, the complete opposite of the witch tending bar before.

"What the fuck do you want, Lionel?" she asks the customer and I watch Asmodeus' jaw drop.

"A fucking drink, that's why I'm standing at this bar," the man I now know as Lionel responds.

The pretty witch gives him a smirk, and I swear I can see her eyes shift color. Suddenly, Lionel's stool breaks, and he goes crashing to the floor. His ass hitting the hard ground as he groans.

"Never mind, I want that one instead," Asmodeus whispers in my ear, and I stiffen.

"Care to make a deal?" I say confidently.

His eyes twinkle when he turns on his barstool. "Whoever bags the witch gets the bragging rights when we capture this fucker," Asmodeus says.

"Deal." We shake hands and gray smoke intertwines between our clasped palms, sealing our bargain.

The dark-haired witch moves from her spot at the bar. She gives me a smirk. She has the cutest beauty mark above her lip and a crescent moon necklace around her throat that I want to grab. While beautiful, she almost looks like she has been crying, or yelling by how flushed her cheeks are.

"What can I get you, boys?" she asks in a raspy voice that shoots right to my dick. I down my drink so that I can order something new.

CHAPTER THREE

BLAIR

4 Hours earlier

When I got back to Hex after meeting with Ryan I went home and changed into something more my style. I pat down the dark skirt and think about how I shouldn't change the way I dress when I meet him, how ridiculous is that? Truly, I want to smack myself for realizing how much I change myself to fit what I think Ryan wants. What should I care what the human thinks of me? Then I remember his nose kisses and the fact he bought me flowers last week. No one has ever been so affectionate with me, and I never realized it was something that I craved desperately.

Pathetic, Blair.

I'm one of the most powerful witches I know, and I'm a shallow puddle for this basic white man. When the fuck did this become my life? Yet here I am, glowing like a schoolgirl over the fact that he wants me to meet his dad.

Swinging open the door to Hex, I'm greeted by my cousin's beaming smile.

"Did you do it?"

"No, he wants me to meet his dad," I say. Plopping my purse and twirling my finger, signaling Stevie to make me a drink.

"Blair! Break up with him. He's turning you into someone you're not. I know you think you crave his signature and I know you're attracted to him. But is his affection worth it, if he doesn't know the real you?"

"I just need some time," I say.

"Well, what do you know about his dad?"

"Nothing, except they don't have a good relationship."

Stevie winces. "Do you think he just invited you to make things less awkward?" I blush and look down at the bar top.

"I don't know."

"Well, does he have any pictures of his dad? Do you know his name?"

I pull out my phone and scroll through Ryan's Facebook. I have to go really far back into some of his albums, as if I didn't feel pathetic enough already. There are some photos from his high school graduation and I pull them up. I recognize his mom and stepdad. He has photos of them in his home. The man I don't recognize is insanely hot. I thought Ryan was good looking, but his dad is the most attractive man I've ever seen.

Stevie snatches my phone. "Holy mother of hot bad boy daddy."

I take my phone back and look at the picture. His dad, Dax, is wearing a leather jacket and jeans. His dark hair is pushed back and there are a few specks of gray on the side. He has the same dimples as Ryan. He looks like he spends a lot of time out in the sun, and I spot the tattoos on his fingers.

"This has got to be like six years ago. No way is he still this hot."

"You never know. Hey, maybe he's his magical parent, and you can upgrade," Stevie jokes.

"Shut up, Stevie."

She puts her hands up in mock surrender. I groan and get up off the bar stool. "I need to log some receipts. I'll be in the back for a few hours until opening."

"Okay, don't forget. Me, you, witch circle under the full moon tonight."

I grumble about stuck up witches but nod my head.

I walk to the back office and take a seat at my desk, locking my purse in the bottom drawer as I pull up our financials. This is the part I hate most about owning a business. I have half the thought of enchanting some financial loser to do this work for me. All it takes is a few suggestions here and there and they are like putty in your hands. Most of the witches in my coven use potions. But I have some spells that make people more captivated by your whims. *It's really not a bad idea.*

Things haven't been adding up lately, and I don't know if it's something that I'm doing wrong or if someone is stealing from me. I feel like my head is going to explode as I enter all the expenses from the last liquor and perishable order.

My phone chimes twice, and I smile, seeing that it's Ryan's name. He said he would text me about dinner with his dad, and that's what I'm fully intending to see in the text messages. But instead I see two really long voice memos.

Ryan rarely sends voice memos, but I shrug and hit play anyway, unprepared for the conversation I'm about to hear.

"Come on, Clover." I only know one Clover. She's in my coven. "You know how bad I've wanted to fuck you? You look so sweet."

"I thought you were dating Blair?" Clover says.

"We go on dates, but I wouldn't seriously date a girl like Blair. She's the type of girl you fuck until you find a woman worth marrying."

"Someone like me?"

"Yeah, someone sweet and innocent like you. Not some goth bitch wannabe."

I'm seething, but I let the next memo start.

"She's a huge bitch. It surprised me you were dating," Clover's annoying voice says.

"Like I said, babe, she's not the one I want. I want your sweet, tight pussy. Not some washed-up slut." I hear a shuffling of clothes and what sounds like crinkling paper, before Clover moans loudly over the recording.

Knowing the recordings will disappear, I record my screen and sit through, listening to them again.

I can feel smoke coming from my palms, and I can't help it when I let out a loud scream, the only way I know how to let out this anger and unfurling magic inside of me. My magic is thrumming under my veins, needing release. It causes the walls to rattle, and it doesn't take long for Stevie to come running through the door. My cheeks feel hot, but I won't cry over the bastard.

"Blair!" Stevie shouts as she answers the door. I'm pacing the small office, kicking milk crates and unclenching my fists. "What's wrong?"

I hand her my phone, and she looks confused for a moment before she presses play.

"Holy fuck," she whispers, and I nod. "Blair, your irises are red. You need to pull your glamour back up."

I let out a guttural noise from my throat as I try to focus. This always happens when I can't control my emotions. I'm usually able to hold the glamour on my eyes without thinking about it. They change color to my emotions, and that's not something I want people to see, supernatural or not.

"I'm going to curse him so fucking hard, Stevie. Make it so no person will ever love him again, that he will go bald, that his dick will never get hard again. I'm going to give him such bad backne that he can't even sleep on his back anymore. I'm going to hex the living shit out of him, that every time he has to pee, a little bit comes out, and he always has piss dribble on his pants. I'm going to make him loathe the day he ever thought to use me like this." I'm still pacing, trying to calm myself down.

"You can't do that, Blair," Stevie says softly.

"And why the fuck not? He deserves it."

"I agree, he deserves it. But you are already on what strike with the council for intervening with the humans?" She shrugs, and I know she's right. I'm just one infraction away from a tribunal with the council. If I fuck up hugely again, the council could imprison me, or worse.

I tug on the strands of my hair. "They won't find out," I say, trying to reason with her.

"You said the same thing about the stockbroker."

I can't help it when I shout again. "He has to pay, Stevie. He made me look like a simpering lovesick idiot!"

She makes a shushing motion with her hands and I try to breathe evenly again. "I know, Blair. Maybe we can think of some human ways to get back at him? As long as you don't use your magic, there's nothing the council can do."

"What? Like murder?" I ask, still seething.

"That's extreme. Maybe some tire slashing. Maybe fuck around with his open houses. I don't know."

"It needs to really hurt him, Stevie. I need him to feel as bad as I did listening to those messages."

"Then we will need to figure out a way to make it hurt. You stay back here for the evening. I'll take care of the front of the house."

I nod and continue my pacing. I need to channel this magic somewhere. It's just bubbling inside of me, and if I don't find some outlet for it, I'm going to burst at the wrong time.

As hard as I try, I can't focus on doing any more accounting for Hex. I plan my revenge on Clover, instead. Since she's supernatural, she's open fucking season. Sure, she can take me before the council. But as long as I don't truly harm her, I should be in the clear. The thoughts of her demise are keeping me level and not exploding this building from revenge.

Maybe I could make her pussy taste like chloroform, so Ryan will never call it sweet again. Or better yet, actually make it chloroform, so he passes out between her legs. So much for sweet and innocent pussy.

Or I could magically curse all of her clothes to have 'traitorous bitch' embroidered into them. Really, the possibilities are endless. They're both going to pay.

I must be back here stewing for hours when Stevie bursts into my office wide eyed.

"You're not going to fucking believe it."

"What?" I say.

"Ryan's dad is here, and he looks fucking hot."

"And? I'm not planning on meeting him anymore." I shake my hand at her to make her go away.

"Blair, you wanted a non-magical way to fuck over Ryan? Fuck his dad, become his stepmom and give him a son he actually loves."

A wicked smile takes over my face and I look at my innocent cousin. "Stevie, I didn't think you had this type of evil inside of you."

"I'm not going to let that asshole hurt you, Blair. Plus, his dad is like, really, really hot. Come and see for yourself."

I do a once over in the mirror, pushing my tits up in my black shirt and doing the best I can with my face. I fluff my wild dark hair as Stevie drags me beside the bar. My mouth waters when I look at the man sitting at the bar. Ryan was merely a weak attempt at creating the gorgeous man in front of me.

My ogling of Ryan's dad is brought to an abrupt end when Lionel bitches about his drinks. My fuse was already short when I spell his stool leg to break and he goes crashing to the floor.

I spin and smile at Ryan's dad and his companion.

"What can I get you, boys?" They both smile hungrily at me and I realize that this is going to be the most satisfying revenge plot I could have ever imagined.

"I'd hardly say we're boys, love," his friend says.

Now that I'm close, I can see how green Ryan's dad's eyes are and then it hits me like a magical brick wall. His magic is strong. It feels like campfire smoke hugging me around my limbs. My eyes widen and he stares at me.

I clear my throat. "No, definitely men. What can I get you?"

Dax downs his empty glass and winces. "Not that fucking drink again. Whiskey?" I nod and turn around, wishing I would have hiked my skirt up higher. I deviously drop a straw and bend over to pick it up, hoping that he watches the motion.

I pour him two fingers of whiskey in a lowball glass and turn and hand it to him. Our fingers touch and I swear to Hecate I feel electricity. My brow arches almost like a question to him. *What the fuck are you?*

"I haven't seen you here before. Traveling for business?" I ask.

"We're detectives, working on a case," his friend says, and Ryan's dad rolls his eyes.

"Oh, interesting. Is it a popular case?"

"No, sorry, confidential," the blonde younger man says.

"You don't look old enough to be a detective," I say, arching an eyebrow at him.

"You flatter me. I promise I'm older than I look. This ugly mug next to me, though, he looks older than he actually is." He nudges his shoulder, and I can see the irritation on his face.

"Well, this is my place. It's probably the best place to eat in town besides Lucia's, the Italian place down the street."

"Noted," the blond man says with a grin. "What's your name, beautiful?"

I roll my eyes. "Blair, and yours?"

"I'm Asmo and this is Dax."

"Dax," I repeat and look at the man's face. *Damn*, he's so hot. His green eyes glimmer and his dimples deepen when he gives me a shit-eating grin.

"Can I buy you a drink, Blair?" Dax asks in his deep, rumbling voice. No way is he just human, there's no way in Hell.

"I'm a tequila girl."

"Your best tequila then," he says, and I smile.

"You two want shots, too?" They both nod and I grab the tequila and shot glasses.

Lionel decides to get rowdy again. "What the fuck, Blair? The pretty boys get free drinks and I can't even pay to be served?"

I mutter a quick *silentium* and Lionel's mouth quickly stops moving. I know it's sloppy to be using this much magic around human customers, but I don't really care, it's been a bad day. Lionel is an obnoxious werewolf who needs a muzzle, or to learn some manners.

"Learn some fucking manners, Lionel, and maybe you'll get served." I give him a glare as I return to pour our shots.

"I love a direct woman," Asmo says.

"It's not going to happen. You can stop flirting with me," I tell him, and his face scrunches up.

"What, and you want this old bastard?" he says, pointing at Dax.

I hand Dax and Asmo their shots and grin at Dax before shooting back the tequila. "Yes," I say, leaning over the bar top closer to Dax.

CHAPTER FOUR

DAX

This is no ordinary witch. When she shoots back her tequila and gives me a beaming smile, I can sense her magic. It's almost like mine is calling to her. It's something I've never felt before.

It doesn't hurt that she told Asmo to fuck off, or silenced the werewolf at the end of the bar. Doesn't he need to get out of here, anyway? It's almost a full moon. She's direct, confident, and from what I can sense from her powers, extremely powerful. A combination any demon would look for in a woman.

"So, Dax," she says my name like she's tasting out the flavor on her tongue. I like that. She looks to be in her late twenties, but witches can be deceiving. She could be in her hundreds.

"Blair," I say her name in return. It suits her. I can't imagine someone named Blair who isn't powerful. I place my hand on my cheek, my elbow on the table. I know women love my dimples, so I give her a flirtatious smile as she responds.

"You're a detective?" she questions, and I know she didn't believe Asmo when he said it to begin with.

"In a sense."

She traces my finger tattoos that say Hate on one side and Love on the other. "I don't know many detectives who have tattoos like these." Her touch has me reeling, but I keep it in check. Asmo is staring at us, pouting as he watches.

"Does it matter what I am?" I ask.

"You have no idea how much it matters," she says in a soft voice. The front door to the restaurant opens and Blair curses. "Excuse me for a moment. I forgot about the band playing tonight."

She gives me one last glance, a warning for me not to go anywhere. As if I was planning on it. I watch as she swishes away in her short skirt and I can't help but imagine sliding my fingers up it and teasing her until she begs for release.

Asmodeus clears his throat next to me. "Well, this is a fucking bust of a night."

"What about the happy witch?" I ask him, giving him a smirk.

"No one is that happy, it's unnatural," he says, rolling his eyes. Waving his hand at the redhead to get her attention. "Love, can I get another whiskey, please?"

"Of course." She perks up and starts pouring him another drink. I spin on my stool and watch as Blair helps the man and woman set up their stage. It takes longer than I would like. I want to talk to her more, see how long it takes until I can take her home with me.

I would be a liar if I said I hadn't been with my fair share of mortals, but besides the fact that she's a witch, I've never been so drawn to someone—ever. What I am causes me to be sexual by nature, but this is the strongest pull I've ever felt. Even if our magic wasn't trying to force us together, her appearance and demeanor would do it for me. I want a woman who challenges me but also will let me challenge her. I haven't been this excited about something since I got my corporeal body. A body that Blair seems to be attracted to. To a mere mortal, we look to have a significant age gap. My human form ages me at around forty five, Blair looks to be in her late twenties.

The couple plays a song. The man strums on his guitar while the woman sings. It's a pleasant background noise, but not so loud that you can't still hold a conversation. Blair smiles at them, and it appears genuine. She seems to have multiple sides of her personality, all of which I'm eager to get acquainted with.

Blair comes and stands between my legs—she's a tiny little thing. She leans over the bar, and I think she's going to touch me, but then she pulls back a cocktail that her co-worker has poured her. She takes a sip and places the drink back on the bar top. *Little tease.*

She leans against my side, not touching, but so I can hear her when she speaks. "How long will you be in town?"

"At least a few weeks. Anything you suggest we do in town while we're here?"

"Oh, I can definitely think of some things."

My hand is on the curve of her waist. The soft black fabric of her shirt rubs against my fingertips. I wish I was touching her skin. I've never felt this magnetic energy to touch someone the way I do with her. I pull her a little closer so her other hip is pushed against my leg. I watch the rise and fall of her breasts as she breathes heavier, but she seems to calm and melt against my touch.

"I'm open to all and any suggestions."

"There's the beach, of course, and plenty of hiking trails. The Halloween festival is coming up."

"What happens at this festival?"

"You dress up, there's food, games, prizes."

"And you want to go?"

"I love dressing up, I love playing pretend," she says, her eyes gleaming like deep pools of honey. "What do you like to do?"

What do I like? "I like my motorcycle, whiskey, and being able to relax."

"Do you like to dance?" she asks, grabbing my hand and pulling me to the dance floor, not even giving me an opportunity to respond.

The band plays their rendition of *Rhiannon* by Fleetwood Mac, and I can't help but laugh. Blair boldly places her hands around my neck and fiddles with my hair. I place one hand on her waist and the other on her back, pushing her closer to me. We're nearly flush against each other. She's warm and soft, and I have to stop all the thoughts of different ways I could position her body against mine.

Her eyes flash pink for a moment until they go back to their honey brown color. I've never met a witch with that ability before. I want to ask her about it, but I'm not sure if I should disclose that I know she is a witch or not. It might lead to her questioning what I am, and the last thing I want to do is scare her off.

One of her hands slides down to my chest against the soft texture of the plaid shirt I'm wearing. She looks up at me and smiles before moving her hand back around my neck.

Lionel ruins our moment by tapping Blair on the shoulder and pointing to his mouth. Blair gives me a wide-eyed glance but whispers under her breath. It makes Lionel leave, and she shrugs.

"What's his problem?"

"He has behavioral issues. Kind of like an untrained dog," she says.

"Mmm, but bad behavior can be fun now and then."

She leans closer to me. "I agree. Too many people think in terms of black and white and not all the shades of gray in between."

"What shade of gray would you be, Blair?"

"On a good day, pewter, on a bad day, charcoal."

"What kind of day was today?"

"It was a charcoal day... until you came into my bar."

"How can I make it better?" I ask her.

She tugs me down by my neck as our lips touch. It's a calmer kiss than I expected from her. I also didn't expect the way my magic would pull me to take her even deeper. Her lips are soft, she doesn't use any tongue, but it's enough to make me want more. I want to devour her. The moan slips out of me as she pulls apart from the kiss, panting and staring at me.

Her eyes are glossy and confused and flash purple before phasing back to brown. She furrows her brow, but still holds me around my neck.

"What are you?"

I lean down to whisper in her ear. "I guess you're just going to need to wait and find out, little witch." I couldn't help myself. Maybe the mystery of who or what I am will keep her intrigued enough to want to see me again, or even let me take her home tonight.

"You can tell?" she asks, confused. I push a strand of her hair behind her ear and she leans into the touch.

"I could sense it as soon as you looked at me across the bar."

"What are you?" she asks again, like I'm willing to lay everything on the table. People don't trust demons, rightfully so. The last thing I want to do is push this fiery witch away when I just found her.

"In due time," I tell her. We walk back to the bar and I pull out a stool for her. The redheaded witch places two drinks for us on the bar top as Asmo tries speaking to me. My attention is elsewhere as I watch Blair spell my drink.

From what I can tell, it isn't a harmful spell, so I act as if I see nothing. The witch is devious, and I like it. Whatever fun she's planning to have with me, I'll allow it. If she thinks I need a performance potion, she would be wrong. The moment she lets me have her, she won't be leaving the bed for days. I'm kind of excited to feel the effect of whatever spell she's cast on me.

She sips her drink, and I can tell she's deep in thought. Blair's curious, and I wonder how much of this pull she's feeling on her end. I place a reassuring hand on her back and it occurs to me she lives in the modern day world and likely follows many mortal customs.

I hand her my phone. "Your number?" I ask confidently. She smiles and puts her number in my phone. "I'm busy tomorrow night, but maybe we could do something tonight?"

"She's busy tonight," the redhead says out of nowhere. Maybe I should take the time to remember her name. She looks down at her phone. "Blair, we need to leave in twenty minutes."

Blair groans and looks at me, like she's trying to figure out a puzzle. "What are you doing tomorrow night?"

"Meeting an old friend." It's a lie, but I don't know her well enough to tell her all of my business. She nods and takes a sip. "Maybe the night after?"

"Plan something memorable and I might consider a date with you," she teases me, placing her small hand on my thigh. I can't help it when I get hard for her.

I lean over and whisper in her ear. "You better stop teasing me, little witch, or I'll pick you up and have my way with you in the back alley."

She whispers her retort quickly. "That's where you're wrong, *Dax*. I'll be having my way with you." She kisses my cheek as she spins off the stool and heads to the back office with her fellow witch. A few other employees are still here and I would imagine they're going to kick us out soon for closing time.

Asmo grumbles next to me. "We need to find a better bar."

"Oh, you're just sad none of the pretty witches wanted to fuck you."

"Hey! I don't see you getting laid either," he says back.

I roll my eyes. "The anticipation and build up is half the fun. Especially with a woman like her."

"Lucky bastard, I bet she's into the nasty stuff."

"We can only hope." We clink our glasses as the women come to say goodbye.

"Heather will close the bar soon, but I guess I'll see you around," Blair says fiddling with her purse, and it's the first time I haven't seen her as the demanding, confident witch that she is. I don't like it. I pull her in close, my hand on her waist.

"I'll be seeing you sooner than you think. Sweet dreams, Blair." If only she knew what I meant.

"Goodnight, Dax." We separate and the two witches make their way out of the restaurant.

My life just got so much more interesting than I imagined it would be when I returned to Hallowsdeep.

"Are you going to whip your dick out and jerk off all over this sticky bar floor, or are we going to go home and work on this case?"

"Someone is a sore loser."

"Fuck you, Dax."

I place a considerable amount of cash on the bar top as Asmo and I leave out the back entrance and we both portal ourselves to the small bungalow we're "renting."

CHAPTER FIVE

BLAIR

"**W**hat did you do to his drink?" Stevie asks as we walk out of Hex. The night is cool but the moon shines brightly in the dark sky. It makes my stomach churn. I don't want to go to this at all. Last thing I need to deal with are dirty looks and whispers from my coven, or my mom's unimpressed backhanded compliments.

"Just a little something to keep me fresh in his mind." Dax might have told me to have sweet dreams, but I think he will be having plenty of his own.

"I don't think you're going to have any problems with that. He was eye fucking you all night. He asked for your number." I can't help it when I blush and Stevie points at my face. "Talking about Ryan never made you blush."

"I just met him, Stevie. I'm not saying that I'm not going to enjoy the seduction, but that's all he is, revenge."

"Yeah, sure, Blair," she says, rolling her eyes as we both get in my Jeep. "I saw your eyes turn pink."

"Shut your mouth, no you did not."

"Sure as shit did. You might be able to lie to yourself, but not me, dear cousin."

I scoff, but she's not far off. I've never felt the instant connection like I felt with Dax tonight. It's concerning, it's too convenient and easy. It doesn't help that he's ruggedly handsome and actually nice. He also seems to get a little turned on by my blunt approach.

"I won't let it get that far. I'll use him to get my revenge and move on."

"Uh huh. Whatever you say, Blair."

"We have a bigger problem at hand, anyway." I drive fast down the back roads as we make our way to the ceremony.

"What's that?"

"That cunt Clover is going to be at this magical circle jerk."

"Well, if you tip her off that you know she slept with Ryan, she will probably tell him and your revenge won't hit as hard. What's your plan with him, anyway?"

"Public humiliation," I reply deadpan.

"And Clover?"

"I've got some ideas." Stevie groans next to me.

"Please, for the love of Hecate, don't fuck up the ceremony tonight."

"No promises."

It takes nearly an hour to get to the opening in the forest where the coven has our monthly ritual to keep our magic strong. It's warded so no werewolves will come anywhere near the ritual. This ceremony is all a bunch of bullshit. I've never participated and felt a surge in power, if anything, I feel drained every time I come to one of these things. It's why I've been avoiding it. To be honest, I'm surprised the council hasn't summoned me to attend. Especially not after my prior transgressions. I wish I could be a nomad, leave my coven, but my mother forced me to join through an irrevocable blood bond ritual when I turned twelve. As far as I know no witch has ever been able to leave a coven when they've joined through blood.

Stevie's small hand tugs on mine as she drags me to the center of the field. Witches are making small talk while the elders put everything in its precise place for the ceremony. The fire hazard is real with the amount of candles these pyros bring to these things.

"Blair," my mother greets me in her sharp voice. My mother's appearance makes her look like she isn't a mother at all. We look around the same age, but she's blonde, blue-eyed and lithe.

"Josie," I reply. I've been calling my mom by her first name since I turned thirteen. We've never gotten along. She's notorious for lying to me and treating me like I'm an idiot. Plus, she's always made me feel like she truly didn't want me. Like having kids was something she never truly wanted.

"Thank you for bringing her, Stevie."

Stevie scrunches her eyebrows at my mom and then looks over at me. "Blair, I feel confused."

I look deeply into my cousin's eyes and I can tell that she's been under a spell. A spell to bring me here, apparently.

"What do you want, Josie?" I look over at Stevie who looks disjointed and shaky. She seemed fine all night. I did find it a little odd how badly she wanted me to come tonight. But she's always tried to help me fit into the coven life.

"It's time, Blair. Time for you to stop being so selfish and take your place as High Priestess."

My eyes are wide as I look at her. "I've never wanted that. You know I've never wanted that."

"It isn't a choice. The magic chooses."

"What? So you and your band of woodland bitches can fuel off my power? I don't fucking think so. Stevie, let's go."

"Blair, I don't feel good." My beautiful, usually lively cousin is on her knees, her fingers reaching for purchase in the grass as she heaves. Her long red hair is like a curtain flowing over her face.

"Stevie?" I get down on my haunches next to her and rub her back. "What did you do?" I shout at my mother, knowing full well my irises are flaming red.

"I figured you would be difficult. I didn't go out of my way to create you so you could be insolent, Blair. Do your duty to your coven and your precious Stevie will be released from the spell."

"Stevie, can you sense what the spell is?"

"Sana. Sana. Sana." I whisper it with intention each time, it heals her momentarily and then she begins vomiting again. The spell must have been cast by the entirety of the coven to not allow me to heal her.

"She's your niece," I say to my mother.

"She's cannon fodder." I look into my mother's evil eyes and I wonder how I got designated as the coven bitch. Maybe it's hereditary, and it just trickled down to me, but I would never do this. I would never hurt Stevie, or try to push a witch into a role she doesn't want.

"Stevie, I'll find another way to heal you. We're leaving." I place my cousin's arm over my shoulder and the farther away we get from the ceremonial site, the more she convulses against me. "Fuck."

I walk her back to the circle, trying to think of ways I can get out of this. I'm not a healer, it's not the magic I'm good at. I'm good at offensive and defensive magic, but not healing or diagnostic. I can't even figure out whose magic is affecting her.

"You're going to pay for this. Stevie...Stevie." I smack my cousin's flushed face to wake her up.

"Get in the circle, Blair," my mom orders.

"Fuck you."

My mom flicks her wrist and whispers under her breath. Stevie falls out of my arms and starts convulsing on the ground. Her eyes are rolling into the back of her head and I watch as her veins start to protrude over her pale skin.

"STOP!" I scream feeling the ground shake under me. My mother doesn't stop and I go to move. It's like my limbs are being held by vines. I look over my shoulder and see coven members chanting.

Stevie starts gurgling on her vomit and I can't take it anymore. I fall to my knees. "Fine! I'll do it. Release Stevie." My mother gives me a cruel smile as she releases my cousin. I crawl over to her and start my chanting.

"*Sana. Sana. Sana.*" This time the healing spell works as her lungs fill with air and she gasps for breath. Her fingers cling to my arms as I watch the color return to her face.

"I'm so sorry, Blair," Stevie whispers to me.

"Shh, it's not your fault," I tell her, petting her hair. Part of me wonders if I could just get us out of here now. She's lifted the spell. But there are too many of them. Stevie is weak right now, and I'm strong, but not strong enough to take on the entire coven. There are a dozen witches to consider. These bitches are going to rue the day they wanted me to be their High Priestess.

"Let's get this shit over with."

"Middle of the circle," my mother directs me, and I take my place as the rest of the witches close their hands together and form a circle around me. Two of the witches force Stevie on her knees to be a part of the circle. You need the entire coven for a ritual like this.

I stand in the middle just thinking about how fucked up today has been. The betrayal tastes like ash on my tongue. It fuels me for retribution. I know becoming High Priestess means the coven will pull from my power, but it also makes me all knowing and the highest power of these witches. My word is law, and they just made me their enemy. I will turn this coven inside out before I let them hurt Stevie and me again. A manic smile takes over my face as the coven starts to chant.

Surge novum. Tempus advenit. Surge novum. Tempus advenit. Sacerdos non decet. Surge novum. Tempus advenit. Surge novum. Tempus advenit. Sacerdos non decet. Sacerdos non decet.

"You all sound like a bunch of mindless assholes," is the last thing that I say before I feel it, the pull. It shakes me to my core and brings me to my knees. My breathing is labored, and it feels like my heart is going to explode out of my chest.

My hands claw at the ground, trying to find anything that will give me purchase. All I can smell is the misty air and the stench of dirt. I can't see anything and all I feel is pain. Their chants increase and I'm flailed onto my back. My chest is rising and falling at a rapid pace. My fingertips clutch at my chest. I feel like I'm dying. My body rises to the air, elevated and held in the midnight chill like a sacrifice.

A sacrifice. *A fucking sacrifice.*

I try to steady my breathing to hear their chanting, and it all becomes clear. They don't want me to be High Priestess at all. They want to take my power from me. I look around the circle, I see Clover's smug face, Jenna's blue eyes are almost as wide as her smile. My mother's eyes are closed as she leads the chant. No, Hell no. I'm not going to let this happen.

Over my dead body.

The scream that exits me is unnatural and loud. I push every ounce of magic out of my body, hoping to end the pain and save myself. I've shaken buildings with my anguish before, but this time I split the earth. Like an earthquake, the rock shifts beneath us, opening the earth's core. I hope Satan makes an appearance and sucks these cunts into the depths of Hell.

The pure damage of my magic causes them to stop their chanting and they drop my body onto the cold ground. Mud and leaves stick to my chilled skin as I try to catch my breath. I'm exhausted. I've never exuded that much magical energy in my life. I roll to my side to see Stevie's wide eyes as she crawls to me. Half of the coven is on the other part of the break in the ground, while the other half is stuck here with me and Stevie. All of them are lying on the ground from whatever magic I cast. They all still look to be breathing, unfortunately.

What I wouldn't give for a goddamn transporter talisman right now.

Stevie makes it to me and she strokes my hair from my face. "We need to get out of here now."

"Fuck, I'm so tired, Stevie." I can feel my eyes drooping. I just want to sleep on this cold soil, just for a little while, until I'm strong again.

Stevie slaps me hard against the face. "Get up!" She huffs and I hear her casting some shielding spells.

"Stevie, I can't."

My cousin weeps over on top of me. "Blair, you will get your ass up. How else will you get vengeance?" My cousin knows me well. I might not be fueled by saving my life, but exacting revenge is the highest form of motivation.

I groan and shift onto my side and Stevie helps throw my arm over her shoulder as she half carries me to the Jeep. She's heaving and out of breath as she pushes me into the passenger door. I can sense the other witches following us before Stevie places a sleeping charm on the group of traitors. They all fall to the ground; I can hear their bodies hitting the soil as Stevie exerts herself to buckle me in the car.

Even though they're all sleeping on the ground, half of the candles have been snuffed out. I can't help but yell at them.

"You bitches are fucking lucky I'm so tired right now," I shout, even though I know they are all asleep and can't hear me. If I wasn't so groggy I would tell Stevie how proud I was of her, that was a lot of people to put to sleep at once. "They're lucky I'm so tired or I would wreck the wards and let the werewolves have them." Stevie doesn't react to my attempt to make things lighter.

She shuts the door, and my head quickly lolls against the glass. I register the slam of another door as the Jeep jolts with Stevie's foot pressing heavily on the accelerator.

"Blair, are you with me, Blair?"

"Yeah," I whisper, but all I want to do is sleep. I haven't cried in years, but at this moment I feel close. I knew my coven didn't like me, but to sacrifice me, *fucking murder me*, for my power. That's beyond anything I ever thought them capable of. If tonight proved anything, it's that they messed with the wrong witch.

Stevie drives like a bat out of Hell toward our house. "They know where we live, Stevie."

"You think they could get through your wards?"

I shake my head no. I've already made sure that Stevie and I are the only magical beings allowed to enter the premises.

"Fuck! Fuck!" I shout in anger and in pain. My head hurts and all I want to do is climb into bed and sleep for a million years. I want to forget that Stevie is the only living person who gives a fuck about me. Am I really that unlovable of a person?

I can't help it, but that thought alone is what makes me cry. Years of pent up anger, frustration, and fear pours out of me.

"Blair?" Stevie whispers in panic. I wipe my eyes quickly and slump into the seat.

"I'm fine, Stevie." I sniffle.

"No, you're not, Blair. It's okay to let it out."

"No, it's not." I sigh and smack my head on the glass of the door and wince. I must fall asleep at some point, because I feel myself being sucked into a dream sequence.

CHAPTER SIX

DAX

Asmodeus and I head to the warehouse where there has been suspicious activity. We got a tip from one of Asmo's vampire informants. It's cold near the import docks, your standard spooky setting for some shit to go wrong. However, nothing feels magical, just gross.

"Humans are fucking foul," Asmo complains next to me as his shoe kicks away the used needles on the ground.

"I don't sense anything, do you?"

"No, just another dead end lead. I'm tired. Let's just portal home."

Suddenly, there's a crack over one of the shipping containers. The air is filled with sulfur and I immediately know another demon has just portaled nearby.

"Funny seeing you boys here," the voice coos.

"Kasdeya?" I respond, taking in the figure before me. Beautiful and deadly, you need to guard every part of your body around her. Her dark hair is in a long ponytail and her outfit looks like she's supposed to be in some sort of action movie. She clicks her tongue and then scrapes it over her teeth as she looks at Asmodeus. She usually spends most of her time in Hell, so I have no idea why she's here.

"I go by Kas now. You truly didn't think our lord would send two incompetent men to do a woman's job, now did you?"

Asmodeus groans next to me. If anyone here isn't happy to see Kasdeya, it's him. They used to have a thing, and then she locked him in the fairy dimension for a few decades. He still doesn't talk about what happened.

"Seriously, he sent you to find out who is doing the possessions, too?" Asmo complains.

"Of course, you two seem too preoccupied with drinking and tasting the locals. But I'm here to make sure the job actually gets done." It makes me wonder how long she has been watching us. Did she see me with Blair? The idea of it causes me to be irrationally angry.

"What intel do you have?" I ask her, tired of her bullshit.

"Why would I share that with you?" She arches a dark eyebrow at me and I groan. I just want this case to be over. Give me the demons that need a simple slap on the wrist. Simple cases like, no ripping angel wings, no telling humans about the supernatural unless necessary, no shifting into demon form in the middle of concerts. You know, the straightforward stuff.

"We've been hunting them for weeks with no luck finding them. Every time we get close, they leave the possessed in shambles."

"I guess we'll just have to see who solves it first." She winks at Asmodeus and portals back to whatever hole she crawled out of.

"This just keeps getting worse and worse," Asmo bitches next to me.

We're about to portal home, forget how unfruitful this evening has been, and start over tomorrow when I hear the whimpering.

"Do you hear that?"

"Yeah, what is that?"

"It sounds like someone crying," I say. Usually I would just ignore it, but the fact that they tipped us off to this location makes me want to check it out.

We walk around a few shipping containers, our steps making slight slopping noises as we walk on the wet pier. The sounds are coming from a woman, hunched over by a shipping container. Likely in her late twenties, she's cradling her head between her palms. Her blonde hair is wet and plastered to her face. She's clawing at her skin as she tucks her body close to her.

"Make it stop, make it fucking stop," she cries.

She slaps her own head hard against the shipping container she's leaned against as she continues speaking to herself. She doesn't even notice us approaching.

Asmodeus crouches down next to her, and she flinches. She stares at him wide-eyed. I can tell she knows what we are by how scared she is.

"Please. Please don't do it again. Just make it stop."

"What did they do to you?" Asmo asks in a soft voice.

"I watched her. I could see and feel everything. With my hands. She used my hands." She holds her hands out in front of her. They're shaking and cold. No evidence of her doing any wrongdoings, but it's clear that she feels responsible.

"Do you know the being who did this to you?" I ask her.

"She called herself Mara," she says and winces after she says the name. She looks around like speaking her name might bring her back to collect her again. "I need to make it go away. I need it to stop." She smacks her head again, hard.

"I could make it go away," Asmo says kindly to her, giving her his dazzling smile.

"You can. Can you make it go away?" The sad woman looks at him with hope in her eyes. I suppose Asmo's methods are better than this woman's suffering as he gets down on his haunches and gets closer to her.

"Is that what you want?" he asks.

"Yes," she pleads, grabbing his shirt. "Make it go away."

I watch as Asmodeus cups her jaw, almost like a tender embrace, as his other hand wraps around her neck. She smiles at him, almost like she knows the raging in her head is going to stop. He quickly snaps her neck with his powerful hands and the woman collapses to the floor.

"Information and a collected soul," he says, sucking his teeth. "Not so bad of a night, after all.

"Luckily, Kas left before we found her."

"No way am I letting that selfish bitch take this demon down." Usually Asmo is a lazy prick and doesn't like doing work. I'm kind of glad Kas came in and lit a fire under his ass.

"Mara doesn't sound familiar," I say.

"We should update Lucifer," Asmo says, and I nod my head. Keeping secrets from the devil is one way to have your soul ripped apart. *No fucking thank you.* I have too much to look forward to. Like a little witch I have devious plans with.

This night went far better than I could have imagined. I've found a new toy and the first real piece of information that will get me closer to shutting this demon down.

I can't help it when a smile takes over my face when I portal back to the bungalow.

It's late, nearly one a.m. when I finally rest my head. I don't need many hours of sleep, but with my corporeal body, I need some rest.

As soon as I'm completely under, a dream sequence starts. Which is odd because I never dream, I only walk in other people's dreams.

Ah, it must be what Blair put in my drink. She didn't want me to forget about her, did she? She's wearing black lingerie, tattoos I can't decipher on her body. I can only visually see the parts of her I have seen in person. The rest is up to my imagination.

She curls her finger at me to direct me to come and sit on the couch with her. Blair doesn't speak, which isn't surprising. It's my subconscious she's in. Blair doesn't actually have the ability to dream walk. I've only met other demons who have this skill, mostly ones with my similar *tastes.*

Knowing the little witch spelled me to dream of her does something to me I haven't felt in a very long time. Usually I'm just interested in fucking, using the body that they present me with and moving on. The energy and ferocity of sexual encounters fuels me, and I want to take what she's willing to give. But right now, with this sexy siren in front of me, I have other plans.

I cup her jaw in my dream and kiss her cheek. "If we're going to fuck, babe, it's not going to be in a dream. Maybe I might pay you a little visit, huh?"

Dream Blair just smiles at me. I've never had someone visit me in my sleep. I don't like the dullness of it. I think it's time I visit Blair in her dream and give her a taste of her own medicine.

It doesn't take me long to find her, fortunately she's asleep. I concentrate as I invade her subconscious.

Her dream is a nightmare.

I watch as they levitate her body in the air. The forest thick around us as other witches chant. She screams piercingly loud and falls to the ground. In the next moment, her dream whirls and we're now inside of her bedroom. She lies on the bed in the fetal position, not crying but her body shakes.

This isn't the type of dream I was thinking I was going to stumble upon. I contemplate making myself known, and take care in the fact that most people don't remember their dreams, so I decide to insert myself.

"Blair?" I say as I go and sit on her bed.

"Seriously, I'm dreaming of you right now?" she groans.

"What happened tonight?"

"Nothing worth mentioning," she says, shifting on the bed. Her eyes are red, and I think she's been crying.

"It didn't look like anything not worth mentioning."

"You saw?" she asks as she plays with her comforter.

"Only a small part."

"Stevie is the only one who cares about me, Dax. You might as well cut and run now. I'm apparently a fucking bitch who isn't worth marrying and my coven wants nothing to do with me either."

"I'm not going anywhere," I tell her.

"Why?"

I ignore her question because I'm not even sure why we're so drawn together. "If you need help with your coven, I can help."

"They're going to pay. I just need to figure out how."

"They were trying to hurt you?" I ask with a furrowed brow.

"More than hurt."

"What can I do?" I ask.

"It doesn't matter. It's just a dream," she replies. I want to respond and tell her that it isn't just a dream. And something about the small, fragile witch makes me want to help her get vengeance.

I go to open my mouth and I'm ripped from her dream. She must have woken up. I gasp as I sit up in my bed, patting down my sweaty hair.

I wasn't planning on stopping by Hex today, but something deep inside of me tells me that Blair needs my help. The realization hits me that tonight is my dinner with Ryan.

Me: Are we still meeting tonight?

Ryan: 7 pm at Lucia's

Me: I'll see you there

Asmodeus walks into my room looking worse for wear. "We're being summoned."

"Fuck, about last night?"

"What else would it be?"

Asmodeus touches my shoulder, and we portal back to Hell. Same boardroom as last time, we take our seats as I notice three other Demons at the board table. Lilith, Milcom, and Toth. Lilith is basically Lucifer's glorified assistant and Milcom and Toth have been his right hand since the beginning of time. All three of them have been blessed with corporeal bodies as well and are allowed to travel between all realms. Milcom is the one who travels the most to Earth. He has long dark hair and is built like a brick shit house. He's built quite a reputation for himself as being Lucifer's prized pet, and he's known to have a major temper issue. Toth is quieter, honestly I'm not sure how he isn't more violent with how long he has been a demon, his ability to keep his cool has saved Lucifer's ass more times than I can count.

Speaking of the devil, Lucifer walks in. He doesn't take a seat but stands before us. A complete power move.

"Update?" he barks. Asmo looks to me like the complete little bitch he is. Lilith, Milcom, and Toth all have their eyes trained on me.

"We found one of the possessed. It's clear that when they're possessing, the mortal is present throughout. The mortal woman said she witnessed evil deeds while she was possessed. Said the demon's name is Mara."

Lucifer flinches at the name Mara and taps his chin. He looks at Milcom, who looks ashamed. What the fuck is going on here?

"When you find Mara, you are to capture her and bring her to Hell. Her soul is not to be destroyed. She is to be brought to me intact. Do you understand?"

"Yes, Lord," Asmodeus and I both say in unison.

Lucifer goes to leave the meeting before he stares at the back of Milcom's head. "Milcom, a word please?" The demon follows Lucifer out of the room while Lilith and Toth both portal out of the meeting space.

"Well, that was weird," Asmo says, and I nod in agreement.

"Let's get out of here."

He clasps my shoulder again and we both portal back to the bungalow. My thoughts are rampant. Before, he didn't care what happened to the demon causing havoc. Now it seems everything has changed.

"We need to figure out who Mara is," I say, and Asmo rolls his eyes.

"No shit."

CHAPTER SEVEN

BLAIR

I wake up feeling like absolute death. It's like I barely slept at all even though it's almost noon. A warm body is next to mine, their hand perched on my waist, and I spin around to see Stevie. Her cheeks are red and it looks like she's been crying all night.

I'm not even sure how I got into the bed.

"Stevie?" I croak. Her eyes flicker open, and she quickly wraps me around in a tight hug.

"Thank the fucking moon. You scared me."

"Sorry," I murmur, tightening our embrace.

"What are we going to do, Blair?"

"I'll handle it, Stevie. First things first. We both need to wear our necklaces I enchanted last summer. They won't allow anyone in the coven to mess with our minds. Besides that, there's no way they can do what they want to accomplish unless it's a full moon. So, for the most part, we're safe for now."

"For now," she says, glaring at me.

"If you think I'm going to let them hurt you..."

"No, I know, Blair. There are just twelve of them and two of us."

"I think we need to figure out why they were trying to sacrifice me and make it so whatever they were after can't happen. If not, I'll wind up murdering them all. More than likely, they're all scared shitless right now and will leave us alone for a while."

"You're so sure?" No, I'm not sure, but if I spend too much time thinking about what happened to me, I'll spiral. Right now isn't a time for spiraling. I need to exhaust this energy elsewhere.

"I'm sure," I kiss my cousin's cheek as I get up to make my way to the bathroom. "I'm going to go fuck up some people's lives and then work at Hex for a few hours. Stay here if you don't feel safe. The wards will protect you."

"I'm supposed to work tonight," she says, looking down.

"I'll close Hex. I don't really care. We don't need the money from the restaurant, anyway. It's more so to keep us busy. Especially now since I'm removing all my financial contributions from the coven's trust."

Stevie nods her head. "Only if you're sure."

"I'm sure, Stevie. Stay home. I'll be back later." I walk over and give my cousin one more hug before I get ready for the day.

The only thing that's going to make me feel better is by making someone else feel worse.

I leave the UPS store with a smile on my face, around three hundred papers in one hand, and packing tape in the other.

With pure glee, I delicately place one of the flyers about every ten feet as I go down Main Street. I receive some glares, but people are reading the flyers and that's all that matters.

Looking down at the bright yellow paper, I smile. Lennon, the bored UPS printing employee, was more than eager to use their design knowledge to help me create this masterpiece. It's a picture of Ryan holding a kitten in one arm and a dog in the other. I took this picture about a month ago when he invited me to an animal shelter event his brokerage was holding. Except both him and the pets have laser beams shooting out of their eyes and the heading above it says 'Ryan Fuller, Hallowsdeep's most untrustworthy realtor. Don't trust him around your house or your pussy.' The laser beams from the cat's eyes are setting homes on fire in the background. Like I said, Lennon has some serious talent.

I'm still angry about everything but, like I predicted, making someone else's day worse is, in fact, making me feel better. The best part is I know he has an open house, so he won't be seeing these for a few hours. Assuming that no one sends him a message about them.

Plus, I have plans for his open house, anyway. I already looked up the listing through Zillow. It's pretty impressive. Bluetooth speakers wired around the home and everything. I looked up the family online, the dumbasses use their dogs name as the password. So gaining access isn't difficult.

I continue my leisurely pace downtown, taking about twenty steps. Taping a poster, twenty steps, and another poster. I must exude don't fuck with me energy, because no one stops me. I even saw Sheriff Clemons drive past. He shook his head but just kept driving. A wise choice, old man.

After an hour of plastering Hallowsdeep with the beautiful yellow flyers, I finally get in my Jeep and drive to the next destination. 7884 Marrow Way, the next stop on my plan to make Ryan's life a living Hell. Checking my watch, it's almost three and the open house is full of at least four different couples. I take this opportunity to walk into the home, connecting my iPhone and playing the second recording.

The sound blasts throughout the house. Clover's wretched voice echoes around the house first.

"She's a huge bitch. It surprised me you were dating." I look to my left and the woman literally clutches her pearls and grabs her husband's hand to leave the home. To me it just looks like Ryan's commission flying out the front door. A realtor is nothing without his reputation.

"Like I said, babe, she's not the one I want. I want your sweet, tight pussy. Not some washed up slut." Then it's the crinkling of paper and loud moans. I don't see Ryan yet, but I just let the sound play repeatedly. The recording starts again, and I can't help but to be proud of how creative I've gotten with my magicless revenge. I've done nothing that could get me in trouble with the council. Human laws might be another story, but I couldn't care less.

"This is the most unprofessional showing I've ever been to," a woman screeches and that's when I see Ryan. He's at the audio panel, trying to figure out how to turn the sound off. Not knowing the sound is spelled and no matter what he does, it won't turn off.

It's at that moment he sees me, and his face falls completely.

"Blair, I can explain." He looks around as his potential homebuyers leave the home, his hand raking through his hair in frustration. I see Ryan clearer than ever before. He cares too much about what people think. While I don't feel like he hid me away, he definitely didn't parade me around as if he was proud to be with me. I look at him now and he's no comparison to his father, looks or otherwise. A simple human man who has nothing to offer me.

"No need, Ryan. The audio is very clear. I'm a bitch, and Clover has a sweet pussy. Does she peg you like I do, Ryan?" His face flushes, and he looks around the room in a bigger panic. "What would the conservative pricks of Hallowsdeep think if they knew their favorite realtor loved being pegged while his cock was caged?" I flick a non-existent piece of lint off my shoulder. I'm not ashamed of what Ryan and I did as consenting adults. I might be a bitch, but I wouldn't use that against him for my revenge. I know it's just him and me in this room and he cares more about his image than anything. He cares more about how people perceive a man being dominated over caring about a man's prostate.

"Blair, did you do this?" Now he looks angry.

"You sent these audio clips straight to my phone. It seemed appropriate to show your clients what kind of man you are."

"Blair, how could you do something so cruel?"

"I'm the cruel one? You led me on, Ryan. You made me think I was important to you, that this was going somewhere."

"Why would you think that, Blair? We were never really official. We fucked, we had fun. But it's obvious I was right. You are a bitch. Clover is so much better than you."

I laugh. Clover is one of the weakest witches in our coven, she will get what's coming to her next.

"Make the recording stop," he bellows, trying to push more audio buttons.

"I've only just gotten started, Ryan. You fucked with the wrong bitch."

I keep the recording playing, knowing as soon as I get out of range, it will turn off, anyway. That felt really nice. So nice that for a few moments I forget about my coven, or the fact that I need to deal with that whole situation. My high slowly leaves me as I get closer and closer to Hex.

I do at least admire the bright yellow posters down Main Street while I park my car and walk the rest of the way to the restaurant.

It's nice having no one here. I closed for the night, which all the employees seemed to be happy about. See—not a bitch of a boss.

Stevie said she might come join me. She's not loving sitting in the house all day, so I leave the front door unlocked as I head back to the office.

It's time to get down to what the Hell is going on with the finances. I'm definitely in a mood as I open up the multiple accounting systems and stare at the numbers. None of it makes any sense. I want to break down, but I keep myself together. If I break down, I won't be able to pick up the pieces. There's too much to do. Stevie is depending on me. I'm great at magic and managing people, I can even cook a decent meal. But when it comes to numbers, potions, and baking, I usually leave it to Stevie. It's like the numbers move while I'm staring at the screen. Supposedly these things are supposed to be idiot proof but clearly not.

I groan and fold my arms over the desk and lay my head down. I'll figure it all out for us. Why the coven wanted to hurt me and used Stevie to do so. Hell, if it comes down to it, I'll move Stevie and me so far away from here that they'll never be able to find us. The deepest, most proud part of myself won't allow it, though. Hallowsdeep might be a cesspool, but it's my cesspool.

There's a light tapping on the door. "Come in," I say, assuming it's Stevie. To my surprise, it is a very hot-looking Dax. He's wearing a heather gray shirt that is so tight I can see his nipples. The short sleeves show off all his beautiful black and gray tattoos. His hair is an organized mess on the top of his head. He looks delicious, and I haven't forgotten that Ryan hasn't suffered enough. Dax is the sexiest piece of vengeance I could have asked for.

"Oh, hey."

"Hey, hope I'm not interrupting anything," he says with a smirk on his face.

"Just sitting here trying to figure out where this money is going."

He walks over and stands behind me. "I'm a bit of a Quick-Books savant. Do you want some help?"

Usually my pride won't let me ask for help. But Dax didn't need to offer, and the amount of time I've spent hovered over these computer screens trying to figure it out is enough for me to comply and agree to his help.

I stand up from the chair, and he sits down. He looks at me expectantly and then taps his knee. "You're gonna want to get comfortable, babe."

I blush. Fucking blush and flatten my skirt out and sit on his knee. His large hand wraps around my waist, holding on to my hip while he uses the other hand to navigate the mouse.

He scrolls through, opening up receipts, not speaking to me but focusing on the numbers. Dax squints and groans. He pulls out a pair of black-rimmed glasses and puts them on. How in the fuck does that make him even hotter? He's like every girl's sexy older hot professor fantasy. I wiggle on his lap a little bit, and his hold gets tighter on my hip.

"Your cash drawer is what's short. But only every three days."

"What?"

He points to the screen, his fingertips digging into my flesh, making me shift a little deeper into his lap. His jeans brushing against the bare skin of the back of my thighs.

"it's small amounts. Like fifteen to twenty dollars. Not enough to notice regularly. It also looks like your produce amounts don't actually match what's being delivered. Looks like it hasn't been going on for very long. Maybe a few weeks."

"So one of my employees is stealing from me?" Just add one more person to the list of everyone who hates Blair.

I can't help it when my back sags against Dax's chest. I'm exhausted, you can only get beaten down so many times before you break. It feels like it's me against the world right now. Well and Stevie, who is so scared of our coven she's afraid to leave the house.

"What color gray is it?" I think back to our last conversation and how we rated our day on the scale of white to black. It makes me smirk a little over the fact he remembered.

"Honestly, pitch fucking black," I say. Vulnerability isn't something I'm used to, but he calms me.

"Can I make it better?" he whispers in my ear. I realize now that both of his hands are on me. One fiddling with the end of my skirt while the other is planted on top of my thigh. His tan skin against my pale tattooed thighs.

"How would you make it better?" I ask, trying to not sound like I'm panting for it.

His face is so close to mine, and his voice is so gravelly and deep when he responds. "I'd fuck your pussy with my fingers so hard your cum would soak through to my jeans."

I moan and throw my head back against his shoulder. *This.* I haven't had this in forever. While I love being in charge and taking control of a man, sometimes it's nice to shut off your mind and just enjoy the pleasure.

I need the release that only letting your mind go and letting someone else take control gives you.

"You want that, little witch? Should I slide my hands up this cute little fucking skirt and see how wet you are for me?"

"Yes, Da—Dax." He groans, hearing his name slide off of my lips. His bearded chin rubs against my throat as he places wet, fervent kisses along my jaw. He adjusts me so my legs are wide and spread, bracketing his own strong, muscular thighs. I feel exposed in the most delicious way possible.

"I love these gods' damn skirts," he says, while flipping the garment up. I'm wearing a plain black pair of panties. I wish I would have worn something cuter. But, I was dressed modestly for revenge, not for a surprise finger fuck.

He slides my underwear to the side, two of his fingers gliding through my wetness as he groans against my neck. As soon as his fingers touch me, I feel exactly what I was missing with Ryan. It's like Dax's magic is calling to mine, making the connection and sexual chemistry that much more intense.

"Is this pussy going to be tight for me, Blair?"

I groan but don't answer, so he lightly smacks my pussy, making me jolt and push harder against his large erect cock that's straining in his jeans.

I huff out a breath but shake my head. "Yes, touch me, please."

"Mmm, didn't take you for the begging type, little witch."

"Fucking touch me."

He smacks my pussy lightly again. "That's no way to ask."

"Please, Dax. Please touch me."

"That's my good girl. I like that, Blair. I want you to be a good girl, but only for me. Only this sweet side for me."

"Yes, touch me." His fingers enter me harshly. Not fucking around, he sticks three fingers inside of me as he uses his palm to rub my aching clit. The sensitivity from his small taps is going to send me over the edge quickly.

I grind my ass against his fat cock, making him groan, and he thrusts right back against my ass.

"Fuck," Dax hisses as he picks up his pace against my pussy, curling his fingers inside of me, hitting my g spot. His other hand wraps around my waist. His hand pushes hard on my lower abdomen.

"I love feeling my fingers fucking your pussy from the outside," he groans, and it's what sends me over the edge. Writhing on top of his lap as I ride out my orgasm, my magic is fully on the surface, making me feel like I'm falling and flying all at once. The orgasm builds and builds until I completely shatter. Collapsing against Dax's chest. Dax removes his fingers and I can feel my center wanting to grab him back in and keep him there forever.

He holds his hand up to my lips. "Suck," he orders, bringing his fingers to my lips, which I suck greedily, tasting my flavor on his large fingers. He slides them out of my mouth and turns my jaw to kiss me on the lips, tasting my essence on my tongue.

"Mmm, next time I'll taste you right from the source," he says confidently.

"What about you?" I ask, pushing my skirt down to where I'm only sitting on his one thigh.

"I've got to go, unfortunately." He shrugs and little tendrils of guilt shoot up my spine. He has his dinner with Ryan tonight. "Can I take you out tomorrow?"

"I'd like that," I say, nodding in agreement.

"You want me to pick you up here or from your place?"

"Text me, and I'll send you my address."

He taps my ass lightly, and I stand up, feeling so much lighter. He leans over and whispers in my ear. "Babe, you better be wearing one of these cute little skirts when I come and pick you up, yeah?"

"Yeah," I reply breathlessly. He kisses the side of my head and gives me a smirk before he leaves my office, shutting the door behind him. As soon as he leaves, I plop down in my chair.

"What the fuck was that?" I whisper to myself. Feeling lighter, and knowing he made my day a better shade of gray.

CHAPTER EIGHT

DAX

A s soon as I shut Blair's office door, I quickly make my way to the restaurant bathroom. What the fuck am I, seventeen? I can't even remember a time when I came in my pants. I wouldn't have been embarrassed if she saw, but I don't need the little witch knowing the hold she has over me. Even that small bit of fun fueled me more than orgies have in the past. I feel upbeat and energized. I'm going to need as much of her as I can possibly get. I can't even imagine what it will feel like when I finally fuck her.

I didn't even come here to touch her. I came to ask her on a date. Like some kind of refined gentleman. But her stress was clear, and I couldn't help myself. I wanted to relax her and make her feel better.

I'm not sure what the fuck is happening to me, and I'm not sure I like it. I'm a demon, for heaven's sake. It's not like this could go anywhere. I don't know any demons who are with any other supernatural beings. It just doesn't work when you're dashing back and forth between the realms.

I groan as I take off my jeans and then my underwear that's wet with my release. With dismay, I take those off and throw them in the trashcan in the corner. I put my jeans back on and the texture against my dick isn't great. I look at my watch, knowing I don't have enough time to go back home and make it to dinner on time with Ryan.

With an odd feeling in my chest, I leave Hex and walk down the street. The place we are meeting is only a few blocks away. I portaled here so I didn't notice the bright yellow flyers plastered all over Main Street on my way here.

I get closer to one and take a look. I'm shocked when I see Ryan's face on the poster, calling him an untrustworthy pussy hound.

I know I shouldn't laugh, but I do. The poster is fucking funny. I crinkle the one in my hands and throw it in the trash with one last chuckle, and I wonder who he pissed off. I wonder if I should ask him about it at dinner, and if he would even tell me the truth. I'm sure that dinner isn't going to be as pleasant as I originally hoped. The flyers probably already have him in a pissy mood. I genuinely consider rescheduling.

My feelings about how I've treated Ryan are complicated enough. I've tried to be there for major events, like graduations and some birthdays. But I didn't feel like he wanted me there, and I hate to say it, I never really allowed myself to deeply care for him. How are you supposed to form a connection with someone you created who you will outlive many life times? If things were different, maybe I could stomach it. Our relationship has been near non-existent out of my own fear. But that's on me, not him. I need to make it right. What that entails, I have no fucking clue. But I need this nagging feeling in my stomach to go away.

The bell chimes over the door of the Italian place as I enter. It's cozy with only about a dozen tables covered in checkered pattern tablecloths. I notice Ryan immediately and walk over to the table and take a seat.

"Ryan, you look good."

"Thanks," he says dryly. He looks worse for wear.

"I saw the posters. If you want to reschedule, we can."

"We're already here," he says, picking up his menu, not making eye contact with me.

"Do you know who put them up?"

"Yeah, I paid someone to go around town and take them down."

"Do you need any help dealing with the person who did this?"

He scoffs and takes a drink of his water that was already sitting on the table.

"I haven't needed you before. Why would I start now?" I nod, because his feelings are valid. I've been absent, unloving, and uninterested.

"I deserve that."

He looks up from his menu with wide eyes, and shock plastered over his face.

"I wanted to meet up because I want to do better by you, Ryan. I know it's too late to ever be considered your dad. I did that, I broke that relationship. It's nothing you did. But I would like it if we could try to become friends."

"You want to be my friend?"

"Only if that's something you want. I would understand if you would rather continue the way things are."

"Can I think about it?"

"Of course," I say as the waitress stops by the table.

"What will it be, gentlemen?" she asks, giving Ryan a bright smile.

"I'll have the spinach ravioli," he says, handing her the menu.

"Veal parmesan, and two beers," I say.

"Was it a girl?" I ask Ryan as the waitress leaves.

"Yeah, some bitch I was dating," he says, taking another sip of water.

"I wasn't joking if you need help handling the situation."

"What are you going to do, whack her?" he says, laughing in his chair. I don't laugh. I'm usually not up for casual murder, but not completely opposed either. At the very least, I could do some demon like shit and spook the girl. "No, she's just upset I left her. I'm sure she will cool down eventually."

"So, how has work been going?"

"Good up until today. Hopefully, not everyone saw the posters."

"I'm sure it will be fine," I tell him. I feel like I'm not in my own skin. This small talk and making nice makes me feel itchy. I still don't feel any genuine affection toward Ryan, and it makes the sloshing feeling in my stomach feel worse. Maybe if he let me do something for him, buy something for him, maybe I would feel better.

The thoughts ease me a little when I realize their selfish nature. It's about how I feel, not Ryan. At least I'm still a selfish demon at heart.

"If not, I'll go after her business." We both hold up our beers that the server dropped off, and it's probably the first time I've felt proud of Ryan.

"Cheers to that." We clink our glasses, and that's when the conversation slows. Neither of us really know what to talk about. I can't exactly explain that I'm searching for a demon who is irresponsibly possessing people. I truly don't want to hear him talking about selling homes. *How trivial.*

We're saved by the server bringing our food, and we eat in uncomfortable silence. Ryan's phone dings mid bite and he smiles widely. "Thank fuck." He looks at me and wipes his mouth with his napkin. "I have to go, one of the prospects at the open house today still wants to write. I thought I was going to lose this deal."

"Sure, of course. Keep in touch."

"Yeah, sure thing. Thanks for dinner."

I continue eating my food and I can't help but think about how I still won't allow myself to feel a connection. What does that say about me? I shake the feeling quickly, and redirect my focus to Blair and what kind of plans I have for the little witch.

Portaling back to the bungalow is like breathing at this point. The small little beach cottage with the light blue siding is becoming comfortable. *Disgusting.*

I can hear it before I see it. The low moans and grunting don't deter me from opening the front door. I'm not surprised when I see Kas, ass up on the couch, and Asmo pounding behind her. If he were with a mortal woman, he could easily shatter their pelvis.

"Well, this is fucking cozy," I say to both of them. Asmo doesn't even stop his thrusts, just keeps pounding into Kas. Her ass jiggles with each thrust as his balls clack against her.

"Join in or get the fuck out," Kas says sharply. Fortunately for her, all I can see is her reddened ass in the air. I'm not really inspired to take a deeper look.

"I'd rather keep my dick fully intact. You're not exactly my type."

"What the fuck does that mean?" she barks.

Asmo smacks her ass sharply. "No talking, you're ruining it."

"On that note, have a lovely evening."

Since they don't seem to be putting any work hours in tonight, I decide to. I've sent multiple letters to demons both in Hell and in this dimension about a demon named

Mara. It's odd, but no one seems to know who she is. The familiarity in Lucifer's and Milcom's eyes was unmistakable when we mentioned her name.

I hear Kas' moans through the wall and I grab my jacket and keys. No way I'm going to get any work done here tonight.

The best place I can think of to get some answers is a local dive bar that is known for housing supernaturals called Eternity. Fitting, since most of these beings live an immortal existence. I drive my bike down the coast. I could portal, but there's something about a motorcycle that I enjoy too much. The cool breeze against my face, the low rumble under my body, the lightness of the bike as it turns a tight corner. It might be one of the best inventions the mortals in this dimension have created.

The bar is located not far from the docks, where Asmo and I found the possessed woman. Even from the outside, I can sense demons, werewolves, and a few vampires. I groan, getting off my bike and making my way inside. The bar is disheveled and disgusting, clearly just enough maintenance is done to keep the place standing. The floor is sticky and the lights are low. I locate an empty wooden bar stool and plop my ass down. The stool creaks like it's crying from supporting my weight, and I wisely decide not to put my arms on the desecrated bar top.

"What'll it be?" the bartender asks. Vampire. Interesting.

"Whiskey." He nods and pours me a lowball glass and slides it over the bar top. No particular person here sticks out to question. Except for one. He's standing in the corner, nearly enveloped by shadows. I'd know this snake of a demon anywhere. I can practically smell his stench from here.

Beelzebub.

Bringing my whiskey with me, I make my way to the corner of the bar, where the little weasel is standing.

"Beelzebub," I greet him, with too much kindness.

"Daxaddon," he replies skeptically.

"Why are you in Hallowsdeep?"

"No reason."

"Hmm, you know anything about these rogue possessions?"

"Of course not, Lord would be so displeased."

"Yes, yes, he would." I look around. No one here seems to give a rats ass about anyone but themselves. I grab Beelzebub by the collar of his shirt and drag him into the back alleyway of the building. I make sure to keep contact with his greasy skin, in case he decides to portal. "What did you do again, to get a corporeal body?" I ask him.

"I—I helped find Archangel Michael."

"Mmm, that's right." I punch him hard in the stomach. If he was human, it would have killed him. "I don't believe you, Beesnatch. You always know what's happening in the underworld, the little rat you are." I hit him again in the kidney. He is sputtering and spitting. "Now, tell me. Where can I find this demon?"

"It's not," he sputters.

"What's that?" I punch him one more time, not hitting him as hard as I was previously. I'm basically holding him up at this point.

"Mara isn't a demon."

"That's impossible. These are clear possessions."

"She's," he says huffing, "a halfling."

"No such thing," I reply, knowing full well no demon has procreated another demon. We're made, not born.

"That's why she can't possess properly, plus she's fucking mad."

"How do you know her? How come no one has heard of her?" I shout in his face.

"Because she's been here, living as a human until recently. I suspect when she turned eighteen, things changed."

"Who is her sire?" I punch him in the kidney, not even giving him a chance to speak.

"Stop fucking hitting me!" he shouts, and I hit him in the nose to make myself clear. "Ugh!" He pushes off my chest, and I let him crumple to the floor.

"Who is her sire?"

"You already know," he says before he portals away.

"Fuck!" I shout. I knew I shouldn't have ended physical contact with him. His words 'you already know.' Meaning she was sired by Milcom, Lucifer? Milcom looked the most guilty during that meeting discussing Mara and he has been kept up to date on these possessions. But how and what is she? Wouldn't she have found a vessel and stayed in it?

At least some of the puzzle is connected. I walk back into the bar and put a twenty on the table before I leave and get my bike to drive home. Unfortunately for me, Kas and Asmo are still fucking. Looks like I will need to catch them up tomorrow. For now, maybe I can spend some time dream walking in the sweetest little witch's dreams.

CHAPTER NINE

BLAIR

I'm still in a bit of a haze when I leave Hex and drive home. My thirst for revenge against Ryan is quenched at the moment. Half due to how good it felt to plaster those posters around town. The other half due to how hard I came around his dad's talented fingers.

Now I just need to figure out what my coven wants and how to make them pay for what they did. Like with any group of weak-minded individuals, you need to find the weakest link and use them to your advantage. I plan on using Clover for that piece of my plan. Partially because she isn't a very talented witch, and because she slept with Ryan. I don't care if she believed his lies, she still called me a bitch and tried to sacrifice me with the rest of the coven.

Then there's the whole someone is stealing from my restaurant ordeal. Normally, that would be high priority, but the way that people are messing with me lately, it's lower on the list. I already have an idea on how to lure the rat out, with Stevie's help. She's the best at potions.

I talk out loud to myself, trying to concoct a plan about the coven. Kidnap Clover, maybe some light torture. Get everything out of her that I can. Maybe cement her feet together and throw her in the ocean. Maybe let her live. It will honestly depend on my mood. Truly, the person who needs to pay the most is my mother. If I can find a way to strip her of her magic, that would be the ultimate payback.

Unfortunately, none of these scared bitches have shown their faces in town since the ritual. The first chance I get, I'm taking one of them and dragging information out of them.

I park my car in the garage of my home, and the door automatically shuts. Stevie is sitting on the couch watching one of her shows when I walk in.

"You didn't leave at all today?"

"No, I've been watching Below Deck all day," she says.

"Fair enough. I have something to keep you busy, though."

"What's that?" she asks, interested. Stevie isn't one to be left idle. While she might have the general upbeat personality of the other witches, she isn't completely free spirited. She loves working at Hex and getting her hands dirty.

"Truth truffles. I need about a dozen."

"Oh, and who are we exacting the truth from?"

"Well, make two dozen, actually. I need a batch for Hex. Someone is stealing. And I might need more if my next plan comes to fruition."

"What plan is that?"

"Locking up one of those traitors in the basement and getting the answers I need."

Stevie is usually sweet and kind, but she nods her head in agreement, completely okay with the kidnapping scheme. I feel a little bad that I'm helping bring this side out of her, but it's necessary. They didn't just hurt me; they used both of us.

"I have a date with Dax tomorrow," I say.

She arches her eyebrow as she sifts through the kitchen cabinets, getting the materials she needs for the truffles. "Where are y'all going?"

"Not sure. He's going to pick me up here."

"Do you need me to disappear for when you come back?"

"With the way things went today in my office, I would say yes."

"What happened in your office?"

"A lady never tells," I say over my shoulder as I walk to my bedroom.

I can hear my cousin say, "You're not a lady."

I ignore her and get ready for the night. There's nothing more to do that I haven't already done. I'm certainly not going to let those hags turn me into a scared shut-in. I'm going to enjoy my date with Dax tomorrow, and figure out the rest as it comes along.

Maybe I'm being stupid for assuming they need a full moon, but that's when everyone's magic is the strongest. They would need that and the entirety of the coven together to attack me again. I have time, and I don't plan on wasting it, but I also don't plan on not living my life in the meantime.

The way Dax made me feel is the most alive I can remember feeling. I deserve to feel good, *right?*

My hands glide down my pleated skirt, straightening the navy plaid material. I'm usually not obedient, but something about Dax makes me want to listen. Him telling me how much he loves me in skirts and how it does it for him makes me want to be a *good girl.* I pair it with a tight black t-shirt. I keep my makeup pretty simple, a black cat eye, some mascara and nude lipstick.

"I'm going over to Bianca's house," Stevie tells me as she leaves the house.

"I thought you two broke up?" Bianca is a vampire, and it was hard for them to make their schedules work with how little night time we get during half the year.

"Doesn't mean we can't still hook up sometimes."

"Fair point. Don't let her bite you, though."

"But I kinda like it," she whines.

"As long as it's what you want, Stevie." I take comfort in knowing she's with Bianca tonight. For the most part, witches stay far away from vampires. So our coven shouldn't give her any issues.

"I'll text you when I'm headed home."

"Okay, be safe," I say to her as she shuts the screened porch door as she leaves. It isn't sunset yet, so I imagine she will need to go underground with Bianca for a few hours.

I check my appearance in the mirror one more time. I almost let my insecurities claw at me for a moment, and then I remember how Dax made me feel. We're going to focus on that, and not the mountain of baggage I'm currently dealing with.

The rumble of a motorcycle engine takes me out of my thoughts as I see Dax driving down my gravel driveway. *Damn, he looks good.*

He parks his bike, taking off his helmet and running his fingers through his hair. He has a deep gray t-shirt on that shows off his sun kissed skin and tattoos.

"Hey," he says.

"Hey, yourself." He kisses the side of my head and tugs on the hem of my skirt.

"Good girl," he whispers in my ear. Yeah, he definitely makes me want to hear that over and over again.

What the Hell is happening to me? I nearly melt against his touch as his hand glides up to my waist.

"Where are we going?" I ask as a rumble of thunder sounds off in the distance.

"I wanted to take my bike there, but it looks like it might rain. Can we take your car?"

I nod my head and look at him. Should I just invite him inside now and ride him like I'm at a rodeo?

"No, babe. I'm taking you out to dinner, then we can come back here for dessert." He winks at me. It's always the worst when a man knows he's hot and the effect that he has on you. *I'm so completely fucked.*

"Yeah, we can take my Jeep."

I enter the code and open the garage door. Dax follows me to the driver's side of the car and opens the door for me. As I climb into the driver's seat, I might bend slightly so he can get a little show of the cheeky lace undies I have underneath.

"Naughty little witch," he says as he shuts my door and rounds the car, getting in the passenger's seat.

"Where to?"

"Start driving toward North Grove."

"We're going out of town?"

"Yeah, unless that's a problem," he asks. Not seeming angry, but genuine, that if I didn't want to leave town, he wouldn't make me.

"No, it's just been a while." I reverse the Jeep down the driveway and press the button, shutting the garage door.

We're quiet for a few moments as I drive toward the highway. Dax's hand wanders over to my thigh and he draws lazy circles on my skin. It's making me crazy.

"So, how old are you, anyway?"

He laughs, and it's deep and gravelly. It has a central line to all my lady bits. "Older than I look, I suppose."

"Hmm, cryptic. Not a vampire, definitely not an angel, maybe a mage?"

"Maybe," he says, the pressure of his thumb increasing on my thigh.

"You're really not going to tell me what you are?"

"Patience, pet." He squeezes my thigh, and I can't help the sound of pleasure that squeaks out of my lips. "Make a left up here," Dax directs, and I turn on my blinker and turn onto the side road.

"Carly's Crabs?" I ask.

"I probably should have made sure you liked seafood, but I assumed from your menu at Hex."

I smile, the memories flooding me a little too quickly. "My Dad used to bring me here on my birthday."

"He still around?"

"Somewhere, I only ever see him on my birthday."

He frowns and his hand stills on my thigh. Probably not the best idea to drop your daddy abandonment issues on a guy who hasn't been the greatest father.

"He sent money, but he just couldn't be a good parent, so he did the best he could," I say, and Dax nods his head. I can't stop myself from the word vomit. "It's not for everyone, being a parent. I know it's not for me. But shit happens sometimes. It doesn't make him a bad person."

"Blair, babe, take a breath."

I do and exhale, giving him a smile. "Ready to go in?" he asks.

"Yeah." I go to open my door and he tsks at me. So I wait for him to get out of the Jeep and walk around and open my door. I was going to hop down myself, but he grabs me by the waist and sets me on the pavement. Carly's is in the middle of nowhere. It's half indoors, half outdoors, with a massive awning to protect us from the incoming rain. Dax keeps his hand firmly placed on my lower back as we walk up to the hostess stand.

"Table for two," he says and the woman frowns, looking down at her table chart.

"It's gonna be an hour."

Dax touches her hand and makes eye contact with her. "I'm sure if you look again, there's an open table." His words are soft and hypnotizing.

"Well, I don't know how I missed that," the hostess says, grabbing two menus and walking us over to the best table in the whole place. It's right on a lake, so we'll get to eat and watch as the rain comes in. Dax pulls out my chair and I take my seat, flattening my skirt under my ass.

Dax sits across from me and smiles. "Mage is still my top choice."

He acknowledges my suspicions but doesn't answer. "Do you want to get a dozen crabs?"

"That sounds good, hushpuppies and calamari, too?"

"Anything you want, babe," he says, giving me a smirk. That fucking dimple makes an appearance and I nearly perish and fall into the lake. "You look stunning tonight," he says.

"Thank you, you don't look so bad yourself."

He smiles and puts his elbow on the table, his jaw leaning against his fist. "You're not like other witches I've met."

"Cunty, or frolicking naked in the woods?" His laugh is loud and booming and it makes me smile at him.

"Fuck, you're cute."

The waitress comes to our table, and she looks a little too hard at my date. I really was making it a resolution to not hurt people who flirt with my date, but if she doesn't stop soon, I'll happily break that resolution. Luckily, she redirects her attention to me.

"What can I get you to drink, sweetheart?"

"I'll have an orange crush, please." She smiles and nods her head, looking back at Dax.

"I'll have the same. We'll do a dozen large crabs, calamari, and hushpuppies. Thanks." We both hand our menus back to the server and she walks away.

"Is there anything you're going to tell me about yourself, Dax?"

"Let's see, I'm a Gemini, my favorite color is green, I hate oatmeal, I like baseball."

"Very vague," I say, as I play with the tablecloth in front of me.

"What about you?"

"Virgo, black, I hate my coven. I like my cousin Stevie."

"What's wrong with your coven?" he asks. The waitress politely sets our drinks down, and I take a hefty sip.

"More like, what isn't wrong with them? They've depended on me financially for the last five years, and then they tried to sacrifice me a few days ago." His eyes widen, but it seems almost like a forced reaction. Could he have possibly already known?

"What are you going to do?"

"I plan on getting some answers before I act."

He nods his head. "Anything I can help with?"

"What exactly do you know about covens?" His green eyes are shiny and his dimple is making an appearance again.

"I'm knowledgeable."

"Hmm," I say as I take in his response. I want help, but the truth is, I don't really know Dax. So bringing him into this drama when I don't know if I can fully trust him doesn't seem wise. "I'll take it under advisement."

"Fair enough," he says. The busboy comes and drops off our crabs and sides and my mouth waters.

This isn't a hot way to eat in front of a guy you like for the first time, but Dax doesn't seem to mind as we pick apart our crabs and eat quietly. The rain suddenly comes in and it hits the metal roof and drips into the lake. Our hands are filthy and Dax has a little Old Bay on the side of his face, but something about this date just feels more intimate than others I've been on. I'm not sure how that's possible when the man refuses to give up any personal information.

We finish our meal, and the rain is still going pretty strong. There's an outdoor sink and I go to wash my hands. Dax is suddenly behind me, his larger body surrounding mine as he washes his hands as well. This shouldn't be attractive, but it is. "Thank you for coming out with me," he whispers. Our hands interlacing and sudsy under the running water.

"Thanks for dinner."

"My pleasure. Do you want to get ice cream before you take me to get my bike?" I turn around, grabbing a towel to dry off my hands. He has a smirk on his face. The way he worded it—giving me a choice, but there's no way in Hell this man isn't coming back home with me.

"That sounds great."

Dax settles the tab and uses his bigger body to shield mine as we run in the rain toward my car. He still opens my car door and waits for me to get in until he gets in the car. We're both wet in my Jeep and the windows are foggy when he leans over the console, gripping my nape with my wet black hair. The kiss is fierce and demanding. Dax isn't asking for any permission. He just takes as his tongue parts my lips. I think that he's going to touch me more, but the kiss continues. His tongue dominates mine and shows me who's in charge. It makes me wet and needy. I rub my thighs together looking for friction.

Dax breaks the kiss, his dark hair wet and sexy. He smiles at me and winks. "Patience, pet."

I want to beg, but I just stare at him for a moment, trying to collect enough brain cells so that I can turn the ignition on and get us home as soon as possible.

CHAPTER TEN

BLAIR

O nce I've collected enough brain power to start the car, I clear my throat and drive back to Hallowsdeep.

"Ice cream?" he asks in a voice. I know he knows what he's doing to me. No man, or whatever he is, should be allowed to be this sexy.

"Seriously?"

"Rain is stopping, why not?" he says, smirking at me.

Why not? Because you've made my panties wet, and you need to do something about it. Instead of saying that out loud, I nod my head and give him a tight smile.

"Cauldron Cones?"

"I forgot everything in this town was Halloween themed."

"You've been here before?"

"Yeah, a long time ago."

I nod my head and don't question him any further. I'm not sure why, but the idea of him bringing Ryan up makes my stomach hurt. Dax is payback. I'm going to enjoy every moment of it, but he can't be anything more than that.

It's dark, but the lights off Main Street are bright as we pull up to the ice cream shop. That's when I see a mass of dark brown curly hair and I know its Clover.

"Fuck," I hiss.

"What's wrong?"

Who knows the next time I'll get a chance like this. Dax isn't human. I'm guessing his moral compass is a little off kilter, too. Maybe he won't think I'm an absolutely deranged lunatic for proposing a kidnapping for a first date bonding activity.

"What's your stance on abduction?"

"Like aliens?" He looks at me, perplexed. We live in a world with vampires and werewolves, if you don't believe in aliens, you're a moron. But, now is not the time to discuss life forms outside of Earth.

"No, like that bitch over there, is in my coven, and I've been waiting to spot one of them to lock in my basement." I look over at him skeptically, this is either the turning point of our date and he runs for the hills. Or I've truly met my match.

He looks at me wide-eyed for a moment. "You are a surprise, that's for sure, Blair."

"I don't need your help. I just need to get her in my trunk."

"How do you plan on getting her into your trunk?" He arches an eyebrow at me.

"I've got furniture strength," I say, and he laughs.

He shrugs his shoulders. "I'm in. What's the plan, boss?" I'm not going to lie, I'm not completely shocked. I feel like Dax is a kindred spirit, people who have been scorned can understand revenge.

I watch as Clover walks down the street and the intrusive thought of hitting her with my car runs through my mind. *Need her alive*, I remind myself. Though the thought of her brown curls stuck in the grill of my car are just as alluring. I physically shake myself, my head is getting to be a scary place lately.

"Think you could get her to walk behind the post office?" I ask.

"Yeah, and then what?"

"I'll do the rest. Just get her behind the post office." Dax doesn't even question me as I park the Jeep behind the post office and he goes out to bring Clover back here. Why am I so turned on by the fact that he's totally okay with helping me kidnap this bitch? Ryan would never, how are they even related? Besides the physical appearance, they're complete opposites, but I guess it shouldn't be a surprise since he didn't have a heavy hand in raising him.

I stay close enough that I can hear the conversation. He gently grabs her by the elbow and I want to punch her in the face, even though he's the one that touched her. Clover has touched enough of my things.

"Excuse me, darlin'," he says in his deliciously deep voice, I swear I feel myself getting wet.

"Uh, yeah?" she asks, turning around as soon as she looks at his eyes. It's like she's transfixed. Just like our hostess was earlier.

"Can you come with me behind the post office?"

"Oh, of course. I'm Clover."

"That's a nice name. What do you do, Clover?"

"No real job right now," she says, and I roll my eyes. *Gold digging witches.*

Once they're close enough to the Jeep, I hop out and grab Clover by the arm.

"Hey, Clover."

Her eyes are huge and she's clearly out of whatever trance Dax put her under. "Bla—Blair?"

"The one and only, bitch. Do you want to do this the easy way or the hard way?"

She goes to scream and I quickly silence her with a *silentium.* She starts thrashing, trying to get out of my grasp. "Night, night, Clover. *Somnum.*" She drops right there on the cement and it definitely sounds like she hit her shoulder pretty hard. It isn't as satisfying as if *someone* hit her with a Jeep, but it's satisfying enough.

I nudge her with my boot and make sure she's out before I open the trunk. I grip her under her armpits and grunt. Her dead weight is too heavy for me to lift. Spells to lift something so heavy run through my head.

"Furniture strength," Dax mutters as he throws her over his shoulder and roughly places her in the trunk. I was already turned on, but the fact that he just threw her in there like a damn rag doll adds to his allure even more.

"I would've gotten her in there, eventually."

"Uh, huh? Are we still getting ice cream?"

"She should be out for at least five hours."

His eyes gleam with excitement as he shuts the trunk and takes my hand in his to walk back toward the ice cream shop. His hand is warm and large. Ryan never held my hand when we walked places. I never realized how much I would enjoy it. What it would be like for a man to be so into you and want to claim you in every direction.

"So you're totally fine with what we just did?" I ask him, checking in.

"You said she hurt you?"

"Yeah," I say and look down at my feet as we walk.

"Then yeah, fuck her." *I need a change of panties.*

I smile up at him and he leans down and places a gentle kiss on my lips as we wait in line for ice cream. Dax orders Moose Tracks and I get a mint chocolate chip cone, the green kind, because the white kind is weird.

We sit down at a nearby bench as we eat.

"The whole kidnapping thing doesn't change me wanting to invite you over tonight," I say confidently.

He grins at me and takes a swipe of my ice cream before placing a quick, cold kiss on my lips.

"Good," he says before kissing me again. "Should we get going?" We both finish up the last of our ice cream and throw what's left in the trash. He takes my hand in his again as we walk back to the Jeep. I check and make sure that Clover is still passed out in the trunk as Dax opens my door and I jump in.

There are butterflies in my stomach and I know I should squash these feelings. They aren't emotional feelings. They're *fucking* feelings. I just want his body on top of mine. *Right?* Right.

Dax keeps his hand on my thigh the whole drive back to my house, and I wish I could just keep this bitch in my car while I have my way with him. But she needs to be locked up and taken care of first. Though, carbon monoxide poisoning is a valid way to kill someone. Why am I feeling so murderous tonight?

When I park the Jeep in the garage, Dax looks at me with an eyebrow raised. "Want me to carry her to your basement?"

"If you don't mind."

We both get out of the Jeep and I open the trunk as Dax throws the traitor over his shoulder. I open the door to the main house. He isn't able to cross the threshold, my wards physically stopping him from entering. I swear under my breath.

He arches an eyebrow at me.

"Wards. Are you okay with me taking a drop of your blood?"

He nods, and I'm glad that he isn't weird about that. Using a conjured needle, I draw both a drop of his blood and Clover's. When it drips over the threshold, I do a few chants to open the wards for my guests. He smiles when I gesture for him to walk through. Leading him to the door to the basement, I turn on the lights and he follows me.

"I was expecting a dungeon, not a fucking finished nice basement," he says, laughing, and I shrug my shoulders.

I open the spare bedroom with the iron cast bed frame and have him lay her on the bed. Taking two silk ties, I wrap them around her wrists.

"I need to do a few spells to make sure she can't get out. Do you want to wait in the living room? I shouldn't be long."

He kisses the side of my face and walks upstairs. Who knew kidnapping could be so romantic?

I spell her ties so that she shouldn't be able to get out of them. I silence the room so no one can hear her screams, and I put a protection on the door so that Stevie and I are the only ones able to get in and out. Fortunately, there are no windows, so that won't be a problem. She will be out for a few more hours, anyway. So I can enjoy the rest of my evening.

It takes me about fifteen minutes to make sure Clover isn't going anywhere anytime soon as I walk upstairs to the living room. Seeing Dax sitting on my couch does something to me. His frame is large, and he looks relaxed with his legs spread as his gaze appreciates my decor. He's licking what looks like chocolate off his fingers, and I gape at him.

"Dax, what are you eating?"

"Those chocolates off the counter, really good. Damn, did you make these?" he says, licking the last bit of chocolate off his thumb. It's sexy as Hell, but I have no idea what to do.

"Dax, babe, how many did you eat?"

"Four," he says as he pats his lap.

"Um, just give me one second!" I run into the kitchen and look at the truffles and groan. I call Stevie and thank Hecate as she answers. "Stevie! Fuck. Dax is here, and he ate four of your truth truffles. What should I do?"

She laughs over the phone. "The right thing to do would be to take one yourself and come clean," she says. I'm not a huge fan of that idea.

"What if I say something about Ryan?"

"Risk, reward," she says as she laughs. I can hear Bianca saying something to her in hushed tones. I hang up, not saying anything else. I take a deep breath before popping a truffle in my mouth as I walk back into the living room.

"Fuck, you're so beautiful. You know that?" he says, patting his lap again. This time, I straddle his lap as instructed. He pets down my hair. "I've been thinking about how you would feel on my lap all night. You're the most stunning little creature I've ever seen."

"You ate spelled truth truffles," I blurt out, the chocolates already taking effect.

"Mmm, is that what that feeling is?" His large hands glide over my thighs, and he squeezes. "These fucking thighs, I can't stop touching them, thinking about them. I want to bite them."

"You've made me so fucking wet tonight," I tell him, feeling lose and happy. Every thought just spilling from my lips.

His grip tightens on my thighs, and he groans. "The indecent things I want to do to you, Blair."

"Tell me," I whisper.

"I want to bend you over and spank your ass until you're begging me to fuck you. I want to fuck you in your sleep and wake you up with an orgasm. You make me want to do things I've never wanted to do before. I want to watch your pretty eyes change color when I lick your cunt so good you can't breathe."

I can't help it as I grind against his length.

"I've never wanted someone so bad. Wanted to take care of someone so badly. I want to spoil the fuck out of you," he says.

"I want that. Touch me, Dax."

His green eyes are so dark as he looks at my face. His thumb sliding between my lips and tugging on my bottom lip.

"What do you want from me, little witch?"

"I want you to be my daddy, Dax. No one has treated me like you have tonight. It's pathetic. I feel pathetic. But I think you could take care of me." I cover my mouth with my hands and groan. I want to die on the spot. How mortifying and embarrassing, no way that's something that Dax wants. I've hardly even admitted to myself that I wanted a man to take control and take care of me, and here I'm word vomiting to the most attractive man I've ever met. My hands push against his chest as I try to get off his lap. His grip is unrelenting as he slides me back up.

He growls and swats my ass. "Not pathetic. My powerful, naughty little witch wants me to be her daddy?"

"Yes," I say breathlessly as my hands grip his shoulders.

"What else does my pet want?"

"I want to know what you are," I whisper, and I can feel him trying to fight the spell.

He groans but answers, "Demon, Incubus." The wanting to fuck me while I sleep tracks better now, and I'm definitely not opposed. "Are you scared?"

"No. I think I would like that. I like that you're a demon." I kiss his beard. "My demon." I can't help but want to kiss and lick him everywhere. His magic is pushing against mine, and it's the most addictive feeling I've ever felt. "Your magic. I've never felt like this before."

"Me either," he says as he stares at me with what looks like admiration. "Show daddy how wet you are."

I grab his hand and slide his fingers over the lace of my panties so he can feel how wet I am for him.

"I came in my pants the other day. Fuck," he blurts out, and I giggle. He looks so irritated about admitting that. I had my suspicions, but it's nice knowing I have just as much of an effect as he does on me. This power dynamic we're dancing with is something I've always wanted. A man who is so confident in how he takes and gives himself to me.

"I've wanted this for a long time."

"What?"

"A man who can take away the decisions, make me feel like I can give them the control." He licks his lips and looks at my chest.

"I'm going to ruin you for anyone else, Blair." I stare at him for a moment and clear my throat. He can't be serious.

"You had a lot of truffles. If you don't want to do this right now, that's okay," I say.

"Blair, if you don't show me your wet pussy in five seconds, I'm going to take you over my knee."

My eyes widen, and I stand up and take my panties off, gently handing them to him. He takes the black lace, bunching it up and bringing it to his nose and groans.

"On your knees, pet."
"Yes, daddy."

CHAPTER ELEVEN

DAX

"Yes, daddy."

Blair slides down to her knees, obediently between my spread legs. I look around her living room and think about how I want tonight to go. I definitely didn't expect to pour my whole soul out after eating some random chocolates on her counter. Her hands go to undo my pants and I grab her wrists.

"One day I'll have your mouth around my cock, but tonight we're taking things slow, Blair. Is there anything you don't like?"

"That your cock isn't in my mouth?" she says and it feels like she's trying to push against the truth truffles. That won't do.

Her eyes plead with mine, in their deep honey color. "Remove your eye glamour."

That gets a rise out of her. "I don't like removing it. It makes me feel vulnerable."

"I want to read easily how I make you feel, beautiful, but if you're not ready, I can be patient."

"Can we wait?" she asks in a small voice, and I cup her cheek. Her skin is smooth and warm.

"Of course. Back to my first question. Is there anything you don't like?"

"Nothing comes to mind currently." Her hands fidget in her lap.

"You look so fucking cute. When are these irritating truffles going to wear off?"

"Probably another hour." I groan, not completely liking the idea of every thought that comes to my head spilling out of my mouth.

"We'll just have to make this last, nothing like the other day in your office. I want to see you. Take your top off."

She licks her lips and slowly un-tucks her top from her skirt. The material is stretchy and clings to her skin as she slides her shirt off of her body. She's wearing a black lace bra, and it's the first time I get a view of some of her other tattoos. She has a mandala of a lotus flower adorned with two moons under her breasts and a sprig of lavender tattooed on her left collarbone.

My finger trails the top of the lace. Her tits are full and creamy white. Basically spilling over the material begging to be touched.

"This too, pet," I say, tugging on the lace. She looks at me while her arms wrap behind her back and she unclasps the bra, sending it to the floor. Her nipples are pierced with barbells through each nipple. The end of each barbell has purple studs. The color contrasts perfectly against her pale skin.

I gently push the barbell to the side, testing her sensitivity, earning me a moan. "So beautiful, Blair." She blushes and looks away. I put my thumb under her chin and force her to look at me.

"Does my fierce little witch not know how to take a compliment?" She goes to look away again, and I grab her jaw more firmly. "Daddy's just going to have to work on that, isn't he? Sit on my lap." I let go of her jaw and relax against her couch, putting my legs closer together so she can straddle me. I'm worried that she's gone quiet and I need to make sure that she's doing okay.

I glide my hands down her arms and can't help it as I stare at her tits, they bounce slightly, when she straddles me. I almost forgot that she gave me her panties and nothing separates us, except the fact that she is still wearing her cute little skirt. That can stay.

"Blair, are you all right?" I ask, rubbing her arms.

"M' fine. I'm not used to the attention, I suppose?"

"Mmm, we'll have to work on that. Because I plan on giving you plenty of attention. So soft and beautiful." I nuzzle against her breasts and she pushes into me. My tongue leaning forward and tracing the piercing before putting her whole nipple in my mouth. I swirl the piercing with my tongue clicking the metal in between my teeth before sucking again. Her hands grab onto my shoulders for purchase as she groans as I suck harder. "Sensitive, pet?"

"Very, don't stop." Her voice is pure sin. If I didn't already know she was a witch, a succubus would have been a close second.

I palm both of her tits and give each one attention with my mouth. Tugging on the piercings with enough pressure to make her squirm on my lap. Then switching it up and taking her whole nipple into my mouth.

My palms drag down to her narrow waist, finally resting on her thick thighs. They look even better pressed down against my legs. I knead my thumbs into them, and Blair leans over to place kisses along my neck. She isn't gentle as she sucks and bites the skin. I like that she isn't meek or shy. She tugs on my short beard as she nips at my earlobe.

"Careful, witch." I grab a handful of her ass and grind her down on my cock so she can feel what she's doing to me.

"I don't want to be careful," she says.

"What do you want?"

"I want to please you." Her words shoot straight to my cock and I groan.

"Where to start with you?" I lick my lips as I look at her tits one more time. I don't know why, but the idea of a quick fuck on her couch just isn't doing it for me. Blair deserves to be devoured. "Bedroom?" I ask, arching an eyebrow at her. She goes to get off my lap, but I hold her still, collecting her ass in the palms of my hands. Her legs wrap around my waist as I stand, and she directs me up the stairs to her bedroom.

Her room is far more feminine than I expected it to be. A mix of dark grays and greens, a large king bed in the center with a soft-looking emerald and black blanket. She has a ridiculous amount of plants along the wall and hanging from the ceiling. Her slate gray dresser houses a variety of crystals and other trinkets. But the most surprising item in her room is a large ball python sitting inside of the wall length terrarium.

She must see my gaze take in the creature, her arms still wrapped around my shoulders. "He's my familiar. Does it bother you?"

"I've never heard of a witch with a snake for a familiar."

She shrugs her shoulders again. "His name is Fez."

"Doesn't bother me. Will it bother him?"

Blair grins at me before kissing me softly. You wouldn't think Blair as being someone soft and needy. An egotistical part of me hopes that this part of her has been reserved for me.

"I believe you mentioned something about tasting me?" she whispers by the shell of my ear, making me smile.

"Is that what you want, babe? You want my mouth on this wet pussy. I bet when I put you down, I'll have a wet spot on my pants."

"Please, daddy," she whispers and I shiver. I place her down on her back on her soft bed. Her tits bounce with the motion and her skirt flips up, covering her waist. I debate heavily on making her take the skirt off or not. *It can stay.*

Blair shimmies further up the bed, propping herself up on her elbows to watch as I lie on my stomach and kiss my way up her smooth calves. She shivers as my fingers graze the back of her knees, bringing myself closer and closer to where she wants me. Her magic nearly radiates off her skin. It's calling to me like a beacon. I've never been so drawn or turned on in my life. I need every piece of her.

I part her legs wider, my teeth grazing the skin of her thigh. My thumb drags her wetness over her clit and I groan.

"So fucking wet, little witch. Such a pretty pussy." She moans at my words and her eyes follow my movements. I kiss her outer lips before taking a slow, deep swipe of her cunt from her opening to her clit. Her flavor hits my tongue, and I hum in approval. I don't think I'll ever get enough.

I push my face harder against her pussy as I savor her with slow flicks of my tongue. Her thighs twitch when I do something she likes and I make mental notes of how to bring her pleasure. Blair has stopped trying to hold herself on her elbows as her head rests on a pillow and her forearm covers her eyes.

I'm about to stop and ask her if she's okay when her nails sink into my hair, pushing my head harder against her, taking that as a sign to continue. I thrust my erection into her soft sheets and groan against her pussy as her cum fills my mouth and drips onto my beard. I unwrap my fingers from one of her thighs and push two fingers inside of her warm cunt. She's so tight as she flutters against my fingers.

"Fuck, Dax. I'm going to come."

My tongue lavishes her clit. I wonder how many times I can make her come like this. How swollen I can make her clit from sucking on it continuously. The idea makes me moan as I suck on her nub even harder. Her back arches above the mattress, her fingers tightly grip my hair and her left thigh is nearly pressed against my face.

"Fuck, fuck. You feel so good," she chants and I don't let up for a moment on her pussy. Fingering her and sucking her clit. I curl my fingers inside of her and her whole body shakes, her pussy gripping my fingers, and she's nearly ripping my hair out with how tight a hold she has on it. Her wetness covers my chin and I only stop when I feel her body go slack.

Blair is panting. Her forearm is still covering her eyes. I remove her arm and she looks at me with wide-purple eyes. I swipe some of the wetness off my face with my forearm as I grab her by the hips and give her a grin. I don't mention her eyes, even though they're gorgeous, it's obvious it's an insecurity for her.

"I'm not done with you, little witch."

"You have too many clothes on," she says while grabbing the hem of my t-shirt. Loving her eagerness, I let her take my shirt off. Her soft fingers trail my chest as she looks at me with awe. Now that she has more control over herself, her eyes have gone back to a soft brown.

She trails a few of my tattoos with the pad of her thumb and licks her lips.

"What do you want, pet?"

"Fuck me, please."

"Mmm, but what if I want to play more?" I slide my two fingers inside of her pussy, and she gasps, making eye contact with me. She goes to look away, and I click my tongue. "None of that, babe. Look at me while I get this pussy ready to take daddy's fat cock."

She faces me again and licks her lips. I can't help it when I lean forward and kiss her roughly. She's so wet that the only sound that fills the room is her cunt sucking my fingers in and out.

"Dax, please," she nearly whispers, and I'm fucking gone. *Playtime is over.*

Groaning, I stop fucking her with my hand. She winces from the loss, and I smirk at her.

"You fucking undo me, little witch." I unclasp the buckle and push my pants and briefs down. My weeping cock springing free. Blair gasps when she sees it. When Satan gives you a corporeal body, sure enough, he's going to give you a nice dick.

I stroke myself slowly as she appreciates my length and lifts her weight back on her elbows to watch me hungrily. I use my thumb to swipe some of the precum and fuck my fist harder. I think I might just come from having her watch me touch myself.

"On your knees."

She does as I ask, turning around. Her perfect pale ass high in the air as she rests on her forearms and elbows, presenting herself to me. Her arousal is sticky on her thighs. My palm rubs a gentle circle on her left cheek before I give it a light swat.

It's the first time I notice the lunar cycle tattoo down her spine. I place a kiss to the full moon on the middle of her spine before I grab a fist full of her skirt and grind my length against her ass.

"Is this what you want, pet? You want me to fuck you hard from behind? Grab your little skirt and ride you until I fill you up with my cum?"

"Yes, please. I've never wanted it this bad." It feels like our magic is intertwining itself, and if I were smart I would stop this. I haven't even been inside of her and I already feel addicted. It's too much, too fast.

Never said I was smart.

I line my cock up against her dripping pussy and rub the head up and down her slit. It's in that moment that reality sinks in.

"Birth control?" I ask softly, pissed at myself for pausing our momentum.

"IUD and I take a potion."

"Thank fuck." I push into her hard and fast. No preamble. "So fucking wet for your daddy, aren't you, pet?"

"Yes, you make me feel so good. Don't stop." With one hand on her hip and the other gripping her skirt, I fuck her hard, her ass smacking against my pelvis and my balls hitting her clit with every thrust. I can feel myself about to come already and that won't do.

I pull out of her and grab the base of my cock hard, making me groan. Once the feeling passes, I put myself inside of her again, but pull her up with an arm wrapped around her chest. So her back is flush with my chest. I have to flip the skirt up so I can lazily circle her clit.

"Your tight pussy was trying to get me to come before I was ready," I whisper against her hair. We're both sweaty and breathless as I fuck her slow—shallow thrusts into her wet, perfect cunt. "I want to feel you come around my cock, pet. Can you do that for me?"

She doesn't answer, and I pick up the pace of my thrusts and the pressure against her clit. "Can you do that for me, Blair?"

"Yes, oh, fuck. I'm coming." Her smaller body shivers against mine, and I feel her clenching around my length. Bright stars flash behind my eyes as my magic tingles under my skin. My magic has never been so present during sex. As her softer magic edges against mine, it pushes me over the edge. I moan into her neck as I fill her with my cum, her body shakes against mine and I can feel my thighs wanting to give out. I continue holding her up against my chest for a moment until her small hands tap on my forearm.

"I need to pee," she whispers, her cheeks blushing.

"Okay," I say, letting her out of my arms and I lie back on her bed.

What the fuck was that?

Hands down the most intense and pleasurable sex of my life. I hardly know Blair, but that was the most euphoric feeling I've ever felt. I should be afraid of getting attached, but like an addict, all I can think about is how to get my next fix of this witch.

CHAPTER TWELVE

BLAIR

I shut the bathroom door behind me and immediately turn the faucet to the sink on. No fucking way am I going to be able to pee knowing he's going to hear me through the door. I shouldn't care, he just ate my pussy like he was on a sniper mission to make me lose all my brain cells.

What the Hell was that?

His cum leaks down my thigh, and I groan as I sit on the toilet. This isn't me. I don't call men daddy, I don't let them see the real me. I'm all hard shells, strap-ons, and a good time.

I'm not a babe, pet, or a little witch. I'm Blair Bellamy, queen bitch, and he's melted me down to a gooey puddle of subbed out bliss. My heart races and my elbows are on my knees as my palms press against my face.

It wasn't supposed to be like this; it was supposed to be in and out. Fuck Ryan's dad, make him feel like the worthless piece of shit he is and move on.

Collateral damage.

I've done worse things to people and felt nothing. But the way I felt with Dax, it was intimate. It was more than a revenge fuck and my head, heart, and pussy are so not on the same page.

I should be thinking about how to kick him out of my bed and how I can best avoid him in the future. But what I really want are his big long arms wrapped around me and his beard pressed against the back of my neck.

What the fuck?

He made me come harder than I ever had in my life. Our magic pushed against each other alongside our bodies. I couldn't even hold my glamour if I tried. Not that I could think with the way he went down on me. The things he said to me, I'm getting wet just thinking about it again.

I'm usually in charge in the bedroom and I had convinced myself that it was what I liked. But actually giving up the control to *him* was a completely different experience. It was the most pleasurable sexual encounter of my life, it's like I'm being awakened to a new facet of myself.

He owned my body, knew what I needed. Made me want to do anything I could to please him, and I enjoyed it. Far more than I ever relished being dominate in the bedroom. I thought that being in charge just proved how everyone views me. Frankly, how I view myself most of the time.

I don't know what I'm doing, but I know that Dax can't find out about Ryan and that I'm not done exploring what this is. Maybe it will fade out and it's just so exciting because it's so new and different. Maybe he will get tired of me. I mean, he's a fucking demon after all, they aren't known for monogamy.

A knock at the door startles me. "Blair, you okay in there?"

"Yeah, just a second." I wipe the obscene amount of cum from my thighs and flush the toilet before washing my hands and turning off the faucet. I open the door and Dax walks in to wash his hands and swish water in his mouth.

I can't help it when I gape at him, this specimen of a man in my bathroom. His tight ass flexes as he shifts his weight on his feet. Dax's hair is a mess as it goes ten different directions on his head. I want to touch it again, feel the soft strands underneath my fingers. I can't even fight with myself internally, I want him so badly.

"Blair, are you sure you're okay?" He turns around and looks at me, his green eyes boring into mine.

I look away and sigh. "It's just never been like that before, I'm processing."

"Do you want me to go?" he asks, and I furrow my brows when I look at him. It's got to be around two a.m. And the truth is, I don't want him to go. I kind of hate that I want him to stay, that I feel vulnerable. What type of badass witch wants to be cuddled?

"I'd like you to stay," I say in a small voice.

"Good, because I'm not done with you yet." He smirks at me as he takes my hand and drags me toward the bed. I climb in, snuggling under the sheets.

"Thank you for staying."

"I wanted to. You know everything I said, I meant, right?" He's behind me and I feel more confident not looking at him when I speak. "This is new for me, I'm usually the dominant one. I feel so comfortable with you and it kinda scares the shit out of me. "

"Babe, did you eat another one of those chocolates?"

"No, it's stupid. We just met. Let's go to sleep."

"Hey," he says, spinning around so I'm looking at him. "It felt different and special to me too, Blair." He kisses my cheek, and I tuck my face against his pec. "Go to sleep, little witch. I'm sure you're going to have sweet dreams."

Sweet dreams don't even compare to how I sleep next to Dax. It's like I get to live out our night together from his point of view, seeing how he views me. It's amazing, the way he looks at me, like I'm sweet but powerful. How much he enjoys himself as he tastes and touches me. I'm not sure how my subconscious knew I needed these affirmations, but I sleep long and hard, not wanting to escape the images my mind has conjured.

"Well, isn't this cute," my cousin coos from my door frame.

I crack an eyelid and see Dax is basically snuggling me like I'm a teddy bear. One of his massive legs on top of mine, his hand draped around my waist, his lips at my throat.

"Fuck off, Stevie," I say, trying to get her to leave me alone. Trying not to shift my weight and not wake Dax.

"No can do. We need to talk about the screeching woman in the basement."

"Is it wrong that I forgot about my captive?"

"It appears you were quite preoccupied," Stevie says, giving me a wink. I notice the bite mark on her neck and roll my eyes.

I point to her throat with my one free hand. "Looks like you are one to talk."

Her hand clamps around her throat. "Fuck, I meant to glamour that before I came home."

"Let me just wake Dax up, and then we will deal with Clover."

"Uh, huh? I'll be in the living room when you're ready." She shuts the door softly behind her and Dax's grip around my waist tightens, and he kisses my throat gently.

"I guess this means no morning sex?"

"I could put up a silencing charm," I say playfully.

He kisses my throat and groans. I can feel his hardness against my hip. "I need to meet up with Asmo, anyway. We have some work to do."

"Care to share?"

"I think we both shared enough last night," he says, placing another kiss on my throat.

"Well, if you don't stop kissing me, there's only one way for this to go."

He kisses me again. "I know, fuck. All right, I'm getting up."

Dax stands completely naked as he collects his clothes and starts getting dressed. Why is that little jump thing they do into their pants so hot?

"Can I take you out again?" he asks, and my stupid black heart grows a little bit.

"Maybe," I say. He doesn't smile. He leans over the bed and cups my jaw.

"I wasn't playing last night, Blair. I want to spoil you, take care of you, make you come so fucking hard you can't think. No games."

"Yes, I would like that."

"There's my sweet good girl, only for me though, Blair. You can be mean to everyone else." He smirks at me and leans off the bed. I grab his wrist so he can't get away.

"Can I plan the next date?"

"Of course, pet." He kisses me, and I grab one of my sleep shirts, tossing it over my head and a pair of loose shorts on underneath as I walk Dax to the front door. Stevie is sitting on the couch staring at us and I assume Dax will feel awkward and just leave, but he surprises me by cupping my jaw and giving me a gentle kiss before leaving the house and getting on his motorcycle.

"Holy fuck, tell me everything," Stevie says as soon as the screen door shuts.

I tell Stevie the fine points of the evening, our date, kidnapping Clover, the truffle mishap and then I tell her how he makes me feel.

"Blair, just because other people have imposed how they feel about you on you constantly doesn't mean that's who you are. I've known you all my life and sure you can be rough around the edges, but I've never felt more loved by anyone than I do by you. You've always protected me and you always make me laugh. Enjoy this," she says, holding my hand on the couch. "I think he's good for you. Don't overthink it. Just spend time with him and see where it goes."

"What about Ryan?"

"Cross that bridge when it comes to it," she says, shrugging her shoulders.

Ignoring the problem is definitely the best way to go about this, so I nod my head and squeeze her hand.

"So I guess we need to go interrogate Clover now?" I ask.

"Suppose so. Are you going straight with the truffles?"

"I think I'd like her to squirm first."

"Obviously," Stevie says laughing. We still bring two truffles down with us to the basement.

I unlock the door and I'm greeted by a red faced Clover sitting in a puddle of her own piss as she screams for help.

"There are wards and my closest neighbor is half a mile away, you dumb bitch. Stevie and I are the only ones who can hear you," I tell her and she scoffs.

"People will come looking for me, Blair, unlike you, there are people who care about me."

I scoff, "Who? Ryan? He doesn't give a shit about you, Clover."

"The coven cares," she replies.

"Do they really, though, Clover? You're probably the least talented of the entire coven."

She gasps. "That's not true! Take it back."

"I don't know. What do you think, Stevie? Is she the weakest link?"

"I mean, she was dumb enough to walk around town after what they did to you," Stevie replies.

"What they did to us," I correct her. I lean against the door frame, seeming almost disinterested in the conversation. "This is how it's going to work, Clover. You tell us what we need to know and we let your home wrecking ass back out into the wild where you can live another pathetic day as a mediocre washed up witch. How does that sound, hmm?"

"I won't tell you anything," she says, trying to tug on her restraints.

"But I think you will. What should we start with, Stevie? Her toe nails?"

Clover sputters on the bed, shaking back and forth. "You wouldn't!"

"Have you ever known me to lie about torture, Stevie?"

"Nope, never. You're a very honest captor," Stevie says with a straight face and nodding her head. Getting the point across that this isn't good cop bad cop. It is double bad cop, so don't fuck with us.

"I'll make you a deal, leftover Clover. You eat this tasty little truth truffle. Tell me what I want, and I'll clean up the bed so you don't have to lie in your own piss."

She looks between Stevie and me, weighing her options. "I'll tell you what you want, but you have to set me free."

"No can do, little three leaf. See what I figure, is whatever ritual you and your gang of merry skanks were trying to achieve required the entire coven. If, I don't know, one little mousey witch was missing, it wouldn't be able to be performed. You're my insurance policy. If you want to continue to be in a piss free bed and fed daily, I think you really need to consider the next words you say to me." I look at her like I could easily make her life a living Hell. She swallows loudly and nods her head and opens her mouth. Stevie plops a truffle right on her tongue. I watch as she chews and swallows.

"Why was the coven trying to sacrifice me?"

"We didn't have a choice."

"Why not?"

"She's powerful. She promised that if we gave you to her that the coven would become powerful, that we wouldn't need you anymore."

"Who is she?"

"I don't know, only your mom met with her in person."

"What does she want with me?"

"I don't know. You know, we just do what Josie says. She said that we needed to do this, that your power would be distributed throughout the coven. That we would be stronger."

"You're sure that there was an outsider? This isn't my mom just trying to get rid of me?"

"Like I said, I didn't meet with the woman, only Josie did. I can't be sure that she isn't making it up."

I groan, frustrated, and tug at my messy, unbrushed hair. "Did you believe Ryan when he said he wasn't dating me?"

She tries to keep her mouth shut. "No."

"Unfortunately, you weren't worth the effort that it took to lock you in here. I hope you find your amenities comforting until the next moon, Clover."

"That's almost a month away!"

"You should have thought about that before you slept with my ex-boyfriend and tried to kill me. You're lucky this is all I'm doing to you."

I wordlessly untie her restraints. I tighten the wards so that she can't leave the room.

"What's the plan now?" Stevie asks me as we walk up the stairs.

"Find out who is stealing at Hex, then we need to track down my mother." The thought makes my stomach hurt and Stevie and I groan in unison.

CHAPTER THIRTEEN

DAX

"Look what the Hell hound dragged in. You need a fucking shower," Asmo says as soon as I walk through the door. I do need a shower, but I also like the idea of smelling like Blair. Her scent is earthly with touches of lavender and femininity. Last night was beyond what I could have imagined.

I'd be a liar if I said I hadn't had my fair share of partners. I'm an incubus and I've been roaming the world for a long time, but last night gave me an energy I've never experienced before. I'm already waiting for when I can get my next fix.

I roll my eyes and toss my helmet on the kitchen table. "Did I miss anything?"

"We have some leads," he says, tapping his finger on the table.

"Care to share?"

"You first."

I roll my eyes again. "Obviously, I spent the night at Blair's."

"Was she a good time?"

"Asmo, if you don't shut the fuck up about her soon, I'm going to lose my shit."

"Calm down, demon daddy," he says, laughing. Never get drunk with assholes and spew your fantasies. They'll only bring it back up at the worst times. "I figured we could work with Kas instead of against her. Her suggestion was to do a search and see who in Hallowsdeep has been listed as missing or went missing and recently was found."

"Does this sudden change of heart have anything to do with you two fucking again?" I don't mention that I think looking into missing persons is actually a pretty smart idea.

"Yeah, it does. Here, these are the people who have been reported missing and still are or were reported missing and then reappeared. It's only three people." He hands me over a file. "First is Paige Taft, twenty-six, works at Inferno, went missing four days ago and randomly showed back up at work yesterday." He licks his finger and pulls out the next. "Louis Jefferson, thirty-five, social worker, missing for two weeks still unseen." Asmo puts the last file down and it's a face I've seen recently. "Last is Clover Cross, twenty-four, known witch, just went missing last night."

"Well, you can take Clover off the list."

"Why?"

I shrug my shoulders. "I helped Blair kidnap her last night."

He lets out a barking laugh and crumples the sheet with Clover's information. "It's abduction when it's an adult. Fuck, she sounds like fun." I don't like him talking about my witch, but I can't let him know that. *My witch.* Fuck, she can't be my anything. As soon as this case is over, I'll be sent on a new one either here or in Hell. I can't form a genuine bond with her, but I also can't keep away.

"The guy isn't the demon's usual MO. Mara seems to prefer possessing women." Only one victim was a man.

"Fair enough. Paige works at Inferno in two days. We can scope it out to see if she's possessed. Even if she's not, it's a supe only club, so maybe we'll be able to get some information."

"Okay, what do we need to get in?"

Asmo grins at me. "Oh, didn't I mention, it's partner entry only. Unless you can come up with a date, it looks like Kas and I will be taking over this one."

I glare at him. "I'll be there."

"You think your mean little witch will be up for it?"

I want to choke the ever-living fuck out of him. "You let me worry about it. Since when is it partner entry only?"

"Since a bunch of werewolves were in there masturbating all over the place, gripping their knots. Made sure that the new policy makes the little subbies feel more comfortable coming." He laughs at his own joke about cum and I roll my eyes.

"Well, if there's no reason to see your annoying fucking face for two days, I'll be on my way."

"Aw, Daxy-poo, don't be such a baby. I'm sure if your precious Blair isn't up for it, we can find you some pathetic woman off the street who'll come with you."

I throw my middle finger up over my shoulder as I go to my room and get away from his annoying voice.

Would Blair actually be up for going to a supernatural sex club? Sure, we had sex and there were power dynamics in play, but nothing like what would happen at a place like Inferno. The only way to find out is to ask. She has enough on her plate, and I don't want to look like I'm a lovesick puppy, so I'll just meet up with her tomorrow to see if it is something she would even consider. The deepest part of me hopes she says yes and that this Paige person isn't actually Mara and we can actually have a good time. Our magic wasn't in play last night. I want her to see what I can do, and I desperately want to see how she would use her magic on me while we fuck.

I sadly shower away her scent and groan as I stroke my cock to thoughts of her sweet pussy wrapped around me.

"What are we doing here again?" Asmo asks.

"I came here, and you were bored and insisted on tagging along," I remind him.

"Yeah, well, I couldn't sit in that shithole anymore and Kas is busy."

"Pussy whipped."

"And proud," he says with a smile.

"Didn't she lock you in a fairy dimension for a decade?"

"Yeah, but I forgave her."

"Pathetic," I say and he shrugs his shoulders.

"Again, why are we here?" he asks, looking at the different products on the shelves. All meant to appear like actual witchcraft, though it's just bullshit for the mortal tourists who come to town around this time of year. With Halloween around the corner, business appears to be doing well. Apparently the shop is owned by a witch who happens to be in Blair's coven.

"How can I help you, gentlemen?" a wispy older woman says. She looks to be in her fifties with long white hair, nearly silver-blue eyes, and pale white skin. Her wrist is adorned with a good two dozen bracelets, and she's wearing a bright yellow maxi dress.

"Great question," Asmo says, and I ignore him, turning my charm onto this woman. Part of my magic is the words of suggestion. I can make just about any suggestion seem like a good idea to the person I'm speaking to. Supernaturals are hard, half of them have protections against my powers. I'm hoping she doesn't.

"I'm looking for a witch who can do a specific spell," I say and I can tell her interest is piqued, but she treats me as though I'm human.

"Surely a man so handsome doesn't need a love potion."

I smirk at her. "Of course not, I'm looking for the High Priestess."

"Oh, such great knowledge of coven hierarchy."

"Who is the priestess?" I ask her, pushing my magic out.

"Josie Bellamy," she replies in a daze.

"Where is she?"

"Hiding."

"Hiding where?"

"She didn't say."

"Why were you trying to sacrifice Blair?"

The witch shows some surprise, but I still have her heavily under my power. "She's strong enough."

"What does that mean?"

The older witch goes to open her mouth when the front door's bell chimes, knocking my concentration off kilter and ending our connection.

She shakes her head and points her finger at the front door. "You need to leave, now."

"Aw, but I really wanted a Ouija board. Got some friends in Hell I need to check in with," Asmo whines and the witch growls.

"Out!"

Asmo steals a lollipop from the checkout table and we both leave the shop. The loud bell ringing with our departure as we head out on Main Street.

"And I'm the one who is pussy whipped?"

"Shut the fuck up, Asmo."

He pops the lollipop in his mouth and licks it obnoxiously. I want to shove it down his throat, even though I know it won't kill him.

"Well, none of what the old bird said made any fucking sense." *Lick.*

"No, but it's more information than what I had before."

"Did she ask you to help?" *Lick.*

"No," I say.

"Pussy whipppped." *Lick.*

"Fucking, give me that." I rip the lollipop from his mouth and toss it to the middle of the street, where a car dramatically drives over the hard candy.

"Hey! You're more on edge than normal. You owe me a lollipop."

"You stole it," I say, looking at him incredulously as we continue walking to an area where we can portal undetected.

"It was still mine."

I ignore him until we get out of the public eye so we can portal. Annoyed with him, we both portal separately to the bungalow. The only thing worse than having to come home and deal with Asmo is coming home and finding Kas sitting on our couch unexpectedly.

I groan as I pass her and Kas clicks her tongue in annoyance. "You really should work on your manners, Dax. You've been alive long enough to know how to treat a house guest."

"I was just saying the same thing," Asmo says, sitting next to Kas and wrapping an arm around her shoulder. I don't trust her, and the amount of time it took her to get Asmo wrapped around her finger is disconcerting.

"Why are you here?"

"Rude," she says, picking her long black nails. "I was here to tell you both that I got us an invitation to Inferno two nights from now. But seeing how you act like an animal in public, maybe Asmo, and I should just go. You don't even have a date, anyway."

"I'll have a date."

"You haven't even asked her," Asmo reminds me.

"I'll go to Hex and talk to her about it. Don't worry about me. Worry about yourself."

"Oh, and pray tell, who will be this date?" Kas asks.

"This mean witch he met the other night," Asmo says.

"Don't worry your evil little heart about it. Just know I'll be there."

Kas arches her eyebrow but slides two invitations to me. "I suggest you read their policies before we go. We can't fuck this up. We need to go in there, hope this is the mortal Mara decided to possess, get the job done and get out."

"I think I know how to do my fucking job," I snap back, grabbing the invitations and heading back to my room. I have a fucking headache, and now I need to figure out how to ask Blair if she will come with me.

I guess I'm taking a trip to Hex tonight, no matter how pathetic it makes me look.

CHAPTER FOURTEEN

BLAIR

Stevie didn't want to come to Hex with me tonight, and I don't blame her. While I was always the black sheep of the coven, Stevie was more widely accepted. The betrayal to her cuts deeper than what they did to me.

I always wonder if there was anything I could have done to fit in better, but I can't figure it out. Why was I always so different? I didn't like the nature aspect of being a witch. I like verbal magic, not potions, which is mainly what my coven specializes in, unless it's group based incantation rituals.

Ever since I was little, I was always a little off. A little too rough around the edges, the other witches were directed to not associate with me. The only reason I have Stevie is because her parents passed and she came to live with me and my mother. Otherwise, I wouldn't have anyone. Even my mother never seemed to accept me, and I wasn't sure why.

I remember one birthday when my father came to visit. I asked him why I couldn't live with him. He told me one day when I was older I could, but for now I had to stay with my mom. At first I believed him until I got older and realized that he was probably just doing what adults do, lie to their children so they stop asking questions.

At least he didn't look at me like something was wrong with me. If I'm being honest, every time I saw my father, he looked at me with awe. But nonetheless his involvement was limited, and it was something I accepted a long time ago. I accepted the fact that it was me and my mother. She never abused me physically, but she was very clear in letting me know what a disappointment I was. She treated Stevie more like a daughter than me. I should have grown up hating Stevie for it, but it didn't work out that way. Stevie put me over my mother, and I've always been loyal to her because of it.

This town has a lot of negative memories and people in it. I've considered leaving Hallowsdeep, but something keeps me rooted here. I'm not sure if it's the magic or the coven, but I have a magnetic pull to this place. It's almost like I can't leave, a petty part of myself also refuses to be the one to leave.

With a little too much force, I grip the steering wheel as I park and grab the Tupperware of truth truffles and make my way to Hex. It's busy and Heather seems to have everything under control. I swear if she's the one stealing, I will be devastated and out of one of the best managers I've ever found. She's part angel, but you would never suspect with the filthy mouth she has on her.

My plan is to get through the late shift and give the truth truffles out and then I'm able to handle business with the person stealing when everyone leaves.

"Hey, Blair. Can you tell Otto we need a fresh tap on the Sam Adams?" Heather asks me behind the bar.

"Sure thing," I say, walking to the back and finding Otto.

When I look at him, he seems like the biggest culprit. He's always tired when he comes to work. As far as I can tell, he's human. I wonder if he's stealing for a habit. His features always look a bit off.

He's robust, with a bald head and dark beard. His white shirt is stained, but he stays in the back so I don't worry much about his appearance usually.

"Otto, we need a new Sam Adams."

He grunts, going over and grabbing it immediately. I'm not sure if he's mute or chooses not to speak, but I've never heard him talk.

I pass him and sit in my office with the truffles. I sigh, looking at the chocolates and remember what it felt like when Dax and I both had eaten them. It was both freeing and terrifying at the same time. I don't like how much I like him, and the way he makes me feel is unfamiliar.

Speaking of familiars, maybe I should turn the thief into a mouse and feed them to Fez. The idea makes me smile, even though I know I couldn't really turn someone into a mouse.

I waste time online, checking and seeing if anyone in the coven has been active or posted anything about my mother. My research comes up with no results. I look down at my phone and realize it's closing time. I leave my office as my employees are cleaning up for the night.

"Oh, I totally forgot. Stevie made these chocolates to thank everyone for picking up the slack while she's out sick." I open up the top of the container, holding out the box and watch as each employee takes a chocolate.

"Mmm," Heather says as she pops it in her mouth, so does Otto, Glen, Lucas, Bethany, and Lilly. The only person who is missing is Jeremy. So if it isn't one of them, then I will automatically know who did it.

Once everyone has swallowed. I don't waste any time. "Who has been stealing from the restaurant?"

"Otto," everyone says in unison, and it doesn't escape me that he can somehow not answer the question. Appears he's not mute by choice.

"Everyone can leave besides Otto," I say and my employees all leave out of the front door. I wait until they're all gone before I stare at the much larger man. If I didn't have magic, I would be afraid of his larger presence.

"Otto, is this true? Have you been stealing from me?"

I can tell he's trying to fight the magic of the truffle. Maybe he needed to eat two because he's such a large man?

Finally, a nod of his head.

"Why are you stealing from me, Otto?"

He looks around, and his gaze is shaky and uncertain. He takes me off guard when I watch his body somehow get larger and he smacks me across the chest, throwing me back against a table and chairs.

It knocks the wind out of me, and I breathe heavily before I can speak. *Cadere,* I chant, hoping to knock him to the floor. He doesn't fall and I check in with my magic, making sure it's still there.

What the fuck is happening?

Otto keeps getting larger and larger in front of me, his form looking less and less human as he grows. He doesn't look like he's made of skin and bone anymore. It's almost like he's made out of clay. His stature is nearly seven feet tall now, his skin a reddish earthy hue. I wrap my brain around his appearance and wonder what he is.

Fuck. A fucking golem. I hired a gods damn golem and had no clue. I'm trying to think hard about what magic I can use on him. He's not a corporeal person, he's not a person at all, really. Before I can come up with anything, his large hand is around my throat, pushing me against the table. Blocking my airway and my ability to speak.

He pulls out a knife from his pocket and starts to cut my wrists. The cuts are shallow, enough to make me bleed, but not enough to kill me. Just enough to slow me down and make me immobile. I can feel the tackiness of my blood dripping down my wrists. I shift in his arms, trying to get the knife out of his hand. My hands are covered in blood and I can barely get a hold of anything. I hear a rumble from his chest with frustration as he continues to try to cut me. I hit him with my fists and he keeps slashing the knife, causing cuts along my forearms and palms. I don't know what to do. He's too fucking strong and I can't say anything with his hand on my throat. Does he want my blood for something? I'm starting to feel woozy, and I need to hold it together, I need to figure out a way to get myself out of this mess.

I try some wordless magic and move chairs and other items in the room to hit him, but nothing fazes him. He's too strong and I can feel my airway giving out. While I'm a witch and can live for a very long time, I can still be killed, and it feels like that's exactly what Otto is about to do to me.

Panic fills my blood stream. I push my magic out of me hard. Willing my hand to burn him. All it does is make his hand harder around my neck. He's staring at me, emotionless, his features muddied. I can see where eyes would go and the shape of a mouth, but he's no longer human.

Someone created Otto to do their bidding, and clearly, their highest order was to take me out. I'm feeling dizzy as my nails scrape against his mucky skin when I hear a feral-like growl from the corner.

Otto goes flying across the room, and I gasp for breath. I feel lightheaded and try to apply pressure to my wrists. I try to use a healing spell, but the lack of blood and exertion of magic is holding me back. Every time I whisper "sana" my arm starts to heal but opens back up again. After this is over I need to spend more time learning stronger healing magic. A clang of chairs alerts me to the corner of the room as I watch Otto hit the floor, Dax jumping on top of him. His fists are powerful as he hits Otto. My hits didn't make a dent at all, but I watch as Dax strikes him hard enough to shift the clay.

"You thought to hurt *my* fucking witch? You mindless piece of shit."

Dax hits Otto again, hitting him hard in the face repeatedly. It's not the same sound as if he was hitting bone, it sounds like an earthquake in the restaurant as Dax's powerful fists hit him over and over. Floor boards crack in half under the weight of Otto's head hitting the wood. The walls in the room shake and the restaurant is being destroyed. My eyes widen in shock as Dax drags Otto across the bar top, glasses shattering loudly against the walls and floors. His strength is astounding. But the moment he takes a chance to look over at me, Otto strikes.

Dax breathes heavily as Otto is able to grab Dax by the waist and run him into a wall, Dax's back hits hard against the wall, all the framed images come crashing to the floor. Otto wraps his hand around Dax's throat, doing the same thing he did to me, but he doesn't try to cut him. Just tries to block or crush his airway.

I feel weak, so weak, but I need to act fast. Think, think. He's basically an inanimate object. Even though he can move, he moves at the behest of his creator, he's clay. *Surge sursus* I say as I watch the golem rise from the floor. It shocks him enough that his grip loosens from Dax's throat, and he falls from the floor as the golem continues floating until he hits the ceiling.

Dax is back on his feet as he comes to check on me. With Otto up on the ceiling for now, we're fine. His large palms grab my face as he looks at my arms and eyes. A low groan leaving his lips.

He takes a pocket knife from his back pocket and I flinch as he pops the blade.

"I'm going to take care of you, you're okay, babe. I got you," he says as he slices his wrist and drops his blood on top of my bleeding arms. He pets my hair as I watch his blood heal my wounds. I still feel so out of it, like I can't think.

"It will stop the bleeding and heal your wounds, but you still lost a lot of blood. How are you feeling?" I don't answer and his palms are on my face. "Little witch?"

"Tired," I say, pressing my face against his palm.

"We need to get the scroll from his mouth and destroy it," he says, and it dawns on me that I don't know shit about golems. If he wasn't here, I would have probably died.

"Why are you here?"

"Doesn't matter. Can you get him down from the ceiling?" I nod and flick my wrist, sending Otto to the floor. The weight of his body breaking even more floorboards. I don't think insurance is going to cover this mess. He's stunned enough that Dax is able to straddle him, his hands shaking as he grits his teeth and pries his mouth open with his powerful fists. "Blair, grab the scroll." I can tell that Dax is mustering every ounce of strength he has to hold his mouth open. Otto hits Dax's side, and he winces, but continues to hold his jaw firmly.

I feel like I might fall over, but I wobble over to where Dax has him pinned, and I grab the scroll poking out from his cakey mouth. As soon as I have it free, Dax lets go of Otto, a small flame appearing from Dax's fingertips as I open the scroll and read the name before Dax lights it on fire.

As soon as the scroll is lit aflame, Otto turns to dust beneath Dax's body, making his knees land on the hardwood.

I fall hard on the ground next to him, my legs hurt, I feel sick. I want to crawl into a hole and sleep for five days. Dax's muscular arms are wrapped around me quickly. Shushing sounds are made into my dark hair as I feel him pick me up and cradle me to his chest.

"You need to get some rest, some blood, too. I'm going to take you home, sweet girl. Daddy is going to take care of you."

"No one ever takes care of me." It's like word vomit as I look up at his green eyes.

"Now someone does. This might make you feel more nauseous. But I promise you'll be okay."

"Wha—"

It's like I'm sucked into a vacuum and my body shifts within itself or is shaken like a paint can as a loud pop cracks through my ears. We're instantaneously in front of my house. Dax puts me down on the grass as I empty the contents of my stomach. His large hand rubs soothing circles on my back.

"Get it all out, babe. You're all right. I'm going to take care of you. You did so good for your first portal. And the way you handled that golem. I'm so proud of you."

I groan as nothing else is coming out of my stomach and Dax picks me up again, my head lolling backward. I want to sleep.

He jostles me slightly. "Stay awake for me, pet. Need to check you out before you go to sleep."

I blink up at him and hear my cousin's screech from the porch. "What happened to her!"

My cousin's soft, small hands feel different from Dax's. "That big bald fucker attacked her at Hex. He was a golem."

"Otto was a fucking golem?"

"Apparently. She lost a lot of blood and used a lot of magic."

"I have some transfusion potions. Take her up to the bedroom. I see the dried blood, but where are the cuts?"

"I took care of that already."

"Come on," Stevie says, leading us into the house, and I can't help it when I fall asleep against Dax's perfect, warm chest. He feels so good, so safe. Who would have thought the most comforting place for me would be in between a demon's arms.

CHAPTER FIFTEEN

DAX

I take two steps at a time as I hold Blair tightly against my chest. I've never truly experienced fear until today. While Blair isn't as frail as a human, she isn't fully immortal, either. Witches can live for an extremely long time; the oldest witch I met was around two millennia. While they can live an expansive life, they can also be killed fairly easily, at least in terms of other supernaturals.

She looks so fragile as I place her delicately on her bed. If that fucker was anything other than a golem, I would have made him suffer. But golems are nonfeeling—they're made beings—their only motivation is the will of whatever being created them.

I was so focused on getting Blair the fuck out of there and getting rid of the golem, I didn't even get to read the scroll. The scroll always has the name of the golem's creator on it. It looked like Blair was able to read it before I set it aflame, but I won't know more until she wakes up.

Her breaths are even, and her chest rises steadily, making me feel better. I push her dark, messy hair from her face and cup her cheek. A sound from the side of the room has me on high alert until I realize it's her familiar sliding from his cage. He quickly slithers over the floor and onto the bed. His body gently constricts her arm, comforting her.

Her familiar narrows his eyes at me and hisses. "Don't look at me like that," I tell him, giving a glare back.

The snake's tongue sticks out, but he rests his head on her palm. What I know of familiars is that they have a direct link to their magical counterpart. Almost like a telepathy of emotions, but I don't think they can actually communicate. Knowing Blair, though, she can probably talk to the fucking thing. She has surprised me at every turn with what I know of stereotypical witches.

Stevie opens Blair's bedroom door and gives me a tight smile. "Fez, calm down, she's fine," she coos at the snake. Her words comforting him as his tongue swipes between Blair's thumb and pointer finger.

Stevie pets the snake, which I didn't even know you could fucking pet a snake. She tilts Blair's chin back with her thumb and pours a dark gray substance into her mouth. "Blood replenishing potion," she tells me as she shuts Blair's mouth and says something under her breath, causing her to swallow.

"For fuck's sake, I've never seen Blair this weak in my life, now it's twice in one week. I don't like this." Stevie looks flustered as she rubs soothing circles on Blair's arm.

"I spoke to the witch who owns that shitty shop on Main Street."

"Martha? What did she say?" Stevie asks, arching an eyebrow.

"She said that Blair's mother is in hiding and something about how she's,"—I nod toward Blair—" strong enough."

Stevie looks down at Blair's sleeping body. "Clover said something about someone telling Josie that the sacrifice had to happen, that if they did it, the coven would be stronger."

"Was the coven getting weaker?"

Stevie nods her head. "It's actually kind of odd. Blair and I are really the only ones who haven't noticed any kind of depletion. But in general, yeah, the coven is weaker. That's why we have the moon rituals. Then slowly throughout the month, the other members of the coven feel weaker."

"How does Blair feel after the ritual?"

Her brows furrow. "Weakened."

"They must pull from her power. Is that bitch still in the basement?" I ask her.

"Clover? Yeah, why?"

"Let's go have a little chat."

Stevie doesn't even question it. She looks down at Fez. "Let us know if she wakes up?"

The snake nods its freaky little head and makes me shiver. I give Blair one last concerned glance as I follow the red-headed witch down to the basement. She opens the door and as I go to enter, I'm blocked by an invisible wall, making me growl in frustration.

"Shit. Blair is so much better at wards than I am."

"Blood?" I ask, just as a guess because that's how I was allowed in the house.

"We can try," Stevie says, conjuring a needle and pricking my finger and saying an incantation as the droplet splashes against the floor.

I can feel the wards open and we walk through the door. Clover looks disgusting, mousey, in the same clothes Blair and I took her in. It smells musty and stale in the room. I grimace at her, and she looks at me with wide eyes.

"You!" she shouts, pushing her body to the headboard. I guess Blair knew her wards were strong enough, and she didn't need to be tied up. "You helped her kidnap me!"

"Actually, you're an adult. It's an abduction," I say, planting my ass on the corner of the bed. "We have some questions for you, Clover." I glare at her.

"I answered her questions, and she promised me I'd be taken care of. All I've had is a sandwich."

"Bad behavior isn't rewarded, Clover." I tell her, picking up an invisible piece of lint from my pants.

"I didn't do anything!"

"You tried to sacrifice Blair. But that's not what I'm here to talk about. It's apparent you're very much on a need to know basis."

"God, why did I sleep with him? It wasn't even worth it. Just help me get out of here. My coven is strong. Whatever you want, we can give it to you."

I tsk at her and stand from the bed. I'm not sure what the Hell she's talking about but that's not the point. "The monthly rituals before you tried to kill her. Were you draining her?"

"I'm not telling you shit."

I'm so fast she doesn't see me coming as my hand wraps around her throat and I push her head back hard against the headboard. I can feel my power radiating off of me and it only takes her a moment to realize it as well. Stevie is quiet in the corner, patiently observing.

"I'd think really fucking hard about what comes out of your mouth next, Clover. There are far worse things than dying. Did you know that? I've got plenty of friends in Hell who are bored out of their fucking mind. They would be so excited to have a little play thing like you. Plain, simple, and most of all, stupid as fuck. I'd consider collecting whatever remaining brain cells you have tumbling in that small little head of yours and answer my fucking questions. Do you understand?" I give her throat a tight little squeeze before releasing her and she nods her head as tears leak from her eyes.

"We were just taking a little of her power. Blair is different. Our coven, we gather our power from the earth. Once Blair was born, everything changed. We couldn't recharge the same. It's like our coven was solely tied to Blair. Most of the elders have been looking for a way to change that. So we used to do the rituals and everyone was happy. But when the possibility of not having our power tied to Blair came up, the coven took it. I'm sorry! Okay, please don't hurt me."

"I don't know what plans Blair has for you. But let me make one fucking thing clear. You attempt to hurt Blair again, you get a whiff of someone wanting to hurt Blair and don't tell me, you're done."

She gulps and cries as she nods her head. I look over in the corner and Stevie is smiling wickedly. Not such a sweet witch after all. Stevie conjures a speaker and pulls her phone out of her pocket.

"This is to help you think about how you weren't honest with Blair and me earlier."

Look what you made me do by Taylor Swift blasts out of the speakers and Clover groans as she continues crying into her palms. Stevie and I exit the room and the sound of the music can no longer be heard.

"You're a deceptive witch, you know that?"

She shrugs. "I've learned from the best. I think Blair will be proud of the song on repeat. It seems like an excellent form of torture."

"How long do you plan on keeping her?"

"Blair wants to keep her till the full moon as an insurance policy."

I nod. "Smart."

"You really like my cousin, huh?"

I groan and scratch my beard. I don't know how to handle these feelings I'm having for Blair. This overwhelming feeling of possessiveness and care isn't something I've ever experienced. Sure, I've had feelings of lust and even enjoyed a few dates here and there. But this connection and need for Blair is wholly unfamiliar. "It's complicated."

"As are most things with Blair. She should wake up in a few hours. Are you planning on staying?"

I should go home, sleep in my bed. But there's no way in Hell I can leave her. "Yeah, I'll stay with her."

"If Fez gets too territorial, just give him chin rubs," she says, walking down the hall to what I assume is her bedroom. I gently open Blair's door, and she's in the same position I left her. Fez is sleeping, wrapped gently around her arm.

She's still wearing her outfit from earlier—a part of me wants to change her so she's more comfortable—but I decide to leave her be as I undress except for my boxers and crawl into bed.

The golem wasn't a huge challenge to me, but the clay fucker was strong. I easily doze off with plans to visit my little witch and see how she's doing in her subconscious. It doesn't take but a moment for me to find her.

She looks stunning in a black cinch dress as she pulls petals off a flower as she sits under a willow tree; the leaves swaying from the wind.

"Dax?" she says in a soft voice. Her eyebrows are furrowed as I take a seat next to her. "Are you a part of my dream for real, or is this something a demon can do?"

"I can dream walk as a demon."

"Is this the first time you've come to one of my dreams?"

"No," I reply and she smirks at me.

"See anything interesting?"

"Mmm, the dreams I've seen haven't been happy ones." She hums in agreement as she plucks another petal from the flower.

Her eyes are pink when she glances back at me, and I can't hold back my smile when I look at her. "I used to come to this tree with Stevie when we were little. It was our fortress. We didn't let any of the other girls come in here. I know I seem like the tough one now, but back then, Stevie would protect me from the other young witches."

My hand rests on her thigh as my back pushes against the strong bark. "Why did they cast you out?"

"I'm not sure. It was always like that. And at first I tried. I tried so fucking hard to fit in, Dax. I held back how strong I was. I was polite and kind, and I tried to get into the potions and the earth side of magic. It didn't matter what I did, so eventually I just leaned into what they thought about me. They thought I was weird and different and I became bitter. If they were going to call me a bitch, I was going to be the biggest bitch they ever met."

"There's nothing wrong with being different."

"No, it's just hard when you don't feel like you have anyone."

"You have Stevie, and now you have me."

Her head rests on my shoulder, and she sighs. "I wish it were that easy."

"We're going to talk more about that when you're conscious."

"Ugh, fine." She picks her head off of my shoulder and looks at me. She's so beautiful like this, I want more time with her at ease and relaxed.

Her dark hair blows in the breeze, and I tuck it behind her ear.

"Promise me one thing?" she says.

"Anything."

She looks at me, her eyes an odd shade of yellow, close to her snake's.

"That you'll never stop looking at me the way you do," she says, and I smile.

"How exactly is that, little witch?"

"Like I'm something precious, someone worth caring about."

I go to open my mouth to respond when I'm ripped from her dream. I open my eyes to a red eyed Blair lying next to me. They quickly change to pink as she catches her breath and realizes it's me and Fez slithers around her arm tighter. She looks down at her forearms before she looks at my face. She lightly pets the top of the snake's head, calming him.

"Were you in my dream?"

"Yes," I say honestly, and she nods her head.

"I'm okay?" she asks, her eyes blinking in confusion. I stroke her hair off her face and the snake hisses at me.

"Yes, your wounds are healed, and Stevie gave you some potions. The golem is dead. Did you see the name before the scroll was destroyed?"

"Mara," she whispers, and my heart stops.

CHAPTER SIXTEEN

BLAIR

"Mara?" Dax repeats, scrubbing his face with his tattooed fingers.

"Yeah, does the name mean anything to you? Because it doesn't to me."

Dax shoots up out of the bed and begins pacing around the room. "Fuck, fuck. Fuck!" he shouts. Fez is so done with the conversation as I rub his chin and he slithers back to his cozy, warm enclosure.

"Dax?"

"She's why I'm in Hallowsdeep."

"Okay?"

"She's a demon who has been possessing people and leaving a serious body count and worse behind. Asmo and I have been tasked with bringing her back to Hell."

"What does that have to do with me?"

"Exactly. *Fuck*. What does she want with you? This is bad." His pacing doesn't stop as his fingers rake through his dark hair. The few gray hairs around his temples seem more prevalent tonight. He seems worried and I don't like it, but I also can't help the warm feeling wrapping around my heart around someone being concerned for me.

I stand up and I'm wobbly. Dax is quickly next to me, grabbing my arm and helping me sit back down on the bed.

My comforter rustling around my body, my hands against the soft fabric, supporting my weight as I sit up.

"Why would a demon want me?" I rub my temple and groan.

"I don't know, but we're going to fucking find out."

I rub my head, a migraine forming right behind my right eye. The kind that makes you want to sedate yourself or scoop out your fucking eyeball.

"Babe, you okay?"

"My head hurts," I say, not liking the vulnerability in my voice.

"Let's take care of you. You need more sleep. We can talk in the morning."

"Dax?"

"Yeah, babe?" he says as he opens my drawers, getting me comfy clothes.

"Why were you at Hex tonight?"

"We can talk about it tomorrow."

"No, we can talk about it now." I pout, with my arms crossed and my lower lip protruding. It's slightly pathetic, I've never been so petulant in my life.

He gives me a stern look. "Listen, little witch, I'm not going to spank your perfect ass when you aren't feeling well. But I will do it when you're feeling better. I told you we would talk tomorrow when you aren't recovering. Now let me take care of you. Got it?"

I sigh but nod my head.

"Arms up," he says, and I listen. He removes my shirt and bra and puts my large Fleetwood Mac shirt on. He gets to his knees and slides off my shoes before his hands glide up my thighs and he rolls my skirt off. "These fucking skirts are going to kill me."

I giggle and then wince at the feeling of my head pounding. Dax stands and cups my jaw. "Is the migraine from today or something else?"

"They happen when I use a lot of power, or when I'm stressed."

He nods his head and goes to my bathroom. It's not long before he's handing me two capsules of Tylenol and a glass of water. I take them quickly and place the water on my nightstand. He eases his large body next to mine, pulling me in close so my head is resting above his arm.

"Two nights in a row. What will the other demons say?" I joke. He stiffens beneath me before he kisses my hair.

"Get some sleep, Blair."

I'm out before I can even reply.

I feel so good, so full, so warm. A soft fuzzy feeling is over-whelming me and I don't want to wake up. I don't want this feeling to go away. The tingling feeling creeps up my spine, and it's when I realize I'm nearly about to orgasm.

I blink my eyes rapidly as I watch Dax devouring my cunt. His thumbs spread my lips as his tongue laps at my clit. His beard grazes between my thighs, and I sigh in contentment as he continues sucking and lapping around my clit. I'm so wet I can hear him swallow my cum.

"Fuck, your tongue feels so good on my pussy, Dax. Please don't stop. You're going to make me come all over your face. You want that?" He hums and he sucks even harder on my clit, his grip on my thighs turning near brutal. A vibration of a growl from his throat makes me jump off the edge as my back arches off the bed and I convulse from the strength of the orgasm.

I expect him to stop and to release my thighs, but he doesn't. He keeps sucking my clit at a pulsating pace. I can feel my clit swelling against his tongue as he doesn't let up.

"Holy—" His lips leave my clit and he smacks my pussy with the tips of his fingers making me come again.

My body trembles as I watch his head raise from in between my thighs. A string of my cum drips from his bottom lip onto his beard. He grins at me, that goddamn dimple making an appearance. He kisses my thigh and wipes off his chin before crawling up my body and placing a chaste kiss to my lips. I stare at him wide-eyed.

"I'm a little shocked how long it took you to wake up," he says, nuzzling against the crook of my neck. Someone is extremely affectionate in the mornings. He fists his cock, lining up the head of his dick against my already extremely wet pussy. "I wanted to fuck you so bad, pet. But I wanted to make sure you were really okay with this. We haven't really had a chance to talk about everything." He swipes the tip of his length up and down my entrance, waiting for permission.

I wrap my legs around him and dig my heels into his firm ass, pushing him against me. He kisses me and we both smile while we kiss. It's fucking adorable and gross at the same time. It's never been this carefree and easy. This is nothing like the last time we had sex. Dax takes his time. It's a lazy morning fuck, and I like it far more than I ever should. His languid strokes and the way his hands gently touch my hair and face. *It's too much.*

Not being able to handle the intimacy, I take matters into my own hands and thrust up from the bottom faster, making

Dax groan. "Are you trying to top from the bottom, little witch?"

"Just fuck me," I say harshly.

It's almost like Dax can taste the lie, but he doesn't call me out on my bullshit. "You need it rough, pet?"

I nod my head as Dax's hand wraps around the side of my throat. I can feel my blood rush to my face and I'm not able to speak. My breaths are shallow and hard as Dax builds up a brutal pace, fucking me relentlessly. It's almost like he's angry, but that can't be right. A hard no strings attached fuck is what every man—demon—would want, right?

"Who am I?" he asks, his grip on my throat loosening. Waiting for me to speak. Deep down I know what he wants me to say, but I feel like saying it will solidify what this is, and I can't have that, can I?

"Dax," I reply. Surely this whole daddy thing was a way to appease me. He doesn't really want that. I don't really want that—I lie to myself. If I let him take that role, I'm giving someone else control. Everything in my life right now is a fucking mess. There's no way he wants to put up with all that.

"Wrong. Who am I?" I look up at his face, gone is the smile from earlier, he looks determined and dare I say, annoyed.

I can tell he's getting irritated with me, that I'm not giving him what he wants. He wanted this sweet early morning intimacy, and I changed the game to give him what I feel comfortable with. I shake my head, and he groans.

He squeezes my throat harder. I can hardly breathe as his pubic hair grinds against my clit. "Come on my fucking cock, right now," he nearly growls. I feel my pussy contract against his impressive length and watch as he shakes and follows me over the edge.

As soon as he comes, he flips over and lies on his back. He isn't smiling or sweet like he was the other night, and I wonder how I managed to fucked this up. Could he actually want something more with me? Should I break down my walls and allow that?

"Dax?"

"Go take a shower, Blair," he says, rolling over to his side. I stare at his form for a moment. I don't want to have these feelings. Maybe it's best if I've pissed him off. He can cut and run now. I'm not worth investing time and energy into. My throat chokes up with emotion and I go to turn and leave for the shower when his hand reaches out and grabs my forearm.

"Come here, Blair," he says, and it's embarrassing how quickly I jump at the chance to be in his arms.

"I'm sorry," I say into his shoulders.

"No, I'm sorry. I was acting like an asshole. This is so new. I think we need to talk through some things."

"Okay," I reply, happy that I don't have to look him in the eye.

"This is fucking intense and has been moving at warped speed. I think we need to let each other know where we stand."

"Okay," I say, playing with his chest hair. Not comfortable putting all my cards on the table.

"This connection we have goes beyond physical. Something with our magic is drawing us together, and I want to see where it goes. I want to take you out, take care of you, treat you right. But I can't do that if you don't let me in, Blair."

I turn to face him. He looks genuine and my heart sinks. This is all built on a lie and yet this beautiful, powerful, sometimes scary man is offering me everything I've ever wanted. I smile at him, a plan forming in the back of my mind on how to give me everything I want. "It's hard for me," I say softly.

"I understand. I just need you to try to be honest with me, okay?"

"I can try," I say and he smiles, giving me a grin.

"That's all I ask. Now, get your cute ass in the shower so we can get breakfast."

I lean over and give him a quick kiss. Before I get up I look at him questioningly. "You never told me why you were at Hex last night. If you weren't there, things could have gotten a lot worse."

He rubs his beard and slightly bangs his head against the headboard. "We have a lead on the human that Mara might be possessing currently."

I furrow my brows and look at him. "And?"

"And she works at Inferno."

I gape at him. I've, of course, heard about it. It piqued my interest, but it's a couple invite only, not that you need to stay with your partner. I haven't dated a supernatural in a long time, and there was no way Stevie was going to be my plus one. "And?"

"And I need a date in order to get access, and I was going to ask you to come with me."

"Yes!" I beam and bounce on the bed.

"But," he says, arching an eyebrow at me, "I'm not sure if that's a good idea now after the golem incident. I don't like the idea of putting you in danger."

I can't help it when I cross my arms and look at him. "If anything, it makes even more sense for me to go. I'm going, Dax."

"Babe, I don't think I've made myself clear on the dynamic of how this relationship is going to go. When you said you wanted me to be your daddy, what did that mean to you?"

I shrug my shoulders and play with the bedspread, not liking the idea of explaining everything. Why does this man have to talk so fucking much? Can't we just have a good time and worry about this shit, I don't know, never?

He shakes his head, noting how stubborn I am. "I'll tell you what it means to me. I've never had anyone call me that before, but I fucking love hearing it from your lips, Blair. It makes my heart race and my cock hard. To me, it means I'm in charge of your pleasure and keeping you safe. I never want you to change who you are, and I don't expect you to be submissive to me all the time. I love that you're powerful and confident, but with me, I want to get to the point where you can trust me enough to take care of things for you."

My jaw drops as I take in everything he just said. He wants to take care of me? But I've always taken care of myself. It's become clear to me that I'm not the domme I always tried to be. Being his submissive in the bedroom will be easy enough. But the vulnerability of his care is terrifying.

"I've never really had anyone take care of me before."

He smirks, *damn dimple.* "Let's just try and see how things go?"

Old insecurities creep in and I can't help it, it's like I've taken a freaking truth truffle again. "You would just be seeing me, right?"

His brows furrow, and his hands cup my jaw. "Little witch, you take up so much fucking space in my mind there's no way I could see anyone else."

"Okay, I'll try."

"Good girl. Now go take a shower and let's go get some crepes." My stomach growls comically, and I pop off the bed and walk to my bathroom.

I'm not sure when my plots got so complicated or when the majority of Hallowsdeep became my enemy. Beyond my coven and some lunatic demon trying to kill me, now I need to figure out a way to make Ryan forget I ever existed.

CHAPTER SEVENTEEN

BLAIR

Dax pulls out my chair for me as we sit at my favorite breakfast spot. Archibald's has been a staple in Hallowsdeep for as long as I remember. Not much has changed since I was a kid, either. All the tables and chairs are mismatched. The round table I'm sitting at is an aged linoleum table top, probably made in the early eighties. Meanwhile the chair I'm sitting in looks like it belongs to someone's dining table in 1954. I swear the man just drives around town seeing who is throwing shit out and uses it to fill up the small breakfast shop.

It's nostalgic and cute. I love it here, and the company isn't so bad either. I'm thankful that Dax didn't hold this morning against me. I knew what he wanted and I was feeling insecure and couldn't give it to him at that moment. He's so patient with me, I just hope I don't wear that patience out.

"Do you know what you want?"

"Brown sugar, strawberries, and lemon preserves, please."

"You got it." He kisses my hair before he goes to the front counter to place our order. Who knew a demon could be so nice? The only time I've seen him slightly irritated is when he was at my bar with Asmo, but honestly, the guy can be fairly annoying. It would be hard not to have a short temper with him. We won't mention the whole watching him rip apart a golem with his bare hands, that was self-defense.

I watch Dax's ass in his dark denim jeans as he stands in line to order our food. The bell to the front door chimes, breaking my concentration and my jaw drops when I watch the most stunning woman I've ever seen strut through the small shop. She makes the place look cheap with how stylish and put together she is. She has long dark hair in a ponytail, tight jeans that shape to the curve of her ass and a black t-shirt that clings so tightly to her torso it's like a second skin.

Her red-bottom shoes click against the worn, aged tile as she places her perfectly manicured hand on Dax's shoulder.

I see red.

The sound of the legs of my chair scraping against the tile is jarring, and nearly everyone in the small shop turns to look at me. I'm halfway to where Dax and this unknown threat are standing when I watch as Dax flicks off her pristine hand.

"What do you want, Kas?"

"A crepe, obviously."

She goes to put her hand on his shoulder and he grimaces. "Don't touch me."

"Oh, Asmo doesn't mind."

"Yeah, well, I fucking mind," Dax replies and my inky black heart grows two sizes larger.

With no care in the world, I stand next to Dax and interlace our fingers together. He smiles down at me before he faces the woman next to me.

"Oh, new pet?" The woman named Kas asks, and my heart deflates back to its standard size. I don't let the irritation show on my face. Not the way she's talking to me, or the idea that I'm one of many Dax has filled this role for. If he was being honest then at least I'm the first to call him daddy, so there's that.

"Oh, are you the old pet?" I ask her in a sharp voice. She gives me a smile so sinister from that alone I know she's supernatural.

She tsks her tongue before she looks me up and down. I've been sized up by plenty of women, and if I'm not mistaken, it's an appraisal of intrigue.

"You must be the mean witch Asmo keeps going on about. I can see the appeal, Daxaddon."

Dax groans next to me and his hand tightens around mine. Kas is clearly testing his patience.

"Asmo has quite the mouth on him," I say. It's glaringly obvious she's a demon if she knows Dax's full name and hangs out with Asmo as well. I know I need to have my guard up with her. But something about her attitude resonates with me. Something inside of me tells me to make this woman my friend instead of my enemy.

"You have no idea. You look like you have quite the mouth on you too, little witch." I don't particularly like Dax's pet name coming from her lips. Dax seems to have similar feelings.

"What do you want, Kas?" Dax asks her, clearly exacerbated by her circling around the conversation.

"Just making sure that everything is going to go as planned for tomorrow night."

"Everything will be fine."

"We can't afford to fuck this up," she says.

"You have no idea. Can you leave us alone?"

Kas ignores him and faces me. "What are you wearing tomorrow?" she asks.

"Uh, probably a skirt, a crop top, or a bra."

Kas taps her chin. "Meet me at Luxe in North Grove in an hour."

"What?"

"If you're coming to Inferno with us, you need to look the part. I'm going to make sure you two don't ruin this by not being prepared."

Dax opens his mouth to answer her, and I step in front of him. "I'll meet you there in an hour."

Kas gives me another evil grin, and I swear I can hear Dax basically growl next to me. "See you there."

She spins on her heel, exiting the shop without another word.

"I don't think this is a good idea," Dax says next to me.

"It will be fine," I say, squeezing his hand reassuringly.

Dax drives me to Luxe on the back of his motorcycle. He's fussing about me meeting with Kas as he takes off my helmet for me and puts it on the bike. He takes extra care in flattening out my skirt, too.

"You really don't have to do this," he says.

"Which part?"

"Shopping with Kas. I like the clothes you wear."

"Kas seems *okay*, and I want to be prepared tomorrow."

Dax shakes out his hair from his helmet and pulls out his wallet, getting his credit card. "Don't worry about the cost, whatever you want to get. I wouldn't be upset if you got a few things for me to take off of you later." He leans in, grabbing two fistfuls of my ass cheeks as he kisses behind my ear.

"Any requests?"

"I'd like to see you in something pink," he says, smiling so widely his dimples are on display. I give him a glare with no heat. If the man is paying, I'll oblige.

"Is there a credit limit on this?" I ask, holding the card up with two fingers.

"Nope, whatever my little witch wants."

"Hm, demon detective pays well?" I say jokingly, placing the card in my purse.

"Mmm. Text me when you're done and I'll come pick you up. If Kas does anything to piss you off, I can come right back."

"I can handle her," I say confidently.

"I know, pet." He leans in, giving me a kiss that probably isn't meant to take place in public, but I relish in it. I'm on cloud nine over everything he has done for me lately. The way he treats me in private and in public isn't something that I've ever experienced before. I feel cherished and honestly, this whole being spoiled thing is pretty nice.

Dax doesn't get back on his bike, but walks a few more shops down the road—doing what? I have no clue. All I know is daddy gave me his credit card, and I'd be stupid to look a gift horse in the mouth. Plus, I want to look hot at Inferno, and even though I might not know how I feel about Kas, the woman has amazing taste.

As soon as I enter the boutique shop, a small man dressed in all black with perfectly styled brown hair greets me. At first he looks at me like I don't belong here, but he speaks to me anyway. "Welcome to Luxe. Do you have an appointment?"

"I'm meeting someone named Kas," I say. His demeanor changes to become more helpful, his gaze less scrutinizing as he smiles.

"Oh wonderful, follow me. My name is Baron and I will be helping you ladies this evening. If there's anything you need, please just let me know. Water, champagne?" Who names their child Baron? I give him a once over similar to the one that he gave me and nod my head.

"Champagne would be great," I say. Baron bows his head and walks away to fetch the champagne. The store matches the name. Everything hanging up is high end and expensive. The shop is pristine white, with lingerie and expensive clothing hanging on the walls and on delicate racks. I walk to the back to the fitting rooms, and I'm greeted by the site of Kas in a full catsuit. I have no clue how she got into the tight fitting leather, but I'd be a liar if I said it didn't look spectacular on her. It shapes her body perfectly, she looks like a combination of evil superhero and dominatrix.

"Ah, you came," she says as she turns in the mirror, admiring her own ass. I can't blame her.

"Figured I could use all the help I could get."

Kas nods her head. "Your style is cute, don't get me wrong. Inferno is upscale, and as Dax's sub, you need to meet a certain requirement."

"Who says he isn't the submissive one?"

Kas throws her head back in a deep laugh. "Don't get me wrong, witch. I'm sure you can play top anytime you want." Her heels click as she walks toward me and turns up my chin. "But the fact is, that feeling that Dax gives you when he takes control, tells you what to do, is stronger than any feeling you got by being in charge of someone else. Am I wrong?"

"You're not wrong," I say with an exaggerated sigh.

"Don't sound too put out about it. If Dax isn't giving what you need, sweetie, I can fill that void." Her thumb is under my chin and she makes me look into her almond-shaped brown eyes. She smiles wickedly again, and it's captivating. So captivating, I nearly need to shake my head to clear it.

"I'm happy with Dax," I say pointedly.

"Well, if you ever change your mind and want a mommy instead of a daddy, the invitation stands." She laughs maniacally as she walks back into the fitting room to try on something else.

Demons are fucking crazy.

I shake my head again and as I go to walk back to the main entrance, Baron stops me, holding out my champagne. I tenderly take the glass, holding the stem between two fingers. "Here you are. Kas and I have taken the liberty of choosing some items for you." He holds back a blush pink curtain. "If something doesn't fit right, just let me know and I can get you a new size."

I clear my throat. "Do you have anything in pink?" I ask quietly, hoping to fuck that Kas doesn't hear.

Baron smiles at me and nods to collect some more garments. I down my champagne in a few large gulps and place the empty glass on the cushioned bench in the changing room.

I grab the first option, and the material feels rich against my fingertips. It's not something that I would normally buy for myself. My wardrobe is comprised of different pleated skirts, a few jeans, and every single type of black shirt you can imagine. While it's not out of the realm of what I would buy, the price tag is more than I would ever spend.

When I put it on, I know Dax will love it and I decide to show Kas, against my better judgment.

Her smile is wide as she looks me up and down. "That's definitely the one for Inferno."

I nod my head, not wanting her to hit on me again or say some other weird shit. I try on a bunch of different bras and lingerie. Baron keeps handing me different things to try on, and I can't help but add nearly everything to the keep pile. People who say money can't bring you happiness have never tried on three hundred dollar bras before. The way the fabrics feel against my skin makes me feel confident.

I've never enjoyed shopping this much and I can't decide if it's because I'm not spending my own money, or that everything I buy will be removed by Dax's skilled hands.

Once my pile is sufficiently high, I put back on my outfit and Baron lets me know he will bring everything upfront for me. I think I could get used to this type of shopping.

Kas comes out at the same time, still as immaculately dressed as she was earlier. Baron also brought her selections up to the front.

"Did you get everything you need, little witch?"

I roll my eyes at this forward demon. "My name is Blair. I'm not your little witch."

"Unfortunately. I've been looking for a naughty little witch to play with. Seems I will need to keep looking."

"Yeah, you do that," I say, and Kas laughs.

"I'm not sure who is touchier about who, you or Dax."

I don't reply to her, and Baron brings up my total. "That will be seven thousand, eight hundred twenty-four dollars and twelve cents."

I give him a smile and hand over Dax's shiny gold card. Kas smiles next to me in approval.

Kas pays for her things, paying nearly double what I did. We both take our shopping bags out the front door. Dax's motorcycle is there, but he isn't, so I text him I'm ready to go.

"Dax should be here any minute," I say to Kas.

"I'll just wait until he gets back."

"You don't have to do that."

"Yes, I do. Demons might have the reputation of being cutthroat and unfeeling, but that's not the case. You're important to Dax, so you're important to me and Asmo. I'm happy for you both, I really am. But I need you to know that there can be no fuck-ups at Inferno. We need to make sure this job is done right."

I appreciate Kas' work ethic almost as much as I appreciate her wardrobe. "Trust me, I want this bitch caught just as much as you do. Anything I can do to help, I'm in."

Kas grins at me. "Such a shame." She shakes her head as muscular arms wrap around my waist.

"Ready to go, babe?" his gravelly voice asks.

"Yeah," I say, as I'm spinning around in his arms, Kas portals to wherever the Hell she lives.

"She wasn't too difficult, was she?"

"No, I think I actually might like her." I make a fake gagging sound as I dig into my wallet and hand Dax back his credit card.

"Did you get lots of pretty things?" he asks with a mischievous smile.

"I did, thank you, daddy," he beams and kisses me roughly. The stubble of his beard against my cheeks makes me smile into the kiss. He breaks away and the way he looks at me, *fuck*. It's like all my problems don't exist when I'm with Dax. "You'll have to wait to see, though."

"I can be patient, pet. Can you?" He asks seductively as he places the helmet on my head and takes my bags to put them in his side saddles.

He puts his own helmet on, getting on his bike first before he gives me a hand signal to jump on the back.

I know I should be stressed. So much is going on that's out of my control. But all I can do is bask in the feel of wrapping my arms around his sculpted abs and breathing in his musky scent. I think Dax just might help me make everything all right.

CHAPTER EIGHTEEN

BLAIR

"This is a terrible idea, Blair," Stevie says to me as I work on getting ready for the night. Dax is going to be picking me up in an hour to go to Inferno.

"He asked me to come. Clearly, this Mara demon is a threat to me. The sooner she's gone, the sooner everything can go back to normal."

Stevie glares at me while she sits on my bed. "You haven't been to Inferno before. You don't know what you're getting into."

"What, and you have?" I ask. She looks away and her cheeks pinken. "Wait, you've been to a supernatural sex club, and you never told me?"

"You never liked Bianca, so yeah, I never told you. We used to go on Thursday nights. It was buy one, get one blood bags." I grimace and stare at her. "You don't understand, Blair. This isn't just some club you can go to and watch and wait. If you don't take part, you look suspicious. You know how paranoid supernaturals are of each other. Especially a witch hanging out with a bunch of fucking demons."

"I can handle that," I say, shrugging my shoulders. I never wear my hair like this, but I feel pretty cute, and I know Dax will enjoy it.

"I don't like it, Blair. She sent a golem after you, Dax said that she's possessing people and scrambling their brains. What if that's her plan for you?"

"Dax won't let anything happen to me," I say.

"You barely know him," Stevie replies, giving me an apologetic look.

"Stevie, have you ever known me to go into something head first like this? I don't know what it is exactly about Dax, but it's never felt like this. I feel safe and cherished around him. You know how powerful I am, and I'll be with three demons who are Hecate knows how old. I promise I'll be careful."

She groans and scrubs her face. "I still don't like it."

"I know."

"Did Dax talk to you about what you are going to do tonight?"

"He's picking me up early so we can discuss it."

"I swear to the moon and back, Blair. You better call me if you feel uncomfortable. I'll come and pick you up right away."

"Thanks, Stevie." I walk over and wrap my arms around my cousin. Her poor face is crushed against my boobs since she's sitting down and I'm standing up.

"Did I mention how fucking hot you look tonight?"

"No you hadn't," I say, pulling back from our hug and looking in the mirror. It's a soft leather pleated skirt. I'm wearing a black lace thong and garter underneath. If I bend over, someone is going to get a view of my pale ass. Black sheer stockings cover my legs up to mid-thigh. The clasps connecting the stockings to my garter have skulls on them. It's adorable. The top could be classified as a bra. It's made of a more delicate lace material, it covers my nipples and crisscrosses around my chest and back. You can easily see the bulge of my piercings through the material. All it would take is one small tug and my boobs would pop out.

My makeup is delicate, just some winged eyeliner, foundation, and a nude lip. My hair is its usual untamed self, dark waves meeting my shoulders. But I put two small buns on each side, pushing my hair away from my face.

I feel beautiful and I know Dax is going to love the look. I already received Kas' approval, and it's clear that Stevie agrees too. One more time, I take a deep breath and look at myself in the mirror. Movement in the reflection catches my eye.

"What is it, Fez?" I ask my familiar as I walk over to his enclosure. He sadly doesn't talk back, but I can feel his stress. "Everything is going to be fine tonight, baby," I coo at him, giving him chin scratches as his top half wraps around my wrist.

"I think he's just jealous there's another man in your life. You never brought Ryan here," Stevie says and I hum in agreement.

"Speaking of Ryan, any ideas on how to make him lose his memory of me?"

"It's a bad idea, Blair. Interference with a human like that is going to get you in trouble with the council, no doubt."

"That's only if they find out."

"Yeah, and if they find out, they might prohibit you from using your magic."

I scoff and roll my eyes. "Losing my magic for a few weeks would be worth it." The council can only do so much. The mere idea of losing magic is abhorrent to most witches, so they stay in line. Truthfully, I dare them to fucking try me. I've never heard of a witch's magic actually being taken away. It seems like an empty threat.

"Wouldn't it just be easier to tell Dax?"

"Uh, no. I think it would be easier to make Ryan forget me and continue whatever it is I have with Dax without having that hanging over my head."

"I think he would understand, Blair."

I shrug my shoulders, ignoring Stevie. What does she know, anyway? I swear Fez rolls his eyes at me as he slithers back into his terrarium, and I hear a light knock on the front door.

"Stevie, I promise I'll call you if anything goes wrong. It will all be fine. You don't have to worry." She gets up from the bed and goes back to her room, irritated with me. "Oh, when's the last time we fed Clover?"

"Oh, fuck," Stevie says, changing directions from her bedroom to the kitchen. It makes me laugh. Poor Clover—*not*.

With major pep in my step, I answer the door and I'm greeted by a huge grin, two dimples, and hungry green eyes.

"Fuck me, you look amazing, little witch."

I can't help it as heat travels up my neck to my cheeks. "Thank you," I say softly.

"I was thinking we could take your Jeep. The portal wasn't so nice on your stomach last time. Plus, I want to make sure we have time to talk."

"Where are Kas and Asmo?"

"They're meeting us there."

"Okay, let me grab my keys." I go to the kitchen to get my keys and watch as Stevie slaps together a peanut butter and honey sandwich for Clover. "I'm leaving, Stevie."

"Please be safe," she says, giving me a stern look.

"I will." I give her a smile and spin on my heel. Walking back to where Dax is waiting for me. He can't stop looking at my outfit.

He gently runs a finger over one of the small buns in my hair and grins. "I like these." His finger slides down the column of my throat before it glides over one of my nipples. "And this." Now both of his hands are on the bare skin of my sides as they drag down the soft leather of my skirt. His left hand tugs lightly at the material. "And I really fucking like this. I don't know whether to put you over my knee and spank the shit out of you for looking so tempting. Or slide my fingers into your tight pussy and reward you for looking so good for daddy."

I swallow loudly. "Both?" I ask, and he laughs. His laugh always shoots straight to my core. It's deep and gravelly, and I don't think anyone gets this same side of Dax that I do, this carefree, happy, and giving side. I know it's quick, but it seems like we both reward ourselves with the most intimate and best sides of each other.

"I'll drive, babe." I nod my head and drop my keys into his large palm. We walk over to my garage and he opens the passenger door for me. His hand is tenderly splayed on my lower back as he watches me climb into the seat. He shuts the door and rounds the vehicle, and gets into the driver's seat. He adjusts the seat back and the mirrors before he starts the engine. I hit the garage door button for him as he reverses out of the driveway. As soon as we're on the open road, he has one hand on the steering wheel, and the other one resting protectively on my thigh.

"Have you been to a club like this before?"

"No," I reply, feeling a little inferior. His thumb rubs circles on my inner thigh as he talks and pays attention to the road.

"I haven't specifically been to Inferno, but I've been to other clubs before. What I've heard about Inferno seems pretty commonplace in other clubs. When we get there as partners you get a wristband to designate what you are interested in. White means you're there to watch and you're open. Blue is for submissive looking for doms, Red is for doms looking for subs. I believe they use purple here for switches. If you're only interested in playing with your partner, your wristband will be white and whatever designation you decide. This lets other people know you are not interested in playing with them."

"Okay," I reply, trying to remember all the color combinations.

"We will have partner bands showing that I'm your dom and you're my submissive. These terms are loose in these clubs, but it helps give you more protection. While we are there, I don't want you talking to anyone who isn't me, Kas, or Asmo."

"I understand." Truth be told, talking to strangers isn't really my greatest strength, anyway.

"If anyone bothers you, I want you to tell me right away. I know you're powerful, Blair. But it's my job to handle that type of shit." I nod my head and he continues. "We will be looking to see if the woman who works there, Paige, is being possessed by Mara. Kas and Asmo are going to be the ones to apprehend her if it is her. We have strict orders to return her unscathed to Hell, so it's going to be difficult. If it is her, I might need to portal you home quickly. I just need you to be prepared for that."

"How will you know if she's possessed?"

"There are a few tells. I wish it was as easy as splashing holy water on a bitch, but it's not. More than likely, she will be able to sense that we are demons and her demeanor will change."

"Paige is a human, working at a supernatural sex club?" I ask, confused about how that's possible.

"No, she's actually half shifter, of what kind we weren't able to pin down. It seems like Mara is upping the ante on who she is possessing. That's why if there's any inkling of danger of her getting near you, I will be portaling you home."

"I understand. Stevie mentioned something about Inferno I wanted to mention." Dax nods his head and kneads my thigh. I lick my lips before speaking. "She said that this club isn't really tolerant of watchers. If you're coming to play, you're expected to play."

"Kas said something similar. I want to make sure that you're comfortable, anything you don't want to do, we won't. I'll be color checking with you all night. Green means you're loving it, yellow means you're hesitant and red means stop. We can also have a safe word if you would like."

It's stupid, but yes, I want a weird safe word. "Planchette," I say and I watch him grin next to me.

"Planchette it is," he says, turning the blinker on and getting us on the highway. It's now that the nerves kick in. "Is there anything you definitely don't want to do tonight?"

"I don't want to share, nothing humiliating. I'm interested in more impact play, but tonight I don't think I want anything other than your hand." His hold on my thigh tightens and I swear his palm just keeps getting closer to my pussy. "Is there anything off the table for you?"

"Fuck, you're cute. I also don't share. As always, I love your sharp tongue, but here, at this place you're mine and being on good behavior is important." He glances over at me, giving me a raised eyebrow.

"I can be good."

"I know you can, pet."

"Is there anything else you want to cover before we get there?"

"Just know if you're ever uncomfortable, you can always tell me. Oh, take my phone out of my pocket. The first photo is a picture of Paige, so you know what you're looking for."

I look at him wide-eyed. A man handing over his phone willingly. He doesn't even have a lock screen as I look at the photo, memorizing the blonde woman's features in front of me. She's pretty. On the one hand, I hope she's the one possessed and this ends tonight, on the other, I hope not. If what Dax said is true, and Mara is inside of this woman, the damage she is doing is insurmountable.

I can't help it when I look at his contacts. There are only two saved numbers in there 'little witch' and Ryan. It makes my stomach sink. Before I can dwell on it any longer, I slide his phone back into his jacket pocket.

Dax pulls into an empty parking spot and I notice immediately that the building is warded. To a human, the building won't even be visible. To me, however, it looks like a warehouse with the beaming word Inferno on the front.

"You ready?" Dax asks me, unclipping his seatbelt. I smile at him and give him a nod. I take a few deep breaths as he exits the car and walks around the front to open my door for me.

I can do this.

CHAPTER NINETEEN

DAX

I take Blair's smaller hand in mine as we walk toward the entrance of Inferno. Fuck, she looks good. I know I was opposed to her going shopping with Kas, but what she's wearing tonight makes it oh so worth it. The outfit she's wearing with the two little buns in her hair had me nearly devouring her on sight. Definitely worth seven grand.

I've considered turning the car around and taking her home and fucking her all night more times than I would like to admit. Mostly because she looks stunning and I want her all to myself. The other part of me, which I'm having a hard time with, is the idea of her being in danger. This whole scheme started with me just needing Blair as a date to get into the club. Now that we know Mara might be going after my little witch, I don't like it one bit.

She looks nervous, but still confident in the way she walks. Part of me hopes she breaks a rule or two so that I can bend her over in that expensive little skirt I bought and smack her perky ass until it's nice and pink.

"Remember, no talking to anyone but me, Asmo, and Kas."

"Yes, daddy," she says, rolling her eyes and kissing my cheek. I must have been decent enough before I was a demon to be blessed with this naughty seductress.

I arch an eyebrow at her, but she holds my hand tightly as we're greeted by Asmo and Kas.

Kas gives her a look of approval but doesn't say much. She seems more eager to get this job done than anyone, and I would be lying if I said I wasn't suspicious of her intentions.

Kas pulls Blair to the side to give her a pep talk or some shit. I keep an eye on her as Asmo comes and stands next to me. We're both dressed more casually as I lean over and whisper to him. "We need to keep an eye on Kas."

"What do you think I do all day?"

"Not that kind of eye, dumbass."

"Listen, I might be nearly blinded by Kas' pristine pussy and life changing ass. But I'm not dumb enough to let her take all the credit for this capture. We're partners. If anyone is going to take credit for bringing this psycho bitch back to Hell, it's going to be us."

"Just want to make sure we're on the same page."

"Won't stop me from letting her top me in front of a crowd of people."

I roll my eyes but shrug. Asmo is going to do whatever he wants, and as long as he realizes that the job comes first and that Kas can't be trusted, that's all I need to know.

"Ready to go, pet?" I whisper against the shell of Blair's ear. She smells like lavender and sage. I want to lick the column of her throat and see what she tastes like.

"Yeah," she mumbles, sparing one last glance at Kas.

Asmo holds the door for us. The lobby is dimly lit; the decor lets you know that it's seedy, but in an upscale way. Debauchery may happen here, but the floors and surfaces you sit on are clean. Kas' heels click against the obsidian tile as we're greeted by the hostess. A vampire female with pale skin and dirty blonde hair stands behind the black hostess stand.

"I'll need your invitations and club payment," she says. Kas hands over two tickets and pays the woman before Asmo and Kas both grab their purple bands.

"Oh shit, they're open to other people?" Blair says next to me.

"Honestly, I don't know who's the bigger sexual deviant of the two."

I hand over our tickets and pay the woman. Getting in here isn't cheap, but most of the creatures who come here live for a long time. I guess they have more than enough money to spare.

I place the white and blue band and put it on Blair's small wrist before taking my white and red one and placing it on myself. Blair gives me a smile that makes me feel like I'm worth something, like the little assurance of only wanting her means the world. If I ever find the fucker who cheated on her, I'll ring his neck.

Taking Blair's hand in mine, I lean down. "You remember the rules?"

"Don't talk to anyone else and don't be mouthy."

"Good girl."

"Where do you want to start?" I ask, walking to the main room. We're greeted by the sight of a woman on her knees, scattered rice on the floor. You can see the indents of the small grains against her pale flesh. Her knees are bright pink, she's clearly been in position for a while. She has no clothes on except the black ropes wrapped around her tightly, showcasing her tits. Her dom, who is clearly a shifter of some sort, smiles at her menacingly as he splatters her tits with tight lashes from a flogger. Their vibe is a little more sadistic than I like. While I like inflicting some pain I don't lean toward humiliation or pain that doesn't lead to pleasure. The wince on her face shows this is more the type of pain not leaning in the direction of pleasure.

Blair's mouth is hanging wide open as she takes in the show. "Holy shit. Is that what you want to do to me?" she asks. Breaking her gaze away from the couple and looking at me.

"No."

She swallows and nods her head. I lead her down the hall. The hallways are dark, our footsteps making low noise against the wooden floor. The hallways lead us to the main stage, with plenty of seating. I sit down first and pull her down to my lap. The seats don't have arm rests but are sturdy oak wood with black velvet cushions. This stage is simple. Lit dimly with a ring bolted to the ceiling and a wall displaying multiple toys for use. There is a couple already in the middle of a scene. I look on, knowing that this is something I would like Blair to see.

"This is more of my style," I tell her. Spinning her around so her perfect ass is pressed against my crotch and her back is pressed against my chest. Her body on mine feels so right. I move her hair off her shoulder slightly so my lips are close to her ear.

I feel her tense as the first smack of his palm meets skin. The man is a reaper I've come across before, Ronan. The little thing taking his hand looks like a fairy. Haven't seen many of them in this dimension. But she looks to be enjoying herself. Her skin is a golden brown and long braids cover her breasts as she stands on her tiptoes. Her wrists are tied with approved rope, but it appears the Reaper is using magic to not strain her wrists.

Blair's hand grips at my thigh as we watch.

"You aren't counting for me, little fairy, should I add twenty more?" Ronan says.

"No, sir," the small woman pants.

Smack. His hand meets her ass cheek again and I watch as her flesh reddens and she attempts to grind her thighs together to get some friction.

His hand cups her pussy as he tsks her. "I own your orgasms for the night, darling fairy. You need to be punished. Once you've taken your punishment, then I'll decide if you get to come."

Blair grinds her ass hard against my hardening dick and I groan.

"Do you like what you see, little witch?"

"I think so," she says.

"I bet if I slid my fingers under this skirt, I would find you dripping wet."

She nods her head in agreement, and I kiss the side of her neck.

"Remember, we're here to play, but we're also here to do a job. Keep your eyes and ears open."

She nods her head again but continues to grind against me, both of us no longer paying attention to the couple in front of us. Except for the sound of him smacking her ass ricocheting in the small space, all I can do is feel the woman who is touching me. I need more.

"Are you ready to play, pet?"

"Yes," she says. I grab her by the waist and place her on her feet. She's a little unsteady as she stands and begins to walk. Right into a firm chest that isn't mine. Hair rises on the back of my neck and I can feel the heat of flames wanting to escape from my palms.

"Oh, and what do we have here?" The large werewolf asks *my* witch.

I can tell that she's really trying to be good and not speak to him. But when he grabs her wrist and looks at her bracelet, he sighs. "What a fucking shame. I could have rutted you to the next full moon."

"Get your filthy fucking mutt hands off of me," Blair says, snapping her fingers, which causes the werewolf to growl and clutch his hand to his chest.

"You fucking cunt," he says in a voice that sounds more animal than human. I don't think, I just grab him by the throat and hold him against the wall. His strength is nothing compared to mine.

"You put your hands on what's mine, dog."

"I—I didn't know."

"What didn't give it away? Her fucking bracelet or the fact that she just got up from grinding on my cock. What exactly didn't make it clear?" I pull him away from the wall and bang his head harder against it. A hand that isn't Blair's touches my biceps and my temper rises. "What?" I bark, looking over my shoulder. It's Kas with a scowl on her face.

"We have a job to do," she says, arching a brow.

"Lucky night, mutt," I say, tossing him down to the ground.

Kas looks at me like I've grown five heads as I go and grab Blair by her wrist.

"That's a broken rule, Blair. Come with me, now."

She doesn't look scared; she looks turned on as she follows me eagerly. I look around at the different rooms and find one that is open, but doesn't have seats for onlookers, but it is still available for public viewing.

"On your knees, pet."

"Yes, daddy."

"Don't go acting all fucking sweet now, little witch. What was the rule?"

"Don't talk to anyone else."

"Not only did you talk to that certified dog man, but you broke his fingers. As hot as that was, we're supposed to be keeping a low profile, not drawing attention. Do you understand?"

Her eyes shift to purple as she looks up at me. Knowing how insecure she feels about it, I tuck a loose hair behind her ear and lean forward.

"Your glamour is down, babe." She shakes her head before she licks her lips and looks up at me from her place on the ground with those deep pools of honey. "You can use magic here. Are you okay with me using mine?"

"Yes."

"Your mouth is going to be full and your hands are going to be restrained. If you want me to stop, just zap me with some magic. Okay?"

"Yes," she says eagerly, licking her lips again.

"Take my cock out, pet."

She doesn't speak, she just uses her small hands to unbutton my jeans before sliding down my briefs enough to release my dick.

"Hands behind your back." She immediately follows orders, placing her hands behind her back and crossing them. I'm not a shadow demon, but I have just enough shadow magic to wrap my smoky mist around her wrists. The magic swirls out of me like they're additional limbs, the wisps of smoke dark enough to notice but easy enough to see through. Securing them so she can't use her hands. I use another tendril of mist to turn her chin to look at me. "Lick the tip, babe. It's fucking messy for you."

The pad of her tongue greedily sweeps across the slit of my dick. Licking up all the pre-cum.

"Suck the head." She eagerly follows directions. Her lips latching around the head of my dick as her tongue sweeps small circles around the ridges. *Fuck*. She looks perfect like this. My magic eagerly and obediently surrounds her while she's on her knees for me. Her perfect tits on display. *Well, almost.*

A tendril of mist slides the lace down exposing her pierced erect nipples and she moans around my length as she licks and sucks as directed. So fucking perfect.

Blair's brown eyes look up at me seductively, waiting for direction. I look to my left and notice we have some onlookers.

"Color?" I ask her, making sure that the exhibition isn't too much. Her lips part from the head of my cock and she smiles at me.

"Green, definitely green."

"Daddy's going to fuck your throat now. You want that, little witch? You want me to use you until I fill that naughty little mouth full of my cum?"

"Yes," she pants, opening her mouth eagerly.

I smack the tip of my cock on her waiting tongue three times before sliding deeply down her throat. I let the shadows I control play with her tits, rolling the piercings of her nipples as I take two fistfuls of her hair and thrust into her hot, wet mouth.

She hums around my length, taking me like she was made for me. "I'm the only one who gets the best of this mouth, you hear me, pet?"

Blair bobs her head on my cock, and I pick up my pace. Fucking her deeper and deeper. I watch as tears fall from her eyes, but she doesn't falter. She just keeps taking what I give her.

"Such a good girl, taking every fucking inch of me. You're *mine*, little witch."

Her eyes turn pink and I don't bother telling her, as I'm entranced in the color and what they mean. I can't imagine they mean anything other than something good.

"Fuck, pet. You're going to make me come. I want you to swallow every fucking drop. Show daddy what a good girl you can be."

Her eyes don't leave mine, pink, alluring, and tears rolling down her face beautifully. I can't hear anyone else, I can only hear the wet sounds of my cock entering in and out of her lips and the choking sound she makes when she takes me too deep.

"That's it, pet, make it nice and wet. So fucking good for me. I love this mouth."

She hums and my thrusts increase in speed as I fuck in and out of her warm throat. I can feel her pushing against my shadows, wanting to free her hands, and it only makes me rut into her mouth harder. Until I can't take it anymore. I can barely stand as my orgasm hits me and I unload spurts of cum down her throat.

I wait until she swallows like she was told, before I release her wrists and bend down to scoop her up off the floor.

"You did so good, babe. Let's go get you a drink before we do anything else."

"I really liked that."

"Which part?" I ask.

"Your shadows, probably the most. But I never thought I would like the idea of being watched, but I did. The idea of people watching and wanting what I have, but they never could."

"Never," I say, reassuring her.

I buy a twenty-dollar water as I sit her down on my lap in one of the aftercare spots. It's two large black soft sectionals. The area has warm low lighting, it's separated from the rest of the club, so the noise level is lower. There's a bar to the right and some people milling about, but in general it's less chaotic than the central club. Her thighs straddle my lap and her head rests on my shoulder as I hand her the water bottle.

Asmo plops down on the couch next to us causing us to slightly bounce on the soft sofa. Both Blair and I give him a death glare.

"Gotta say, mean witch, you're much nicer with your mouth full."

"Shut the fuck up, you towheaded cunt," Blair bites back. I hear Kas laugh next to Asmo while he sputters slightly. Damn, I really like it when she's mean to other people. Asmo especially.

"Keep being so fucking mean to me, and I'll fall in love with you. Why do you think I'm still with Kas?" Asmo says.

"I'm with Dax," she says and I squeeze her ass in approval.

"Yeah you are," I reply, kissing the side of her neck as she picks up her water bottle and takes a drink. A slight trail of water drips from the corner of her mouth, and I use my thumb to wipe it away. I grin when I see Blair's blush. Sucking my cock in front of people doesn't make her blush, but my tenderness in private does. It makes me more eager to break down her walls and find out other ways I can make her blush. I know she's mine, it's just a matter of figuring out how to keep her.

"Any signs of Paige?" I ask Kas more so than Asmo.

"No, not yet. Asmo and I were going to play and see if we can find anything out after."

"Sounds good, we will be in here for a little while."

Kas looks longingly at Blair, and I don't like it. "You can go now," I say sharply. She rolls her eyes at me before grabbing Asmo by the collar and dragging him to do whatever the Hell they plan on doing.

"I think I'd like to do more tonight," Blair tells me sitting up more firmly on my lap.

"What do you want? I'll do my best to give you whatever you desire." She blushes and looks away for a moment before meeting my gaze.

"I think I'd like to try what we were watching earlier."

"You want me to spank this sweet ass, little witch?" I squeeze and knead the tender flesh emphasizing just how on board with that plan I am.

"Yeah, I think I'd like that."

"Drink your water, and I'll think about it." She pouts, and it's cute as Hell. *I'm done for.*

CHAPTER TWENTY

BLAIR

I straddle Dax's lap. His thighs are muscular and I feel small pressed against him. I think I could live here forever. What we did in the first room didn't feel like a punishment. It felt like a relief—it's odd. I've always felt like I was a rule breaker. That I didn't like when people told me what to do or being punished when I did something wrong. With Dax, it feels different. His rules when we came here were for safety, and I broke that rule, so he showed me who's in charge. I loved every single moment of it, especially his magic touching mine. Our connection is so deep, I know that I'm falling fast. I push all of those nagging thoughts out of my mind as I just relish in the now. In his body heat warming mine, his firm hand gripping my ass and his eyes focused on me finishing my water.

"You good, babe?" he asks. His green eyes watching every move I make, making sure that I'm okay.

"Really good," I say, sliding down so I'm pressed against his length, which is already getting hard again.

He smiles as he nuzzles his beard into my neck, his hands fisting my skirt and ass. He groans in my ear as I grind against him. I need him to relieve some of this tension for me.

"Does my little witch need to come?"

"Please," I say.

"Please what?"

"Please, daddy." He moans and abruptly picks me up, my ass in his hands and my legs wrapping around his waist.

"I'm going to make you feel so good," he says, nothing but a promise sliding off of his tongue. I know without a doubt this man is going to wreck me, this time with a bigger audience.

He carries me further into the club, to the portion we haven't been yet. The halls all look the same here, so I'm not sure which way he's going. His boots click on the hardwood floor as the black walls pass me. Every now and then my eyes travel to a different room we pass. Each of the rooms has a similar decor, but with different intentions. I watch the other club goers as he carries me, a mix of all different supernaturals. We pass a room with a wall with hooks, each of them holding a different strap on. It would be nearly impossible to miss the scene of Asmo lying on his shoulders, his back supported by some piece of furniture, his ass up, arms wrapped around his thighs, cock fully erect as Kas pegs him. She strokes his length as the purple dildo retreats in and out of his ass. Her fingers grip tight on his thighs and they both smile at each other as she takes control. Lowkey, wish Dax wasn't carrying me right now so we could take a brief pit stop and watch the rest of the show.

I sigh when I can no longer see them. Maybe after Mara is caught, we can come and do this again and I will actually get to really take in the sights. I could sit on Dax's lap and he could touch me as we watched them touch each other. While there's no way in Hell I'm willing to share Dax, it's crystal clear that I don't mind people watching, and I quite enjoy being watched.

The room he takes me to is more publicly centered. Larger than the one I gave him head in, and there are six chairs that allow onlookers.

The room is simple. There's a wall with different floggers, paddles, and instruments hanging menacingly. A deep purple chandelier is in the middle of the room, dimly lighting the space. But the showstopper of the room is the bench in the middle. Made from oak wood with five sections of burgundy padding. There are restraints on all four outer padded sections, clearly there to restrain your calves and forearms. I realize that this is a spanking bench. I have never seen one in person, but now that I have, I feel intimidated, especially as I look at the restraints.

"Don't worry about those. We won't be needing them," Dax says, making me turn my gaze from the bench to his face. He looks like he wants to devour me, and frankly I'd let him eat me alive with how he makes me feel. "Panties," he says, holding out his palm face up.

Without hesitation, I hitch up my skirt and go to roll down the thong. Problem is, my garter is in the way. Dax tsks but gets down on his knees and it's such a beautiful sight. He smiles at the skull clasps, but undoes them, releasing the cord that tethers the stockings to the garter. His tattooed fingers slowly glide along the pebbled flesh of my thigh as he tenderly rolls my thong the rest of the way down my legs. He places one small kiss on the Hecate tattoo on my upper thigh before rising to his full height and pocketing the panties.

If I wasn't already wet before, I am now.

"On the bench, little witch." I eye the piece of furniture and think about the best way to get on. Dax smirks and taps one of the lower sections designated for my legs. "Legs first, pet."

I place a knee on the first padded section. The leather is cool against my skin. Before raising my next leg. I look over at Dax for approval as his hand pushes gently at my back, making my chest press firmly on to the large centerpiece of the bench. "Forearms here," he says, taking my arms and putting them on the two last pieces. My face is flat against the cool leather as I look to my left, where two couples have sat down to watch the show. "Color?"

"Green," I reply, and his hand slides down my spine.

"So sexy like this, pet. Ready and waiting for me to spank your sweet ass and make you come, is that right?"

"Yes, daddy," I say and I watch the reaper grab his cock from the outside of his pants as he watches. It's the same man I watched earlier. Now that I get a closer look at his wrist, it's solid red. The woman he was playing with earlier isn't the only person he's willing to interact with, and it seems like he's enjoying watching my and Dax's show just as much as we watched him earlier.

"Such a good girl for me, but I think you need a reminder to follow the rules. Is that what you need, Blair? You need me to spank you and show you who is in charge of you?"

"Please."

"So sweet when you ask nicely." His fingertips glide down my spine and the anticipation looms over me. He leans in so only I can hear. "Use your safe word if it's too much. Just my hand tonight." I nod in agreement as his palm reaches under my skirt, flipping it up and baring my ass to the room. It's not embarrassment that heats my cheeks, it's desire. The want I see in the eyes of those watching, viewing what they can't have. Knowing that Dax wants this as badly as I do only adds to the anticipation and want.

Dax toys with me, his fingertips gently gliding down my back and over my ass. It takes a moment to realize the cool sensation that's greeting my limbs isn't the cool air of the club. It's Dax's shadows coming out to play again. I get wetter from the feeling of them against my skin, holding down my forearms and calves to the lower part of the bench. My torso is free, but I can't move much with my arms and legs tied down by his magic. You wouldn't think of a smoky substance as being strong, but the grip is firm, and it holds me down tightly.

Impatiently, I wiggle my ass at Dax. I hear a dark chuckle before the first slap hits. *Smack.* His palm hits my left ass cheek and I feel the sting immediately. It's not a wince or a hiss that leaves my lips, it's a delicate moan. He kneads the skin in his hand, relieving some of the sting.

"I want this cunt dripping, pet. Only then will I give you what you need. You understand?"

I don't answer immediately and a whoosh of air alerts me to the next spanking headed my way. The audible cracking of flesh meeting hits my senses before the actual sting does. I can't help but make eye contact to the supernaturals watching my punishment. The woman who was spanked earlier with the long braids sits next to the Reaper. His hand is playing with her pussy and hers is wrapped around his cock as they work each other. They're touching each other while watching me and Dax. Why is that so incredibly hot?

Lost in the show in front of me, the loud crack of another smack makes me groan and attempt to shift on the bench. I'm nearing sensory overload, my need for Dax to make me come builds inside of me. The anticipation of when he will let me come is consuming my thoughts.

"Do you understand?" Dax repeats.

"Yes, daddy," I reply automatically this time.

"Such a good witch for me. Do you think if I spank you hard enough, your magic will come out and play with mine?"

I groan at the idea. My mind is working overtime on how I could play with him. His shadows are impressive, but I can move objects without the need of shadows. I keep that thought in the back of my mind.

Dax hits me where my thigh connects to my ass, his fingertip ever so slightly grazing against my cunt. I feel myself getting wetter and wetter for him. He's so all-consuming. Even with people watching us I'm completely enraptured by Dax and his magic. His shadows tighten around my limbs—*smack*—eliciting another groan, and I attempt to move my torso to get any friction.

Dax's finger slides from my wet core, and he rims my asshole. "This ass looks gorgeous with my marks. Next time I'm going to plug this sweet ass when I spank you. Make you beg me to fuck you in the ass after your cheeks are nice and pink."

I groan at his words and try to push myself closer to his hand. "Please, Dax. Please."

"Begging already, pet? I told you what I wanted. You're wet, but not dripping. What do I need to do?"

I make a petulant noise, not sure what he wants from me.

"Mmm, I think I know what you need." His hands glide up my thighs and his touch is blazing, so warm that I attempt to pull away from his palm. The smacks rotate between each cheek and they're rapid in pacing. I lose count but at least ten unearthly hot spankings to each cheek. My ass feels like it's on fucking fire. It's painful, but in a way that makes me want to beg for more. I'm panting and overwhelmed when Dax slides his fingers from my clit to my entrance, his fingers no longer hot, humming in approval. "There's my dripping girl. Time for your reward."

I wish I could see him. All I can do is watch our onlookers. Their eyes rotate between my reddened ass and whatever Dax is doing. My breaths are heavy as the anticipation lingers in the air. One of his shadows releases one of my forearms and tenderly pushes my hair back and strokes my spine. It feels sweet and caring. Who knew shadows would be my new thing?

"Dax," I say in an impatient tone.

"I'm always telling you about patience, pet."

A low growl vertebrates from my chest. My ass is hot, my cunt is dripping, and I need him to do something about it *now*. Dax's large hands grip my ass, spreading me apart, and I wince at his touch. Without even seeing him, I know he's smirking. His hot fucking dimples likely on display. I want to tell him to fucking choke on razor blades, but before anything can leave my mouth, Dax's magical mouth is on my clit.

I'm so wet I can hear him slurping up my wetness, devouring every last drop of me as his tongue lavishes my clit. His lips create the perfect amount of suction on the overly sensitive nerves. The tenderness of my cheeks as he grabs them only amplifies the pleasure.

"Yes, please don't stop. Holy fuck."

He hums against my clit and doesn't stop. His nose nuzzles against my entrance and I wish I could have it all, have his mouth on me, his shadows surrounding me, his cock filling me to the brim. I want everything he can give me.

Dax stops licking me, and I groan in frustration. "Time to flip you over." He doesn't even give me a warning as his shadows flip me onto my back. The smoky tendrils holding my legs wide and spread as he grins at my needy pussy. I'm not sure when exactly Dax got naked, but I'm guessing when I was waiting for him to touch me. He's devastatingly perfect. His chest is scattered with tattoos and chest hair. He's muscular, but not in an overly cut way. I lick my lips as I take in every inch of him, including his perfect cock that curves up ever so slightly.

I meet Dax's gaze, our eyes locking, and I know this is the moment I want my magic to come out. "*Propius,*" I whisper, flinging Dax's body into mine. He has to use his hands to catch himself on the part of the bench that was previously holding my forearms. The bench groans from the sudden movement, rocking us backward as his body weight crushes against mine.

Dax groans, bringing his lips to mine. The kiss is hard and passionate, our tongues fighting for dominance. His shadows squeeze my thighs as his hands hold my torso tightly. Dax kisses down my jaw and teasingly tugs on one of my nipple piercings with his teeth before sucking the erect nipple into his warm mouth. The glide of the head of his cock against my wetness makes me moan. He smirks as he thrusts into me brutally, causing the bench to creak.

No one else in the room exists. It's just Dax and me as he fills my pussy and holds me with his magic. I scrape my nails through his hair as he enters in and out of me. He has one hand holding my throat lightly while he uses the other to rub my clit.

"Need to feel you come on my cock, little witch," he says, tightening his hold on my throat, making my eyes roll back as my orgasm hits me hard. His shadows hold steady as my legs shake and I grip his length. The hand on my throat loosens as I come down from my release. Dax's green eyes watching in awe as perspiration covers both of our bodies and we pant lightly. "I want another one, pet." I think I die just a little.

Dax looks over at someone in the audience. I can't even look away from Dax. He's the center of everything right now. It's only when the Reaper from earlier hands him a toy do I realize he somehow communicated to the man what he wanted.

The buzzing breaks my attention, and I watch as Dax places the wand on my overstimulated, swollen clit. I lurch as soon as the device touches me and he smiles. His thrusts have slowed, but he still fucks me deeply with each one.

My hands are pushing against his chest, and he tsks at me. His shadows pulling them away and above my head. "I can't," I say.

"Yes, you can. Give daddy one more."

Fuck me.

His thrusts increase and the buzzing of the toy is so loud it feels like my brain is muffled by static. The orgasm builds slowly. It's like it takes over my whole body, my vision blurring, my hearing going out. My fucking face is numb. My pussy clenching tightly against Dax's impressive length as he fucks me harder. It's only when his body leans over mine do I realize he's coming.

"Fuck, this pussy is perfect."

It's sudden when his magic disappears, and my legs and arms drop suddenly, making me wince. Dax pulls out and looks at me apologetically. "Sorry, babe. Lost my handle on them for a moment."

"It's okay," I say. Totally ready for him to bundle me up in a soft blanket and snuggle for a good ten hours.

He bends my legs for me, so that they're now resting on a lower part of the bench. "You good?" he asks, stroking my skin and pushing my hair back.

"More than good," I say, grinning at him.

His firm hands grip at my torso to sit me up. I feel a little dizzy, but I get my bearings and I finally look at the crowd. My jaw drops when I see the person walking past our stage.

"Stevie?"

CHAPTER TWENTY-ONE

DAX

I t's a really uncomfortable feeling when the woman you just had the best sex of your life with calls out her cousin's name as soon as you pull out your wet dick.

Looking over my shoulder, I'm shocked when I see the red headed witch on the arm of a vampire. The woman she's with has olive toned skin and dark curly hair; she's lean and towers over Stevie.

"Why the fuck is your cousin here?" I ask, looking at Blair. She's completely blissed out. I was looking forward to holding her and taking some time to relax, but now it seems someone has decided to ruin my plans. I quickly grab my clothes and start to dress myself.

"I have no idea." She says it in an airy way. Like she wants to take a nap, not deal with this shit. We probably went a little too hard considering we were supposed to be doing a job. But holding back around Blair is proving to be impossible. I want to give her everything, explore each other and the world together. Shit, I'm really getting ahead of myself. Can you blame me? She's special. Not just the way our magic connects, but it's like we fit well together, what each other has been searching for.

She goes to get off the bench and is a little precarious, I watch her slightly grimace as she shifts her thighs. It shouldn't feel so good knowing my cum is currently dripping down her thigh, but it does. I grab her hand and steady her. I push down her skirt, making sure she isn't exposed as we walk down the hallway after her cousin. I'll clean her up as soon as we get back to the more relaxing rooms. Blair grabs her cousin's arm roughly, turning her to face us.

"What the Hell, Stevie?"

The witch's cheeks heat, and the vampire she's with doesn't look amused. "What bullshit is this, Stevie?" the vampire asks. "Fuck this. Find your own ride home," they say before walking away from Stevie. The witch looks more irritated than upset.

"I guess she got the hint that I used her to get in here tonight." Stevie rolls her eyes and I see the similarities between her and Blair in their mannerisms. Though they don't look much alike, it seems spending so much time together has caused them to pick up a few things from each other.

"And why exactly is that?" Blair asks her.

"I had to make sure you were okay, which, from what I saw, you're more than okay."

"Ew, you watched?" Blair asks.

"For like five seconds, I barely saw anything."

"I didn't ask you to come, Stevie."

"No, you asked Dax for that." Blair looks like she's about to smack her cousin. "God, you're so fucking difficult, Blair. You're the most important person in my entire life. Excuse me for being worried about you and wanting to make sure that you were okay."

Blair seems stunned by her cousin's words, not replying right away.

"Thank you for caring about me, Stevie, but there needs to be a line. I think watching me get railed by my demon boyfriend and his shadows needs to be that line."

Boyfriend sounds so trivial, but I'll take it. The public claiming by Blair does something to me. A possessive rumble of approval spurs in my chest as the cousins continue talking.

"Boyfriend?" Stevie asks for me, arching her eyebrow and looking between us.

"Yeah," Blair says, shrugging her shoulders and looking at me for reassurance.

"As her boyfriend, I need to take her to wind down. You can come with us if you want. I imagine Asmo and Kas will be there too."

"Sure, now that I don't have Bianca with me and I just have the blue wristband on, I'd rather not be wandering the club alone," Stevie says. I nod my head. She's important to Blair. If someone tried anything, I would need to step up and put them in their place.

Sure enough, as soon as we enter the room, Asmo has his head on Kas's lap as she strokes his messy blonde hair.

Her eyes brighten as soon as she sees Stevie. "And who is this beautiful creature?" she asks.

Stevie smiles at her and waves. "I'm Blair's cousin, Stevie," she says.

"She's a normal nice witch," Asmo says snarkily and Stevie glares at him.

"And you're the less attractive demon that Blair turned down at the bar. Are you still butthurt about that or from the treatment Kas just gave you?"

Asmo gapes at Stevie while Kas gives her a devious smile, patting the spot next to her. "Come sit here, sweet witch."

Stevie beams at her request and eagerly sits down next to her. Asmo groans as Kas stops petting his hair to focus her attention on Stevie.

"Not so nice of a witch after all," Asmo says with a new-found interest in the not-so-nice witch.

"This is fucking nauseating. Will you hold me?" Blair asks.

I nod and sit down on the soft cushions, bringing her down with me back to our favorite position of her straddling my lap. My hands rub up and down her thighs, slow circles around her back.

I speak lowly enough so the assholes next to us don't hear. "You good, babe? Do you need anything?"

"No." She sighs, pressing her cheek against my chest. Nuzzling against the soft material of my shirt. "Any sign of Paige?"

I shake my head and continue rubbing her back. My hand wanders down to her ass, and she winces at the touch. "Sorry," I say, even though I'm not sorry for a single fucking second. Watching her pale ass get pinker with each smack. Seeing how much she liked it when I heated my hands and hit her in fast strikes. She was made for me and she's wrapped in this beautiful package that I want to peel layer by layer. What makes Blair tick? What does she love to do in her free time? Does she like to travel? All the questions I have for her churn in my head as she pops up from leaning against my chest dramatically.

"Over to the left, standing by the bar, is that Paige?" she asks me quietly.

"It sure is," I reply and snap my fingers to get Kas and Asmo's attention. Asmo looks like an old dog who just got replaced by a cute new puppy, as Kas has a tendril of Stevie's long red hair between her fingers. Kas' eyes meet mine and

I tilt my head in the bar's direction. Her eyes widen for a moment before she puts her cool facade back on.

"Sweet witch, I'd love to continue this conversation, but I have something I need to take care of."

"Uh, okay?" Stevie replies. Kas and Asmo both stand, as do I, removing Blair from my lap and placing her gently on her tender ass. She winces and shifts her weight.

"Why don't you stay here with the witches and Asmo and I will handle this," Kas says. I give her a glare.

"No fucking way am I letting you handle this," I reply. Stevie and Blair both watch the conversation like it's a tennis match. I stop paying attention to them when Kas claps her hands together while trying to make her point.

"Like Hell I'm going to let dumb and dumber handle this. If you want a job done right, you send in a woman. That's why Lucifer assigned me to this case, to make sure you incompetent dick folds didn't screw it up," Kas mouths back.

My temper is on the surface, and I can't help it when my finger is near her face. "There's a fuck ton more on the line with this case than you realize. I'm not letting her get away. I don't even give a shit if you're part of taking her back to Hell, but this needs to be done right."

"You think there's a lot on the line for you, you have no idea!" Kas shouts back at me. Both of our demon tempers simmer on the surface.

"Yeah, and what the fuck do you have to gain, Kas?"

"Like I would tell you, you wouldn't understand, anyway."

"What does that mean?" Asmo asks her pleadingly. Hell, this man is pathetic. He touches her arm, and she shucks it away.

"You two are assholes and if we don't do something soon, we're going to miss our opportunity," Asmo says.

Kas and I are trying to calm down as we glare at each other. Asmo in the middle of us like he's our kid and we're in the middle of a custody drop off.

"Can we just get this over with?" he asks, and Kas and I both huff.

It's at that moment that we hear a loud yelp to the left of us. Stevie's red hair is in the clutches of Paige—Mara.

"What do you want? How did you find me?" she says. Her eyes darting between the three of us and finally landing on Blair.

"Let my cousin go, now," Blair says calmly, standing from her seated position.

"Only if you come with me," Mara says back, her eyes now unmoving from Blair. I go to take a step toward Mara and she growls at me. She pulls a blade from under her dress and holds it to Stevie's throat. "Any closer and I'll do it." I can't tell from here, but it looks like it may be a dark object. The damage that could do versus a standard blade is severe.

Kas' hand gently touches my arm, letting me know to stay back. Not the usual indifferent demon that I'm used to.

"You can't have Blair," I tell her.

"Blair, Blair, Bair, fucking Blair. She's really everyone's favorite, isn't she? I didn't ask for this. But this skin suit is meeting its expiration date."

I watch as Blair's irises turn black. She looks like a demon with her eyes changing to that color. Smoke billows from her fists. Mara grins at Blair.

"Perfect, you're perfect," she nearly coos at Blair. She's so distracted that she isn't paying attention to Stevie. Who stomps hard on Mara's toe and runs into Kas' arms. Kas immediately portals Stevie out of the club, while I'm standing with Asmo next to me.

"Portal her to Hell, and I'll portal Blair out of here," I whisper to Asmo. He looks irritated that Kas ditched us, but nods his head in agreement. Mara watches in fascination as little embers of flame crinkle from Blair's skin. It's clear that Mara thinks she would be the perfect vessel, and what's terrifying is, I don't think she's wrong.

"Blair," I say gently, trying to get her attention. I'm a little concerned if she's fully present and takes her magic out on someone besides Mara. "Fuck, all right. On the count of three. One, two, three."

At the same time, Asmo and I lunge. My arms wrap around Blair, her touch burning my skin, and I wince. I watch as Asmo attempts to grab Mara, but just as he grabs her, deep inky black smoke shoots from Paige's mouth. I watch as it spirals through the air toward Asmo. Without even thinking, I portal us to the front yard of her house.

We land roughly on the grass as Blair heaves and I stroke her back. My skin repairs quickly from the burns she left on my skin, and I hope that they're healed before she's completely back to it.

"What the actual fuck? Can I have a normal fucking day?" she says, standing up on her own and looking over me, easily seeing the char marks on my shirt as my skin heals the burnt flesh. "Did I do that?"

"It's fine. I heal fast."

She comes over and picks up my arm. And she gasps. "Where's Stevie?"

"Kas portaled her out before anything could happen. I really need to see where she is and if Asmo got out of there."

She nods her head. "My wards are strong. I should be safe here."

I look at her and the house, not liking leaving her by herself one bit. "As soon as I know that they're okay, I'll come right back."

"The black smoke. Was that her true demon form?" she asks.

"Yes, Satan doesn't hand out meat suits freely. You have to prove yourself if you want to travel to other dimensions and fit in."

"So you think she's an older demon who came to earth, to what? Find the right vessel?"

"No, I think it's more complicated than that."

She walks and winces. "You all right, babe?"

"My ass hurts, and so do my hands." I look down at the skin and watch in awe as the skin grafts itself back together from the flames she conjured. It's not the same as my own. My own flames don't burn me. "This has never happened before," she says, looking up at me, her brown eyes full of concern.

"Go inside, shower, get cleaned up. I'm going to find everyone and bring them back here."

"Okay," she says, I can see that there's a little tremor in her hands as she goes to walk away. Blair always tries to be strong. I sigh as I wrap my arms around her and hold my back to her chest tight.

"Daddy's going to take care of everything, okay?" She nods her head against my chest, holding back tears, as I give her one more squeeze before stepping away and portaling to the bungalow.

I open the door and scan the living room and luckily find her cousin and Kas. I watch as Stevie straddles Kas' lap. Kas' hands wrapped around the long red locks as Stevie cups her jaw as they kiss.

"This is fucking sweet and all, but where's Asmo?"

Kas pops her mouth from Stevie's quickly and she looks at me like I'm hiding the blond-headed dumbass in my pocket. "He's not with you?"

"No, I had to portal Blair out when Mara left Paige's body."

"Fuck," Kas groans.

"Is Blair okay?" Stevie asks.

"She's worried about you, and I think she's a little freaked out about what happened."

"I've never seen her eyes go black like that before, only other colors," Stevie says.

"She's back at the house waiting for you. I can portal you there while Kas and I try to find Asmo."

Stevie nods her head and attempts to get up off of Kas' lap, who eagerly pushes her back down. "We'll all stick together."

"Whatever," I reply as Stevie tells Kas where she needs to portal to. With two quick pops, we are right back in front of Blair's house.

Stevie and I both walk through the front door and as soon as Kas attempts to walk past the threshold, she's held back by Blair's wards.

"Sorry, Kas, Blair is so much better at wards than I am. She will have to give you access."

"Or not," I say, walking up the stairs to find Blair. Her snake is coiled around her wrist. She hasn't changed from her outfit to the club as she lies on her side, facing away from the door.

"Babe," I say, going to sit next to her. Fez gives me a shitty look, well, a shitty look by snake standards.

"Dax, I don't think I'm completely a witch."

I sigh and nod my head. As soon as the smoke came out of her hands, I knew she wasn't fully a witch. "I know, but you're still my little witch."

She rolls her eyes and scoffs. The snake sticking his tongue out and licking her forearm.

"What do you know about your dad?" I ask.

"Not much. He usually just lets me talk when he visits me for my birthday."

"When's your birthday?"

"Friday," she replies.

"Your birthday is in a week and you didn't tell me?" She shrugs, cradling her head further into her pillow. "Are you supposed to meet your dad?"

"Yeah, on the dot, every birthday. He never misses it. He always gives me money, takes me out to eat and gives me the longest hug at the end of the night."

"Maybe your mom knows something?"

"Seeing as she tried to sacrifice me and she's gone into hiding, I'm not sure how I'm supposed to ask her."

"Kas and I need to find Asmo, and after that's done, I think we need to track down your mom. Mara seems more powerful and calculated than I thought. Maybe if we know more about why she wants to use you as a vessel, the easier it will be to take her down."

She nods her head, and I lean over and kiss her temple. Fez doesn't like that at all, but I ignore the moody fuck. "Oh, do you want Kas to have access to your house?"

"No," she replies, and I smile.

"Get some sleep. I'll be back as soon as I find Asmo. Maybe change into some comfier clothes?"

She nods her head, and I put the blanket on top of her, in case she decides she doesn't want to get up. I spin on my heel, leaving her house with a pit of worry festering in my stomach.

CHAPTER TWENTY-TWO

BLAIR

A slight squeeze around my wrist wakes me up and I look down to see Fez wrapped around my arm. I thought maybe Dax would have come back at some point in the night, but the other half of my bed lay cold and empty.

Last night was—I really don't know how to put into words how last night felt. On the one hand, I felt completely sexually liberated, had the best orgasms of my life, and I'm in the middle of what's clearly a sexual awakening. The second half terrifies me. After Mara—Paige—whoever the fuck grabbed Stevie, it's like I blacked out. Like something dark was seeping out of me and I had no control of it, like I wasn't the one driving the wheel. One might compare it to being possessed. That train of thought has me freaking the Hell out.

I've always been a witch. It's who I am, what I am. But now... now, I'm not so sure. Maybe I'm something else too, and that's why I never fit in. Why my coven never truly accepted me and why I've never felt like I belonged. Maybe I belong with some other group of supernaturals.

The chances of my mom speaking to me, or me being able to find her, are low. But there's someone who might be able to help. Stevie isn't going to like it.

When I walk downstairs, I hear crying from the basement, and I roll my eyes. Who knew keeping a human alive was so much fucking work? Honestly, it's not surprising so many kidnappers kill their victims. If Clover didn't have an eviction date for after the full moon, I might just strangle her.

Against my own volition, I make her a cup of noodles, grab some crackers and a bottle of water, and carry them downstairs. I had to take the silencing charm off the room because we kept forgetting to feed her when we couldn't hear her.

The low tone of "Look What You Made Me Do" by Taylor Swift plays, and I smile. It's been a few days since Stevie just let it play on repeat. When I open the door, I find Clover huddled in the corner, her arms wrapped around her knees.

"Brought you breakfast," I say.

"Please turn the music off. I'm begging you."

I place the food on top of the dresser and tap my finger to my chin a few times, contemplating her request. Logically, I know that maybe I've taken this too far. But she fucked my boyfriend and tried to kill me, so I squash that negative way of thinking quickly.

"What information can you give me? If it's good enough, maybe I will turn the music off."

Her eyes scan the room like a crazed person as she tries to come up with something valuable.

"I think I might know where your mom is," she says, looking down.

"Why don't I believe you?"

"I said I might. Not that I know for sure."

"What do you know?"

"Ryan helped her purchase a cabin in North Point, all cash, and I don't think it's under her name."

I tap my chin again, irritated with this little bitch for not telling me this sooner. "Why are you telling me this now?"

"Because I fucking love Taylor Swift, and you psychos are ruining everything for me."

"You know what, Clover? I think I might just believe you. The downside of this means I'm going to need to talk to Ryan."

"The sex really wasn't worth all this," she says.

"You're definitely not wrong there," I say before I turn around, silencing the music and leaving the basement.

When I return to the kitchen, Stevie has her hip pressed against the kitchen counter as she blows the steam from her tea to cool it down. Her hair looks like a rat's nest, and she looks like she hasn't gotten much sleep.

"You look like shit," I say, pouring myself a cup from the kettle.

She ignores my comment but rolls her eyes and places her mug on the counter. "You turned off the music?" she asks as she puts two pieces of bread in the toaster.

"Seems little Clover has decided to actually be useful."

'Oh, yeah?"

"She said Ryan helped my mom buy a property in North Point." Stevie arches a brow at me and pushes the mechanism to make the bread disappear.

"So you're going to have to talk to Ryan?"

"Looks that way, but I had an idea first, maybe to get some insight into what happened last night."

"Your dad?" she asks.

"I wish, but you know he just always shows up on my birthday. I was thinking Adelaide."

"Are you fucking kidding me?" she asks as the toaster pops and she ignores it.

"Listen, I know how you feel about divination, but you can't deny that she's good at what she does. In a world full of things that don't make sense, you really don't think there's any value in what she might know?"

"It's not that I think divination is shit, it's just Adelaide." She turns so I can't see her face. My cousin is easy to read, so her turning away tells me enough.

"You fucked her," I say confidently, more like a statement, not a question.

She squeaks and turns around. "Maybe, a few times, and maybe I didn't call her back."

"Stevie, you little bitch."

"Maybe she won't be mad. Maybe she saw me ghosting her in the cards." Stevie shrugs and tilts her head, like she's trying to make herself believe her faulty logic.

I can't help it when I bark out a laugh. "You don't have to come if you don't want to."

"I think we should stick together."

"I think so too."

"Any word from Dax?" she asks while she spreads jam on her toast.

"No, maybe I should tell him where we're going?"

"I think that's a very mature response. Look at you, growing up being a good little girl."

My eyes widen, and I glare at her. "How much did you see last night?"

"Enough," she says before she shrugs and takes her tea and toast in her room.

"We leave in a half hour."

She garbles some sort of agreement, and I huff. Grabbing a muffin from the counter and walking back to my room to get dressed. I text Dax, not expecting a response.

Me: I'm going to North Point today. 4573 Terrace Place, just wanted to let you know.

Dax: Thank you for letting me know, babe. Sorry I couldn't come back last night.

Me: Have you found Asmo?

Dax: It's complicated. Call me if you need me, and stay safe. Check in with me so I don't worry about you, okay?"

I smile down at my phone.

Me: Yes, daddy.

He doesn't respond, and I don't expect him to. It's clear that even though Asmo gets on his last nerve, he cares about the annoying demon. I place my phone down and get ready for the day. Looking forward to what Adelaide sees, not looking forward to seeing Ryan. Will he be able to tell I'm fucking his dad? If you asked me a few days ago, that would have been the plan. Get under his skin. But now, I don't like the idea of Dax feeling used. It makes me feel guilty, and guilt isn't an emotion I'm familiar with. I need to plot with Stevie on how to make Ryan forget all about me.

But with Mara lighting a fire under my ass and our safety on the line. Ryan is at the bottom of the list. At least Heather is taking care of the employees at Hex while renovations are being done from the fight with the golem.

Honestly, as dangerous as everything has been, the amount of action I've seen lately has given me a new purpose, the idea of running a restaurant almost feels trivial.

We had to take a ride share to pick up my Jeep from the club, fortunately it was on the way to where Adelaide lives, on the outskirts of Hallowsdeep. Technically it's North Point.

Adelaide's cabin is secluded and small, you would only know where to find her if you are a part of the community. It's a one story log wood cabin, surrounded by wild flowers that she clearly doesn't maintain. The chimney has a plume of smoke creeping out, even though it isn't cold out. I'm thankful that Adelaide is a nomad, if she was a part of the coven, there's no way in Hell we could have come here.

The door opens to the cabin, and the witch looks at Stevie first before her gaze reaches mine. Her skin is a light brown and her hair is cropped short to her head. She's wearing black yoga pants, and a cropped white t-shirt. Not the usual visual you would have of a fortune teller. But she's the best at what she does on this coast. I just wonder how vague she's going to be about the answers I need.

"I was wondering what time you would come," she says.

"What, the cards can't tell specific times?" Stevie mumbles next to me. Adelaide gives her a pointed look, and I want to poke her in the ribs. Why is she being such a little shit?

"I see you are still upset about your reading, Stevie," Adelaide says as we both walk into the small living room. Adelaide gestures for us to sit on the cream-colored loveseat. There's a square table with a black tablecloth between us as Adelaide takes a seat across from us. "I told you I can't force a reading, Stevie."

"That's enough," Stevie says, glaring at Adelaide. What the Hell happened between these two?

"Fine. Blair, you're the one here for the reading, anyway."

"Yes, I'm focused on the present and the future."

"The present and future is nothing without the past." She tsks as she shuffles the deck. The cards are gorgeous, hand painted. The backs are all black with foiled intertwined snakes. She shuffles as she hums, her deep gaze never leaving mine. Adelaide places three cards on the soft tablecloth in front of us.

Past. Present. Future.

I watch as her long, dark, purple nails flick over the first card. Indicating my past. "The Moon," she says. It's a beautifully detailed card, black with gold, just like the other side. A moon at the bottom and two koi fish circling each other on the top. The card doesn't face me and I already know its significance. It's negative. "Someone in your past has misrepresented something, or has created a misunderstanding. There's a lot of fear and anxiety in your past."

I nod my head, not wanting to say aloud how misrepresented I felt as a child and how much more needs to be cleared up for my past to make sense.

The middle card is glaring at me, the golden snakes taunting me, like I'm a joke. Adelaide flips the card.

"Justice," Adelaide says, humming, her eyes gazing up at me. The black and gold card faces me, the sword prominent in the middle with scales equaling out to each side. "It seems the cards have not decided if your justice is validated. While karma is meant to be yours, accountability on your end needs to be the payment."

"Well, that's horseshit," I grumble.

"The cards don't lie, much like your tongue does," Adelaide bites back and I sit up straighter.

"Will my lies catch up to me?"

"Don't they always?" Adelaide says, looking at the last card, the most daunting of the three. As soon as the card flips, the silence in the room is palpable. The gold of the card almost looks fuzzy as I stare at the image facing Adelaide and not myself. "The hanged man," she says. She doesn't immediately go into her representation of the card.

"This is bad," Stevie whispers, "we shouldn't have come here."

"It isn't irreverently bad," Adelaide says. "The hanged man means many things, the lack of sacrifices, or the need for sacrifice. But it also means the need for apathy. The sacrifice isn't always literal. It's sometimes a sacrifice that cuts so deep, you would rather die than make it."

"Well, that's comforting, and not really what I came here for."

"I can't tell you what you are, Blair. Those are not questions I have the answers to, but we can consult the cards."

As badly as I want to tell her to go fuck herself with her cards, I nod my head. She flips the card and places it lengthwise against the present card. "The empress." The card with the queen stares at me. I don't need Adelaide's divination to tell me what this means. "Find your mother, and you will know all."

"Where is she?" I ask.

"My cards are not a GPS. That, you will need to resolve on your own."

"Well, this has been riveting," Stevie says snidely next to me.

"Don't blame the cards for your possible misfortune. And don't be rude to the woman you ghosted when you didn't like what you heard."

"Let's go, Blair," Stevie says, tugging at my arm.

"What did the cards tell you?" I ask Stevie.

"Ugh, the hermit, that I would be alone. Isolation."

"That could mean so many things," I say to her.

"Blair, you're all that I have. If I was truly alone, that would mean that you weren't here." I stop in my tracks, staring at her. Stevie's card claiming that I will no longer be around, and me drawing the card for the hangman. *Sacrifice.* There was already a sacrifice in my honor, will there be another one?

"Fuck divination," I say, forcing a smile for Stevie.

"Yeah, fuck divination. Now, let's go find your sack of shit, cheating ex-boyfriend."

"Yeah, let's go do that."

As hard as I try, Adelaide's words follow me throughout the day. It could be a sacrifice so strong that you wish you would have died. She couldn't have given me one decent fucking card. *Fuck divination.*

We figured the first place to look for Ryan would be at his brokerage. Unfortunately, he wasn't there, fortunately his assistant is a man and easily persuaded. He has another open house today. I'm a little ticked off that my posters didn't at least slow down his business a little bit.

It's a smaller house than the last open house I attended. The on goers are a little less stuck up and there's no sound system to blast provocative sounds from.

"Maybe I should ask him?" Stevie says. Not a bad idea, he's not likely to give me any information.

"Sure, we will call that plan A," I say, and Stevie smirks at me.

I hide in the foyer as Stevie meets with Ryan in the living room.

"Stevie, hey. Are you looking for a new house? I don't blame you for wanting to move out of Blair's." *Dick.*

"Yeah, honestly, living with her has been really tough lately."

"Has she been crying nonstop?"

"Something like that," Stevie says. Yeah, crying with passion from taking your dad's giant demon cock.

"Well this is a three bedroom, two bath, new HVAC system." Ryan starts listing off the features of the house.

"Actually, I was thinking about staying with my Aunt Josie for a while. Her phone isn't working, and she sent me the address to her new place in North Point and I just haven't been able to find it."

"Oh, I can't give out private information."

"I understand. Oh, I just baked these chocolates. They're to die for. Do you want one?" Stevie asks. I love my cousin.

"I'm trying to cut back, but those do look amazing." He picks up the chocolate from the small container that Stevie brought. I'm not surprised he took it, he's had plenty of Stevie's baked goods before. "Damn, these are amazing."

"Thanks, they're a new recipe. I hate to ask again, but that address?"

"7867 Marrow way," he says, shaking his head, confused as to why he told her the address.

"Thanks, oh, and why did you cheat on Blair?"

"She intimidated me, and I wanted to feel like a man in control again."

I roll my eyes. That's what he thinks deep down. But I know the truth. He's just a greedy asshole.

"That's sad, Ryan. Wishing you the best. Not!" Stevie says as she meets me in the foyer and we dash to the car.

"Looks like we're driving back to North Point," I say.

"Looks that way," Stevie replies.

CHAPTER TWENTY-THREE

TAX

"I can barely feel him," Kas says when we portal back to the bungalow.

"What do you mean, *feel* him?"

"Don't be dense, we blood share," she replies and I roll my eyes, wanting to burn the imagery out of my mind. I won't lie and say that I didn't enjoy giving Blair my blood. Even though she has no idea that it means that I can always sense her. I'll tell her, eventually.

"What are you feeling?" I ask Kas.

"He's weakened for sure. Not dead, well, as dead as a demon can get, anyway."

We can be sent back to Hell, and our souls can be destroyed there. But here on Earth, there's not much that can do a lot of damage. Our bodies heal. We can't be exorcised when you have a corporeal body. There are some dark objects that can send you back to Hell. But they're hard to come by. Most were confiscated and brought back to Hell a few centuries ago.

"Should we go to the club and see if anyone saw anything?"

Kas nods, gripping my forearm, and we portal back to the club. The event space doesn't hold the same appeal as it did a few hours ago. Not when I had my cute little witch on my arm, under my palm and on top of my lap. I should let Kas handle this and crawl back into bed with her. I know she's stressed about everything that happened tonight and it's my job to take care of her.

The look in Kas' eyes is deadly though, and I need to make sure she doesn't do anything crazy. There aren't as many people in the club as there were earlier. It's died down. Though the acts happening around us seem more intense than they were earlier in the night. Seems that later in the evening, the more sadistic the club goers get, I think it correlates to how many more vampires are now here.

I scan the dimmed space and see if there's anyone I know. Luckily, I see Ronan, the Reaper, from earlier. He has a new sub tied up in the same standing position. This dude clearly has a lot of stamina.

"Ronan?"

"What?" he asks before he flogs the tiny blonde in front of us. She whimpers but pushes her ass back to his touch.

"Have you seen Asmodeus?"

"The annoying blonde? I'd whip him into good shape, that one. That boy wouldn't have such a sharp tongue after I'm done with him."

"Yeah, that's the one."

"The demon that was exorcised portaled out of the room with him."

"They *what*?" Kas asks from behind me. I swear I can see steam billowing from her ears.

"Don't shoot the messenger," Ronan responds, flogging the woman again.

"Any idea of the portal location?"

"Looked like a shitty bar," Ronan replies.

"Eternal," I say, looking at Kas then back to Ronan. "Thanks for your help, Ronan."

"No, thank you for that beautiful show earlier. If she ever wants anyone else to play wi—"

My hands are around his throat. "Don't finish that sentence." I release his throat and he guffaws.

"I really don't know how demons got this reputation of being the big bads of the supernatural world. You all are a bunch of lovesick puppies."

"Whatever. Come on, Kas, I know where we need to go." She doesn't ask any questions as we portal to the shit hole bar I visited not that long ago.

"This place is disgusting," Kas says as her red bottom shoe sticks to some sticky substance on the floorboards. "Why would she bring him here?"

"I have someone who might know," I say, scanning the room, looking for the greasy fuck. "Beelzebub," I whisper over to her.

"I hate that guy," she says, lifting her shoe, inspecting the bottoms and groaning. "Is that Erlik?" Kas asks, pointing over to the Thor-like man in the corner. Erlik is too pretty for his own good. I'm really not sure how Lucifer matches the body to the soul. In this case, he got it right. Pretty on the outside, stupid as fuck on the inside. "You stay here. I'll go talk to him." I nod my head, wanting nothing to do with him. I'm going to kick Asmo's ass when we find him. Taking away precious time I have with Blair. Instead, I'm at this smelly bar, trying to find out where some crazed demon has taken him. All he had to do was portal her to Hell, yet somehow she got the upper edge on him.

I can hear their conversation but don't watch, not wanting to give myself away.

"Erlik, it's been so long. How are you, sweetie?"

"Kasdeya? Looking beautiful as ever."

"Aw, thanks doll," Kas coos. "Listen, I'm kinda looking for someone. Have you seen Beelzebub or Asmodeus by chance?"

"Haven't seen Asmodeus in decades, but Beelzebub was just here. He left like ten minutes ago. Buying some artifact off of some rich guy."

"Any idea on who this rich guy might be?" Kas asks. I can tell she's making her voice as sweet as possible, it's probably a real challenge for her.

"Douglas, something? He was bragging about it. Said his boss is going to be so happy once he has the item."

"Hmm, boss, as in, not Lucifer?" Kas asks. I can hear him shuffle uncomfortably in his seat.

"I mean, I'm sure it's something freelance sanctioned by the lord."

"Very well, we will keep this a secret between the two of us. What do you say, Erlik? I don't tell Lucifer you didn't turn in a traitor and you tell no one I was here tonight. How does that sound?"

"Sounds good to me," he says.

The clicking of her heels makes me turn around. She's irritated and probably trying not to strangle Erlik. "Does the name Douglas ring a bell?"

"Douglas Cummings is one of the richest men in town. He owns a real estate company." I don't tell her it's the company my son works for.

"You know where he lives?"

"Yeah, I know where he lives. But"—I look down at my watch—"it's nearly 5 a.m. We're going to have a hard time accessing his house."

"Why?"

"He's a human who knows all about supernaturals. A collector of sorts."

"You know this because?"

I shrug my shoulders. Not wanting to admit that I took the time to look up this man and see who exactly my son was working for. The way I felt affection for Ryan was making sure he was safe from this world. That he could live a happy and healthy life, one that didn't include me or my baggage.

"All I know is he could be holding other supernatural beings in his house or have weapons against us. We need to be smart."

"We need to act fast, is what we need to do. Beelzebub might know where Asmo and Mara are. If we don't follow him now, we might lose our chance."

"Fine," I grumble, "we shouldn't portal directly onto his property."

"Okay. Well, let's go," she says, grabbing my arm, intending to hitch a ride. This is the most time I've spent with Kas in over three decades, and I gotta say, I'm not enjoying it.

Douglas Cummings' house is one that reeks of I'm a rich white man with a tiny dick. It's perched on top of a hill just on the outskirts of Hallowsdeep. A wrought-iron fence surrounds the house and property, which is easily three acres of perfectly manicured lawn. At the top of the hill sits his atrocious ten thousand square foot house. It's white and gaudy with what looks like marble pillars holding the front awning of the house.

"This place is tacky," Kas says before jumping the fence. I do the same as we walk up to the main house. It's unlikely that Beelzebub did anything besides portal here. So we take our time, being cautious as we walk around the home. Kas and I have excellent hearing and it seems that there are around two to three people in the home.

"Let's just go knock," Kas says, and I glare at her. Wanting to get this over with, I shrug my shoulders and follow her. Wondering how the back of her heel doesn't divot into the grass with each step.

Kas' perfectly manicured hand raps against the all-white door, the golden lion door knockers banging slightly with her knock.

A mousy-looking woman answers the door. "May I help you?"

Kas puts her finger under her chin and looks deep into her eyes, putting her under a wave of cognitive persuasion. What Kas wants, this unsuspecting maid will provide. I use it as needed, but Kas, she has mastered this skill beyond any other demon I've ever seen.

"Take me to your boss," she says, and the maid spins on her heel. The maid wears flats, which makes sense with cleaning a house this large. Her steps make no noise, but Kas' heels click against the opulent marble floors as the maid opens the pocket doors to the study. Revealing a devious Douglas handing a dagger to Beelzebub. A dagger that I recognize immediately.

I give Kas a look that I hope insinuates what I'm thinking. I don't even wait for her to understand the context as I get as close to Douglas Cummings and wrap my shadows around his throat, wrists and the blade—very delicately around the blade. Kas doesn't even hesitate as she pushes Beelzebub to the ground and begins punching him in the face.

"You brought more filthy demons into my house?" Douglas yells. I've had about enough of him. With minimal effort, my shadows tighten around his throat, the rolls on his neck not deterring them from choking him. We hold him with such little effort it makes me smirk. I watch as his eyes bulge and he turns purple. Until he's no longer breathing.

The maid stands starkly in the corner as Kas hits Beelzebub with murder written in her expression.

"Kas, have the maid make a devil's trap," I say.

"With what?" she says, crawling off Beelzebub. I clamp a hand on his shoulder so he can't portal anywhere. I hand her the blade and look over at Douglas' lifeless body.

"I'm sure you can get creative."

Kas hands the blade to the maid. "Here's what you're going to do, darling."

CHAPTER TWENTY-FOUR

BLAIR

My hands fist the wheel of the Jeep as we drive back to North Point. I haven't seen my mom since that night in the forest. The look on her face was something I'll never forget. She looked like she was doing the right thing, like the idea of finally getting rid of me would be the best thing to ever happen to her.

While I haven't given much thought to matricide in the past, it's completely on the table now. I need to do what I have to, to protect myself. It's clear that unconditional love isn't a real thing. At least when it comes to my parents. A semi-absent father and a mother who would have killed me given the chance.

"Do you think she'll be there?"

"Maybe," I say, trying to concentrate on the road.

"Do you want her to be?" Stevie asks.

"I'm not sure. What do you say to your mother after she tries to sacrifice you?"

"Good point."

The cottage is basically in the middle of nowhere. It's a bumpy ride as the Jeep handles the gravel driveway. It's desolate, and it's honestly a great place to hide. I have no idea why she hired Ryan to be her realtor. Not that she took much of an interest in my life, or that we spoke often, she at least had to be privy to the fact that we were dating.

This driveway has to be at least three miles long before we reach the cottage. It looks unkempt and decrepit. If you walked past it or stumbled upon it during a hike, you would think no one lives here. Her car isn't out front and since it's daytime, I can't tell if there are any lights on in the house.

I sigh as I park the car, and both Stevie and I get out.

"Do you sense anything?" she asks and I shake my head. I would have assumed she would have put wards up around the home. At least something.

We walk up the porch of the cottage, curving my hands to look in the windows and not seeing anything. The plank porch creaks as I reach the front door.

Chancing my luck, I turn the knob and see if it's locked. It's not, the cool metal of the gold feels daunting on my palm as I turn it. The door creaks eerily as I open it all the way. The inside is completely polished, looking nothing like the exterior. It's simple and not high end, but it's clean and modern enough.

The foyer is small. There are rain boots and a single jacket hanging on the hook. Straight ahead is an open concept living room, dining room, kitchen combo. There's a TV on mute with the captions playing and a small purple couch in the living room. The dining room space has nothing and the plain wooden kitchen is spotless.

There are three doors to the back of the cabin. I would imagine two bedrooms and a bathroom.

"Let's stick together," Stevie says, grabbing my wrist. I don't want to sound like a scared little bitch right now, but something feels off. Ominous, almost. My mother might be a raging bitch, but she's the High Priestess. Seemingly the most powerful in the coven. She wouldn't leave her home open like this. She would have at least had wards up. At a bare minimum, the door would have been locked. Josie is a lot of things and paranoid sits pretty high on the list.

A low thump makes both Stevie and I jump. We hear it again. *Thump. Thump. Thump.* The noise is rhythmic and almost like someone is knocking on a door.

"I think it's coming from the door on the left," I tell Stevie. She nods her head, her grip nearly bruising my wrist.

"This is so fucked," Stevie says.

"*Perspicuss,*" I whisper. It's a defensive spell. Anyone who is looking at us will see us, but not clearly. It will confuse them and at least give us a chance to escape if need be. I'm prepared to do what I need to if it comes down to it.

"Good idea," Stevie whispers. The thudding noise doesn't stop. It only gets louder and louder. Stevie and I walk toward the door where the sound is coming from.

I don't want to tip off whoever or whatever is in that room to our presence. My hand slowly grips the brass door handle. As slowly as I can manage, I twist the knob and I crack the door. The noise never stops, still on pace with before, so I open it even further. Stevie's grip is tight on my upper arm as we both look into the room.

What I find was not what I was suspecting at all. It's my mother looking haggard and exhausted. Her hair hasn't been brushed, and she's wearing a nightgown. Her feet are black and disgusting, like she's been running around outside for days. She bangs her head violently against the wall of the bedroom. I can see her lips moving, but I can't hear anything she is saying.

"Josie?" I say. She looks over, confused, obviously not being able to see anything. She turns her head back to the wall and continues to hit her head. A trail of blood beads from her hairline, down her cheekbones and jaw until it drips onto the floor.

"*Perspicuss finis,*" I whisper. Stevie's hand is nearly cutting off the circulation to my arm. "Josie?" I ask, calling my mother's name again.

She turns and looks at me and Stevie. Whoever is looking at me, isn't fully my mother. While I can sense the presence of her magic, it's been significantly weakened.

"Make it stop," she says, looking at me. There's a crazed glimmer in her eye.

"Make what stop?"

"The pain. She took it all. I was good for a while. She said I was good. But I wasn't good enough. Not strong enough." She's pacing, looking at the wall again. There's a smear of her blood against the off-white paint.

"Who said that?"

"Ugh! Don't be fucking stupid!" she screams before she paces again. Her eyes dart back to the wall and she hits her head again.

"What the fuck do we do?" Stevie asks.

"She needs you, not me," my mother mumbles. She hits her head really hard then on the wall. The blood gushing from her head more steadily now. "We'll just have to call her."

Collecting her blood, she begins to draw a symbol against the white wall.

"Fuck, you need to stop her," Stevie shouts and I'm moving. My hand wrapping around her forearm, pulling her hand away from the wall.

My mom thrusts her head backward, hitting me in the face, making me wince and groan. She continues to draw on the wall.

Stevie tries to stop her from writing and she grabs Stevie by the throat and hauls her across the room. I hear a crack and look over and see that she isn't moving. Her arms limp around her sides as her body lies precariously against the dresser.

The words escape my lips before I can even think about how I feel about saying them. "*Mortem a suffocatio.*" I watch as my mother's hand lifts from the wall, no longer creating the symbol that I'm pretty sure was created to summon Mara. Her hands wrap around her throat as her body restricts the airflow from her body. She falls to her knees, as her lungs can't take in any air. The veins in her neck and face turn blue and her eyes bulge from her head. Until there's nothing but silence in the cabin, the last noise I hear before I run over to Stevie is my mother's dead body hitting the hard wooden floor.

I should feel more, there's a price to pay for death magic, my soul should be fractured. I should feel cracked in half. My magic should be revolting against the evil I just used, but it doesn't; it sits calm and content within me. It shouldn't be possible, witches have died casting death magic before. It's probably a part of why they are so docile now. I look down at my hands which are shaking heavily. Though I know I didn't use my bare hands to kill my mother, I might as well have with how this feels. My magic isn't revolting against me, but my mind is spiraling.

My eyes are watery, but I hold back the tears. I'm on my knees in front of Stevie, cupping her pretty face in my hands.

I can tell she's breathing. Thank Hecate. "Stevie, sweetie, you need to wake up. We need to get out of here."

I'm not sure how much of the design needed to be completed. If what she has now was enough to alert Mara. I just know I need to get my cousin the fuck out of here now.

Stevie groans and shifts her weight slightly. Her eyes still haven't opened, and I'm panicking. The adrenaline is wearing off. I just killed my own mother. Her body is right over there. I'm not sure how much was left of her inside of that shell, but it was still her to some degree. While I might not have loved her, she tried to kill me. How does someone conceptualize killing the person who brought them into this world?

"Stevie, please, we need to go." She doesn't move, and I'm just lost. I don't know what to do.

With shaky hands, I take my phone from my pocket and dial Dax. He picks up on the first ring.

"Hey, babe, what—" he starts.

"Dax," I say, knowing it comes out as a croak.

"Babe, where are you? What's wrong?"

"Can you portal to me? I need help, Stevie, she's—" I can hear the tears in my voice, but they still haven't leaked from my eyes.

There's shuffling. "Dax can't come, but I will." It's Kas' voice, and I lamely nod my head, thinking she can hear me. She hangs up the phone, and I wonder how she's going to know where we are. So I text the address to Dax's phone.

I have to retype the numbers of the house twice before I get it right and shoot off the text. It's not even two seconds later that I hear a large pop and the front door banging open.

Kas storms in the room, looking at my dead mother on the floor and Stevie's crumpled body against the dresser.

She doesn't speak, she just picks Stevie up like she weighs nothing. Apparently demon strength is a universal thing.

I follow her outside where we stand in front of the Jeep. "Your keys," she says.

"What?"

"Your keys, little witch. Sit in the backseat with her, and I'll drive your car home."

I nod my head and place the keys into her perfectly manicured palm. Getting into the backseat, she slides Stevie in next to me. I pet her long red hair between my fingertips as Kas gets in the front seat and drives like a bat out of Hell back to Hallowsdeep.

She doesn't say a word until we're on the highway. "Is she okay?"

"Yes, I'll give her some potions when we get home. I think she just hit her head pretty hard."

"Who was that back there?"

I look out the window and sigh. "My mother."

"Oh, fuck," Kas says.

"Yeah, it's been a pretty shitty week."

"Listen, as soon as we get back, I need to leave. Dax needs me."

"Is everything okay?" I ask, worried about Dax and also selfishly wanting him to be here with me.

"No," Kas replies, giving me no details and my thoughts begin to spiral. How does someone kill a demon? Are there worse things that could happen to him?

It's not long before Kas is basically pulling the e-brake on my car and jumping out and taking Stevie in her arms. I open the front door and she begins to follow, but she's blocked by my wards. I can't carry Stevie, so now I'm going to have to give yet another demon access to my house.

"I need your blood," I say, and she holds out her hand. I prick her finger with a conjured needle and allow her within my wards. She gently places Stevie on the couch, kisses her hair, and is immediately gone. I have a sick, deep, horrible feeling about what is happening to Dax, but right now I need to take care of Stevie.

I leave her unattended to gather the supplies from the kitchen. Thank Hecate she labels everything with retentive detail. I pop the cork on the pain reliever, muscle relaxer, and bone growth potion and toss them all into her mouth. She doesn't swallow, so I have to hold her mouth shut and plug her nose until she thankfully swallows every drop.

I sit next to her body for hours until she finally wakes up.

"Blair?" I pop onto my knees and pet her hair.

"I'm here. You feel okay?"

"Yeah, how did we get home?"

"It's a long story. Let's get you up to bed."

She nods and puts too much of her body weight on me to support. But eventually, with my arm looped around her waist, we're able to get her into her bedroom. I plop her on her bed and her familiar, Gary, purrs and cuddles next to her chest.

"Watch after her. Come get me if she needs anything," I tell the cat. He blinks at me three times, which I take as confirmation and understanding. Fez is incredibly intelligent, Gary, not so much. But he's Stevie's familiar and will be in touch with her emotions.

I huff at the exertion and can't help it that as soon as I get to my bedroom I fall on top of my mattress, not even bothering to change my clothes. I know there are a few splashes of blood on my top. Tomorrow's problems are going to be tomorrow's problems.

Facing the fact that I killed my mother doesn't need to come today, nor do the negative thoughts about what could be going on with Dax. He probably can't afford me distracting him anymore than I already have.

As much as I try to pep talk myself into not spiraling into a panic attack, I can't sleep. I open my night stand and take a swig of ever sleep potion. It hits me hard and fast. Removing any impending thoughts from my brain and lulling me into a deep slumber.

CHAPTER TWENTY-FIVE

DAX

I'm feeling fucking murderous; we've been at this for hours and the little pig still hasn't squealed. My eyes stare at Beelzebub tied to a chair in a devil's trap. Careful to leave him in the center and that my footing doesn't step over the line. The pentagram is drawn in blood, courtesy of Kas. I think she might have had too much fun opening up Douglas' gut and having the maid draw the trap on the floor. The poor maid stands in the corner, eyes glazed, blood on her fingers and apron.

Beelzebub was hoping to make a deal with Douglas for the dark item that the maid holds. The blade was created by Archangel Michael after Lucifer figured out how to give demons corporeal bodies. They wanted a way to send us back to Hell and cause real damage. I want to know why he wanted it, if he was giving it to Mara and where the Hell Asmo is. I need a nap, a good fuck, and a bagel sandwich.

He can't portal, but since he has a corporeal body, there's no exorcism to be had. He's stuck here until we release him. The chair he's strapped to is a wooden and leather desk chair. Blood runs down his face as Kas instructs the maid to slice it up. The knife exhumes dark magic, easily tearing through his flesh.

"Where's Asmodeus?" Kas growls at Beelzebub.

"I told you already. I don't know shit."

"Darling, would you mind slitting his throat just a tad?" Kas instructs the maid. The woman, who just was at the wrong place at the wrong time, nodding her head to Kas' instructions.

The silver blade is tightly pressed in her hand as she slits his throat, enough to burn and bleed, not enough to kill.

"Why were you getting this blade?" I ask him. He grins, his snaggle teeth covered in blood. It's clear to me that Lucifer gave him a body as ugly as his personality.

"Like I would tell you two mindless flackies?" he asks Kas, coughing and sputtering. He looks more disheveled than usual.

"Says the guy who is tied up and in a devil's trap. I think our little maid friend needs to get a little more creative."

"I'm not telling you shit."

"Darling, open his pants for me, will you dear?" Kas says, speaking to the maid. Beelzebub's eyes go wide. The maid's hands shake as she unbuckles his pants. "Tell me something valuable or our lovely friend here is going to chop your pathetic little dick off. That's a dark object, Beelzebub, meaning only Lucifer himself could help you. Do you really think he would be so willing to help you regrow a pecker when you had information about Mara and didn't tell him?"

"Stop, wait!" he shouts.

"You can stop, for now," Kas says to the maid.

"I don't know where Asmo is, but I know where Mara lives. Well, has lived. Sometimes she lives in the homes of people she possesses. She probably took him there."

"Spit it out," I say, getting annoyed.

"Above the coffee shop on main," he says.

"That's two doors down from Blair's restaurant. You've got to be kidding me. What does she want with her?" I ask him, holding myself back from stepping into the devil's trap.

"She wants her to be her vessel. It's time that Lucifer is overthrown. Mara is powerful enough to do it. I've just been helping her reach her potential."

We already knew about the vessel. But this far-fetched plan to overthrow Satan himself? Kas and I both laugh at the deluded demon in front of us. Many have tried to take over Hell as their own and failed monumentally. To think a demon with no form stuck on Earth could overthrow him is comical.

"Do whatever you want with the maid, but let's go," I tell Kas.

"We should kill him, it's what our Lord would want," she says.

"Agreed," I reply, grinning at her blood thirst. She might seem like she doesn't give a shit about Asmo, but it's clear that's far from the case.

"Darling," Kas coo's at the maid.

"Yes," she replies in the trance.

"Strike him right in the heart."

She lifts the blade, and Beelzebub rocks his body in the chair. "Tell Lucifer we said hi when you get back to Hell, fucker," Kas says before the maid drops the blade down on his heart. His black inky soul drips to the ground like volcanic sand as it drags him back to Hell. His body following suit and crumpling to a no longer usable meat suit.

The maid leaves the circle and walks to Kas. "You did so good, darling." She strokes the maid's hair, smiling lovingly at her before Kas snaps her neck. The crunch is quick and quiet, her body rumbling to the floor. "Let's go." She rips the apron off of the maid and wraps the blade around in it before handing it to me and I place it in my pocket.

"Did you really have to kill her?"

"She wouldn't have been able to live with what I made her do. She'll enjoy herself in whatever resting place is chosen for her," Kas says. I won't admit it, but she probably has a point.

We leave the mess of this mansion behind us, three dead bodies. Detectives will have a field day with the case. I'm sure they'll speculate about satanic rituals, and they won't be too far off.

Kas and I both portal to the coffee shop. My elbow hits the windowpane of the door before sticking my arm through and unlocking it. No alarm sounds and we head to the upstairs loft of the shop. When I try to open the door to the room, it gives resistance.

"Fuck," Kas says next to me.

"What is it?" I ask and she growls lowly.

"Something's wrong with Stevie," she says.

"You gave her your blood?"

"Like you didn't give any to your little witch."

I shrug my shoulders, knowing that I did give Blair my blood. But it was to heal her wounds, not to track her like she's a microchipped animal. My phone buzzes and it's Blair's number. I answer immediately.

"Hey, babe, what—" I try to ask.

"Dax," she says, sounding like she's on the verge of tears.

"Babe, where are you? What's wrong?"

"Can you portal to me? I need help, Stevie, she's—" She's definitely on the verge of breaking down, I'm about to portal right to her. Kas snatches the phone from my hand.

"Dax can't come, but I will." She hangs up the phone and I look at her like she's insane.

"Your witch is fine, Stevie isn't. I will go to them and bring them back to their house. You investigate this. I'll be back as soon as I can. I can feel Asmo getting stronger anyway. It's probably best that you find him and not me, I might murder everyone on sight."

"Make sure she's okay," I say, knowing deep down that there has been no physical harm to her, but something isn't right. She nods her head before she portals to wherever Blair and Stevie are. I swear to Satan if she went somewhere without telling me and put herself in danger, I'm going to fucking lose it.

I push my shoulder hard against the door and the wood splinters as the top hinge falls off and the door bursts open wide. The room is empty, a mattress on the floor with a patterned quilt on top and two pillows, and a fuck ton of blood staining the sheets. It's ominous how quiet it is here, but someone has very clearly been here recently. There's a wooden rocking chair next to the bed and a suitcase of mismatched clothes. It looks like there's a trail of blood on the floor, starting from the bed and heading over to the dresser..

My phone dings, and I hope it's Blair or Kas with an update.

Ryan: Do you want to get dinner tomorrow?

Fuck, now is when he decides to reach out? If I don't get some of these issues resolved, there's no way I can make this happen, but refusing his invitation makes me look like I don't care.

> **Me:** I'm busy with work, but I'm sure I can
> make it work.

> **Ryan:** Great, same place as last time.

> **Me:** Sure. See you tomorrow.

What's one more obligation on my plate? Beelzebub is dead, Asmo is still missing. No one knows who Mara is possessing right now, and my girl is under duress. How did I go from the best night of my life to the worst?

I'm about to say fuck it and go home to make sure Blair is okay, when I notice the blood droplets flow to a bigger pool splattering on the ground. That's when a card on the floor catches my eye.

Adelaide Forten, Augur to the inhuman. The card is black with gold foil and a single bloody fingerprint lays on the corner. I dig around the room and find nothing else seems amiss. I portal to the address on the card, a small dainty cabin in North Point. My fist doesn't even hit the door before the door swings open.

"Was wondering when I would be seeing you, demon," she says. If I'm being honest, I've never seen a more laid back looking fortune teller in my life.

"Do you know why I'm here?"

"You picked up my card, and I know where you found it."

"Mara," I reply.

"Yes, just one of the many powerful demons I've had the displeasure of meeting lately."

"Was one of them a blonde man who looks to be in his early twenties?"

She arches an eyebrow and nods her head for me to follow her. We enter the front of the house where she clearly meets clients. She pushes the black curtain, and I walk through where there's a living room and kitchen. Her decor is simple, but it's not till I see the bloody mess that is Asmo lying on her couch do I get suspicious.

I grab the witch by her arm. "Why is he here?"

"I found him in my front yard like this. Don't fucking touch me, demon," she hisses, pulling her arm away.

"You're lucky I didn't just leave him out there. Not that I think he can bleed out. But something's wrong with him."

"He isn't healing. What the fuck?" I take my knife out, making sure it isn't the dark object and cut my arm, dripping my blood over his wounds. Which causes them to heal. Really not pleased about being able to feel this fucker for the foreseeable future. This makes little sense. "I'll take him home."

"Good, and you can tell the rest of your demon friends to fuck right off. Bunch of ungrateful cunts."

"I don't have any other demon friends," I say, and she rolls her eyes. I grab Asmo by the waist and portal us to the bungalow, where Kas is waiting.

"What happened?" she asks, looking at Asmo's pale face as I place him on the couch.

"He wasn't healing. He lost a lot of blood."

"You gave him yours?" she asks and I nod my head. She strokes his bloody, matted hair, taking a knife out of her pocket and cutting her own arm, dropping some of her own blood on his tongue. I'm not sure if it's a possessive move or hoping she can help him heal quicker. Whatever it is, it quickly works as he blinks his eyes up at us.

"Asmo?" Kas asks.

"Baby, fuck. That bitch is insane," he says as he sits up. "Crazy ass tried to possess me, tried to clear me of my body. I guess she doesn't understand how corporeal bodies work. She had a dark object, some sort of scalpel, kept bleeding me, hoping my soul would go back to Hell and she could take the vessel."

"She told you this?"

"Yeah, she's actually really chatty. Really crazy too. Said what a shame it would be to take over my body because she would like to have more demon friends."

"What else did she say?" I ask.

"Said that she was raised as a human, but about a year ago she kept doing bad things that felt good. Slowly it felt like her body couldn't hold her anymore and then she was free from the confines of her mortal form. She's been possessing people since then. None of the vessels can hold her long, ejecting her."

"You mean, she isn't possessing and leaving them, she's getting pushed out?"

"Yeah, or the vessel dies, and she has to leave," Asmo says.

"And she thinks Blair will be the perfect vessel?"

"She said she's been blessed."

Kas and I both furrow our eyebrows. "Blessed?"

"Not in the Jesus, Hallelujah, sense. I'm not really sure what she meant by it, but she thinks she's perfect and she won't stop until she gets her. She's strong, Dax. We need to get her back to Hell fast."

"How did she take you, anyway?"

"She held the dark object to my throat," he says.

"How did you get to Adelaide's?" I ask him, hoping he still has enough strength to answer.

"I found it in the room. I couldn't hardly think straight enough to portal. But with the address there in front of me, I was able to focus."

He dozes off and I look between them.

"You got this covered?"

"Yes, but I will need to check on Stevie later." I nod my head and look at the way she looks at Asmo. Something sinks in my gut, making me realize that it's the way I look at Blair. "Blair is probably going to be upset when you get there," Kas says.

"Why?"

"Probably best to hear it from her."

CHAPTER TWENTY-SIX

DAX

Again, I find Blair in her bed, sleeping in her clothes. Fortunately, not the same clothes I left her the other night. Her hair fans her face against the pillow as she breathes heavily. She's curled up on her side, no blanket on top of her. A tight black shirt clings to her chest and she's wearing a black skirt.

I love looking at her like this. Her face relaxed and her mouth pouty. Nothing bothers her when she's like this. She's peaceful and pliable. While sleep takes her, no one is after her or disappointing her. Blair deserves everything and I'm here to make sure she gets it, that I give her the best and the darkest parts of me to her, knowing full well she wants them both.

I've seen the gleam in her eye when I talk about things I want, and how she admires my violence. We were made for each other and there's no way in Heaven or Hell that I'm going to let her go.

As I push her hair off of her neck, I notice a few splotches of blood. It looks like she may have been scratched. Anger and fear rip through my chest and I take my shirt off while panting heavily.

She's mine.

Fucking *mine*. And someone hurt her, touched her. I wasn't there. I was too fucking busy finding Asmo, torturing a demon, and finding dark objects. Is this what our life would look like, me constantly away, not able to be there for her while I do Lucifer's dirty work? There's no getting away from what I am and who I work for. But for the second time in my life, I wish I could be something else, something better.

I remove all of my clothes, my breathing heavy as I stare down at my witch. I try to push my dark desires down, knowing that this isn't the time. But for me it is. I need this proof that she's mine. That in any state she belongs to me.

She doesn't even move as my knee hits the mattress and my body follows suit, crawling behind her. Her body is cold from not being covered, and I grab the blanket and cover us. I know I should just sleep, my body needs it, among eating and showering. But at this moment, my craving for her— like this—sweet and content is all consuming.

My fingers graze the soft fabric of her skirt, flipping it up, revealing the delicate texture of the lacy panties she's wearing. I lift the blanket to look at her ass. The panties are pink and look stunning against it. There's some slight bruising on her right ass cheek, but nothing that won't heal in due time. I'm pretty sure if Blair wanted to, she could heal it with a potion or a spell. But she didn't. She chose to wear my mark, wear my panties that I bought her, in the color I selected. It's like she's beckoning me to touch. I'm a demon, an incubus at that. This is my fantasy. She knows this is something I want, and she agreed to, wanting it. There were no complaints when I woke her up by tasting her.

Knowing that she wants this just as bad as I do, my body moves before my mind does. A demon only has so much restraint and mine is gone as my fingers dip into her panties from the front, pushing her plush ass against my hard erection. I grind against her soft cheeks and she doesn't even stir. I slide my fingers next to her clit, knowing I need to get her wet and ready for me. The idea of her unconsciously knowing that it's me, that she knows that I need this makes me harder.

I remove my hand and lick my fingers before I begin gently rubbing her clit. I expect her to wake rather quickly, but she doesn't. Slowly I insert two fingers inside of her warm cunt, feeling a slight clench as she becomes wetter for me. My motions are slow and measured, lazy even. I just want to enjoy touching her like this for as long as possible. I wonder if I can bring her to the brink of orgasm and she can wake up right as it rocks through her body.

I don't expect her to stay still and let me continue touching her, but she does. She's slowly soaked my hand, ready for whatever I give her and I do. Stoking her clit a few more times, she finally stirs, but doesn't wake. I need more. I need to be inside of her. I push her panties to the side; the bruised curve of her ass on perfect display for me as I slide the head of my cock back and forth over her wet entrance. Blair still doesn't wake. With reverence and care, I slowly slide myself inside of her. She's so wet and warm for me. It's like she was made for me, for whatever I give her, she's *mine.*

My arm wraps around her chest, holding her tightly as I slowly fuck her. I'm in no rush for this to end any time soon. I never want to leave this bed. It's warm and safe and nothing is in here that can hurt her. Hurt us.

I tweak her pierced nipple between my thumb and forefinger and hum in approval as her pussy clenches around me. I hear a rush of air and Blair's breathing picks up.

"Dax?" she says it so quietly.

"It's me," I say, not stalling my thrusts, still long and deep, enjoying her.

"I missed you," she says, her arm clamping down on my own, her nails digging into my forearm.

"I missed you too, babe."

We stay like this; me fucking her tenderly with devotion, her grabbing my arm and pushing her ass against my pelvis. Her eyes are closed. I know she's awake but still tired.

"Do you want to come, little witch?"

"Please, Dax."

I pull out and she whines slightly at the movement. Placing her on her back, I look at her bright pink eyes and smile, pushing her hair out of her face before grabbing her cheeks and kissing her frantically. I'm breathless and overwhelmed by emotion when our lips part, her eyes still pink as I enter her again. She has a small smile on her face, and it's like tension is leaving her body as my lips and hands touch her reverently. This time, rocking my pelvis hard against her clit.

She still seems out of it and groggy, the friction not doing enough for her.

"You got any toys, babe?"

She haphazardly points to the nightstand. I sadly have to pull out again to lean over and open the drawer. She's got quite the haul in here, lots of things I hope to explore in the future. But right now, I find what I want. A small pink bullet. I test the settings and it seems like my girl charged it. *How fortuitous.*

Placing myself in between her creamy thighs, I hold myself up on my shins as I begin to fuck her and hold the bullet against her clit.

"Holy shit," she moans. Her back arching off the bed, one of her hands clutches the bedspread under us, the other grips hard around my wrist. She moves me so that the bullet is right where it needs to be.

I feel and hear her getting wetter, the obscene sounds of our copulation urging me to go faster. I watch as my dick becomes wetter with every thrust. "So fucking wet for me, pet. Are you going to come for daddy?"

"Yes, gods, you feel so good."

"No gods here, little witch, just your demon."

"Don't stop."

"I'm not stopping until I feel you come around my cock. Even then, I might not stop."

I turn the setting up even higher, the buzz of the toy loud in the room. Her grip on my wrist tightens, her head thrashing back as her pussy begins to milk me. Sending me over the edge. I keep the toy on her over sensitive clit as I fuck her with no mercy, showing her what she does to me, that she's mine, that she needs to take better care of what belongs to me.

She nearly screams in my ear as I come, the sensation of the toy and how hard I was fucking her too much. We're both panting when I look her in the face. She gives me a sleepy smile and holds her arms out at me. Not mad, not scared, but with want. This smaller, more fragile witch, who has been through who knows what, wants to comfort me. When is the last time I felt or desired comfort for myself?

I lie down, my head on her soft breasts, arms wrapped around her waist as her small arms wrap around my head. This, *this* was what I needed.

Clanging of pans is what wakes me up, my face pressed against the most perfect tits I've ever seen. I kiss them delicately and there's a soft giggle above me. I can't help it when I pull back and smile at her.

"What time is it?"

"Around nine, I think," she says. "Do you want to shower before breakfast?" I nod my head. I feel disgusting after the past couple of days. My feet hit the hardwood floor and I walk to the shower first. I can see in the mirror that Blair is watching my ass as I move.

"Are you watching or joining, little witch?"

"Both," she says, walking behind me and slapping my ass. She turns the spray of the shower on, holding out her palm to test the temperature. The shower is small, but it will do: a simple glass shower with white tile, a toilet and a small vanity covered in products. "Is everything okay with Asmo?"

"Yes, we found him. He's with Kas."

She nods her head, still holding out her palm under the spray. We don't speak, a million words hanging between us waiting to come out. Once the water meets her requirements, she takes my hand and pulls me into the shower.

She likes the water hot. She would do well in Hell. The thought churns in my stomach over the fact that I could never take her there. That this can only last for so long. I can't think about this, about everything I'll lose because of what I am.

The warm water hits my chest and the back of Blair's head as she presses the side of her face against my chest. I wrap my arms around her. One on her lower back and the other wrapped in her wet hair.

"I killed my mom," Blair whispers.

"Are you okay?" I ask her, because I'm not sure what else I could say.

"I feel like I should be feeling more. It's like how is my first emotion relief? My soul should be tarnished, I should be in physical pain from using that spell. I killed my mom, came home, went to sleep, and then had sex with you. That's not normal."

"Were you protecting yourself?"

She places her head against my chest again and nods her head. "She hurt Stevie, and I'm pretty sure she was summoning Mara to the cabin."

"You did what you had to do. Not being human means we feel things differently. Even though we're surrounded by them, our expectations of our emotions shouldn't be the same."

"I wish I could be human sometimes," she says.

"Me too," I say, surprising her. Her face pulls back from my chest so she can look at me.

"Why?"

I sigh loudly. She just told me something that she did, and what I have to say has been weighing on me. "I have a son," I say. She looks a little perturbed. "He's grown, probably around your age. Lucifer had this whole idea that he could create more demons, and sent us to this realm to impregnate humans. So now I have a son, who is biologically half demon, but really isn't. He's just plainly human."

"So, why would you want to be human?" she asks, eyebrows furrowed.

"I've been a shitty dad. I see him now and then, but I always keep my distance. The idea of outliving my son by multiple thousands of years made me sick. How could I let myself care about someone I knew was going to die? And in a timeframe that is in a blink of an eye to me?"

"You care about him?"

"The most I've allowed myself. I'm supposed to meet him for dinner tonight."

"Why don't you tell him what you are? Tell him what you just told me?"

"I've always worried that having a demon for a father would have been worse than having an absent one."

She places her head back on my chest, breathing softly. "Tell him what you are, Dax. I think you'll be surprised how he would act if he knew the truth."

"The truth is really difficult sometimes."

"Yeah, it really is." She holds me around my waist tightly. Neither of us have washed, but I'm content holding her here. It's nice to have someone like this, someone you can be open and honest with. When it comes to other demons, I always hold my cards close to my chest, never wanting to express vulnerable emotions. With Blair it's different, like I can be more than what I've been conditioned to be.

The warm spray continues to hit us, and I plan on taking her advice and telling Ryan as much as I can.

CHAPTER TWENTY-SEVEN

BLAIR

D ax, Stevie and I all sit quietly around the table eating the breakfast Stevie has made. I know it's wrong, but I really enjoy when Stevie is stressed because she makes a ton of baked goods. I have a chocolate croissant, bacon, and waffles on my plate. All three drizzled in syrup. The only thing breaking the silence is Clover's crying in the basement.

"Maybe we should let her go?" Stevie says.

"I mean my mom's dead, so the coven isn't really whole any more. I don't think they could do anything." Stevie looks at me like I grew five heads as I brazenly discuss my mother's death, and the fact that I killed her.

"Oh-kay. So you want to let her go?"

"Yeah, we can talk about it later."

Dax's hand is on my thigh, the touch always comforts and grounds me.

"I'm going to go work with Kas and Asmo to see who Mara has possibly possessed next. I think it's best for you two to stay at home. If you need to leave for any reason, will you please let me know?"

"Yes, I can do that," I say, as I snag a piece of bacon off of his plate. I dip it in my river of syrup before taking a bite.

"You're sure you're okay and don't need me to stay?"

"I'm sure."

We finish the rest of breakfast. The silence is terse and awkward. I'm not sure why Stevie feels uncomfortable. Maybe she heard us fucking, or the fact that she knows I killed my mother. Dax probably doesn't know what to say after unloading on me what he most likely thought was a bombshell. I almost blurted it out, took Stevie's advice, and told him everything. But after hearing the softness in his voice, how he wishes he would have been better, how he didn't allow himself to love Ryan, I couldn't do that. How can I possibly be responsible for hurting Dax. So, today is going to be for potions, experimentation, and the start of setting the world back on its axis.

I walk Dax to the front door once we finish our breakfast. Both of his large palms cradle my jaw. "I'm going to fix everything. I just need you to promise me you will stay safe."

"I promise," I say as he places a tender kiss on my lips, his thumbs gently circling my face.

"Remember to let me know if you leave the house." He gives me a stern look that does things to me.

"I will not leave the house. Go catch that psycho bitch who is trying to body snatch me." He glares at me before he creates a portal and steps in it from my front yard.

I walk back to the kitchen where Stevie is sitting, hands perched under her chin. "What's the plan?"

"Create a potion that makes people forget, test it on Clover and then give it to Ryan so he will forget me."

Stevie sighs and nods her head. "You sure you don't just want to tell him the truth?"

"After last night, there's no way. He told me about how much he would like to be human, so he wouldn't feel the way he does about having a son."

Stevie gapes at me as she takes down her grimoire, leafing through the pages. "You know this is something that will get you in trouble with the council, right?"

"It's worth the risk," I say. Leaning over her shoulder.

Her pointer finger follows a few lines of texts. "I think if we modify this potion for reinstating someone's memory, we might make it work."

"I knew I could count on you," I say as I start collecting some of the ingredients. Lavender, alder cones, elderberries, frankincense, graveyard dirt. "I gotta say, I'm impressed you already have all of this shit in the kitchen."

Stevie is unmoving, with her hip propped against the counter. "I think we should talk about last night."

"I think *we* should forget about it."

"Blair, you killed your mom. You used death magic on another witch. Something else that can get you in trouble with the council. You might not care about your life the way you're going about things. But I fucking do. I need you to care. I need you to take care of yourself."

I place the jar of graveyard dirt on the table and look over at my cousin, her red hair a mess, bags under her eyes. "She tried to kill me first, and she was going to do it again. She rendered you unconscious, for fuck's sake. What was I supposed to do?"

"I'm not saying it was unjustified. I'm saying you're being careless and acting like it doesn't affect you. I don't even know how you're up walking after using a spell like that." Stevie looks me up and down, like maybe my flesh is falling off or there's some sign of wear that she can't see.

"I'm fine, Stevie."

"That's the whole fucking point, Blair! You shouldn't be fine. Not after killing your mother, both psychologically and physically."

"I'm sorry that I'm not weeping in a corner or that my soul isn't tattered into shreds, Stevie. This is who I am. Now, are you going to help me with this potion or not?"

"You know what, do it yourself. If you can't find it in yourself to care about your safety, why should I?" Stevie turns on her heel and goes up to her room. It's the first time I've seen my cousin genuinely pissed at me and it feels like acid down my throat and stomach. But I'm too stubborn to apologize. Potions might not be my specialty, but I can make this work.

Grumbling and irritated, I pull the cauldron from underneath the sink and place it over the stove. It's 2022 but you still have to use a fucking cauldron, riddle me that. An electric stove is fine, but if you don't use an ancient conduit like this thousand year old hunk of junk, you might as well not bother brewing anything. I follow the directions. Adding in the flowers, moon water and a drop of my blood. Once it comes to a boil, I add the dried ingredients like the graveyard dirt, elderberries, lavender, and alder cones.

The directions say to let it simmer for fifteen minutes, not touching or stirring anything. I make sure the stove isn't too hot and watch as it bubbles and slowly turns a disgusting shade of olive. Frankly, the potion looks like shit. At least I have the perfect test subject in the basement to administer the potion to. It will be beneficial to all of us if Clover forgets her little mini vacation here.

After fifteen minutes, I have to do some incantation over the potion. *"nunc obliviscere me, obliviscere me in aeternum."* I repeat the chant five times as instructed before straining the potion into a glass container. Honestly, it seems too easy, but I'm not about to ask Stevie for her help.

Clover is crying in the basement, huddled up on the bed, when I open the door. "Well, Clover, I hate to break it to you, but today is eviction day."

"Really? You're letting me go?"

"Assuming this potion works, then, yes."

"What is it?" she asks.

"If I told you what it was, then you wouldn't know if it works or not."

"Will it kill me?"

"Sadly no, now are you going to drink, or would you like to continue being a freeloader in my basement?"

I hand the vial to her outstretched hand, her fist clutching it tightly before she downs the amount that I gave her. I watch as she gags slightly as the sluggish potion drips down her throat. A smear of the green liquid is in the corner of her mouth and it looks foul.

After a few minutes, Clover looks around the room questioningly.

"Do you know who I am?"

"Blair," she states. Hmm, maybe it doesn't work.

"Do you know why you're here?"

"Where am I?" she replies, and I try to hold back my smile.

"What's the last thing you remember?"

"I really wanted ice cream," she says.

"That's right, and you bumped your head and I brought you here to make sure you were all right."

"That's nice of you," she replies, and I smile and nod my head.

"I think your head is fine now. Do you want to go home, Clover?"

"That would be nice. I feel tired."

"Hitting your head will do that to you. I'll call you an Uber," I tell her as we walk upstairs.

I put in the address of Clovers' home into the app, only five minutes out, thank god. I need this girl out of my house.

"You have a nice house," she says.

"Thanks, Clover."

"You don't come around the coven much."

"The coven doesn't really like me," I tell her.

"Only because your mom told us to stay away." Another ding on the side of not feeling guilty about my recent parricide.

"Here, you can stand out here. Your driver's name is Jeff, and he drives a gray Honda Civic. Nice knowing you, Clover." I shove her out onto the front porch and lock the door behind me. This house is eerily quiet, and I consider telling Stevie that I did it on my own and that I didn't need her help. That her advice was shit and magic can help me solve all my problems. I don't think so, at least I'm mature enough not to do that. What I really need to do is give Ryan this potion before he meets with Dax tonight.

I know I promised Dax I would tell him if I left the house, but how do you say 'I left the house to poison your son with a potion so he would forget I existed so we could be together'? I don't think there's a Hallmark card with anything like that on it. I look down at my phone, knowing that Ryan will probably be getting to the restaurant at any moment. How the Hell am I supposed to get him to eat it?

I park my car in the parking lot of Lucia's, just waiting for Ryan to get here. My plan is faulty and I know that, but desperate times and all that. I watch as Dax hops off his motorcycle, looking hot as fuck. I made sure to park in the corner so he wouldn't see my Jeep. When he takes off his helmet and shakes his hair out, I almost want to come out of hiding and tell him to give me a ride and forget about dinner.

With what could be the worst timing of the century, Ryan pulls up in his BMW and parks right next to Dax and gets out of his car.

Okay, plan B. I watch as Dax and Ryan enter the restaurant. Knowing I will need to put it on his food somehow. Here's to hoping that he orders something with Pesto.

I wait about five minutes until I know they're seated and I enter the establishment from the employee entrance. Shockingly, I don't get any questions as I glance through the kitchen door to see where they're seated.

"What table number is that? I forget," I ask one of the sous chefs.

"Table twenty-one."

"Thanks," I reply, nodding my head before I grab an apron to fit in.

"Who are you?" one of the workers asks.

"Filling in, Hex is shut down for renovations. Lucia asked me to come fill in."

The man looks down at me. He's skinny, tall, and he literally looks down at me over his large nose. His dark eyes looking at me menacingly.

"This is my kitchen, don't fuck anything up."

"You got it," I say. As soon as he walks away, I wait for the waitress to bring their order to the back.

My hands are shaky, and I wonder if I can pull this off. I'm desperate to make this work. Maybe I'm more desperate to make something in my life seem less chaotic. It seems like nothing has gone right. I need this one thing. I need Dax.

The risk is worth the reward. If I can make Ryan forget me, then I don't hurt Dax, and we can keep being with each other the way we have been. If he finds out I've lied to him, he might never want to see me again. It's at this moment that I realize Stevie had merit to what she was saying. If I were honest upfront, I could have saved myself this embarrassingly desperate adventure.

I'm not sure how Dax would have reacted, but knowing now that I've lied all this time to him, when he's been so open with me. I can't let it happen, I'm in too deep.

The order is up, and I sigh, looking at their order. Fuck, I don't know who ordered what. I grab the waitress by her sleeve before she can leave. "What did the younger guy order?"

"The penne alla vodka," she says, looking at me like I have five heads.

"Thanks," I say and groan. Of all the things to hide this murky green potion in.

The chef snatches the order out of my hand and looks down at me again. I'm seriously going to set this asshole on fire if he doesn't stop doing that.

I watch as he makes the dishes, fully intending to make my move when the meal is ready to be expedited. I have the potion lid open, ready to make it work. It takes a good eight minutes before their food is ready. The chef dings the bell as the waitress comes to grab their plates. I'm fast, dumping the green mix into the Penne and mixing it in with the sauce as best as possible.

I grin with satisfaction as the waitress takes his plate and puts it in front of him.

"Does this color of the sauce look a little off to you?" Ryan says to his dad.

"I mean, it still looks good," Dax says. Thank you, Dax.

Ryan takes a fork full and puts it in his mouth. I feel an overwhelming sense of accomplishment. Until an enraged frizzy haired Clover storms into the restaurant and smacks the fork out of Ryan's hand, making it splatter to the floor and catches the attention of everyone eating dinner.

"Clover, where have you been?" Ryan asks.

Dax's eyes go wide as he looks at Clover and his gaze rakes over the rest of the restaurant.

Clover looks down at Dax and grimaces. "I've been locked in Blair's basement."

"Shit," Ryan says.

"She tried to poison me, but she's shit at potions. I pretended to forget. Psycho bitch doesn't realize how thin her walls are, either. She—"

The frying pan clutched in my grip hits her head and she crumples to the floor.

"Blair?" Dax asks, looking between me and Ryan. No one really caring about the girl I should have kept locked in my basement, out cold on the floor.

"You know Blair?" Ryan asks Dax.

"She's my girlfriend," he replies proudly, until he sees the look on Ryan's face.

"You've got to be fucking kidding me, Blair. You fucked my dad? What, to get back at me because I didn't want to be with you? How pathetic."

Dax puts his fork down and his brows furrow as he looks at the table.

"It wasn't like that, Dax," I say.

"It wasn't?" he asks. His hands clenched into fists on the table.

"I mean, it started out that way, but that's why I'm here. I thought it would be easier for Ryan to forget me so that way everything would be fine."

"Wait, make me forget? How does someone use food to make someone forget something?"

"That's not the point, I want to be with Dax. That's why I'm here to make things right," I say. I watch as Dax looks down at the table, I can almost feel the disappointment looming off of him.

"You're nothing but a bitch who does things that are in your best interest," Ryan says.

"Don't call her a bitch," Dax growls.

"So that's it then. You choose her? You couldn't be a good parent to me my whole life and now you come back saying you want a relationship and then my ex-girlfriend seduces you, and now you're ditching me?"

"No, just don't call her a bitch," Dax says, raking his hand through his dark hair. I see how conflicted he is. How I caused this. How I made more problems for him. He was trying to be better, more than a demon. He wanted this relationship with his son and I've gone and fucked it up.

Dax looks at his son pleadingly. And I can't take the look on his face.

"Dax, tell your son everything. I'm so sorry that I put you in this position. Ryan, you need to know that he didn't know we dated before we started things. That doesn't change the fact that we have feelings for each other. I'd like to make this right." I look at Ryan pleadingly. I hate this asshole, but I'd be willing to make a deal with the devil to keep Dax.

"No, fuck this. Choose," Ryan says and my heart sinks. Dax looks destroyed as he looks between us.

I make the decision for him. "Talk to your son, Dax. I'm so sorry."

"Blair..." Dax starts.

"It's okay, Dax. You know where to find me. Make things right with Ryan."

"You're going right home, right?" Dax asks, still concerned for my safety. My heart aches, and I nod while holding back tears.

"This is just fucking rich," Ryan says, and I try to stop my eye roll. Clover groans on the ground, and Ryan helps her sit up.

"Can we go somewhere more private to discuss some things?" Dax asks Ryan, and I force a smile as I turn on my heel and leave Lucia's. Unshed tears fill my eyes as I walk out the front door. I still have hope that we can fix this, but I don't see how thanks to the position my selfishness has put us all in.

I hear Ryan agree to talking with Dax, but that he needs to take Clover home first. Clearly I should have hit her with the frying pan just a little harder.

The bang of the heavy wooden door clears my thoughts as does the fresh air. Fall is right around the corner and the air feels cooler and dewy against my skin. As I look up, a handsome man with blonde hair and bright blue eyes wearing a dark black coat approaches me. "Are you Blair Bellamy?" he asks.

"Who's asking?" I reply.

Someone stealthily approaches me from behind, placing heavy iron shackles around my wrists. "Blair Bellamy, you are under arrest for the kidnapping and attempted poisoning of Clover Simmons as well as attempted interference with an *exsul*'s memory. You will be brought in front of the council in approximately three hours."

It's the last voice I hear before everything goes to black and all rational thoughts escape me.

CHAPTER TWENTY-EIGHT

BLAIR

My eyelids are heavy as I blink rapidly a few times. I go to move my hand to rub my eyes but cold heavy iron shackles prevent me from being able to reach my front. They clank as they fall back to the ground. My arms are sore from being bound behind me, and I groan, taking in the appearance of my cell.

Classic witch bullshit, all flare, no class. I'm in what I would consider a dungeon. There's cold cobblestone flooring; it feels wet and musty down here. There's a mattress that isn't fit for any human to lie on in the corner, and a basin right next to it. There's a trickle of fluid that drips against the cobblestone, and I shut my eyes just listening to the rhythmic patter of water splashing against the stone. *Drip, drip, drip.*

I've really gone and royally fucked everything up. Who isn't mad at me at this point? Fez is really the only person I can think of, and he isn't a person at all. At this moment, sitting in this cold, dreary space, I feel more alone than I ever have in my life, and that's saying something. My stubbornness and selfishness has landed me in my worst fear: Irrevocably and depressingly alone.

I should be more upset about the fact that I'm about to be set forth in front of the council and whatever punishment they dish out. The fact is, I probably deserve it. Magic has checks and balances and I've been teetering on the edge for too long. Acting like I'm better than everyone else because my mother and coven scorned me. I've used my trauma to justify my behaviors, and realizing that makes my stomach churn. I didn't think that there would be a day where retribution didn't drive me, but I don't know what could motivate me. My self-reflection has tears dripping down my face. I stop the waterworks quickly and have to use my shoulder to wipe the tears away.

Hope that at least Stevie will still care about me and love me is the only thing holding me together right now. If I even dare to think about the regret and sadness written on Dax's face from earlier tonight, I'll spiral. I just need to get through tonight, answer the council's questions, accept my punishment, and move on.

"Let's go," a voice barks beside the wrought iron bars of my cell. I look up and it's the same man who accosted me outside of the restaurant.

For the first time in my life, I keep my sharp tongue locked down, rise to my feet, and walk to the bars. He unlocks them with a ridiculously large skeleton key that's held on a ring with at least twenty other keys of different shapes and sizes. They jingle as he walks me to wherever we're going. The jingle echoes in the halls of the stone we're walking through. Almost like a taunting noise, like '*ha, bitch, time to finally face the music*.'

We walk through multiple narrow paths. It's cold and clearly underground where we are. The man holds me by the elbow as he ushers me to a large open area. There's still the same cobblestone floor, but the room is massive and there are stained glass windows at the top of the room, easily seventy feet high. The man places me on my knees on the hard, cold, uneven flooring. Damn, you can't even get a chair during your sentencing?

There are three thrones in front of me and I already know who will come out before they do. I've met them before, not here but previously when I got my first two strikes.

The first woman walks in, Elizabeth the true. She appears to be in her early thirties, but you would be mistaken. She's easily one of the oldest witches alive at nearly two thousand and ten. Her black hair is in a loose chignon, her pale face is makeup-less and challenging. Her face shows she doesn't take shit, and she doesn't know what smiling is. She's petite, but terrifying.

The next witch is Hadiza, with no last name. She's the most warm of the bunch in appearance, anyway. She at least smiles. Her skin is a dark brown, her hair in long braids reaching her waist. Her dress is bright orange and reads friendly, but I know better. Hadiza can be the most cruel with punishments out of the three.

Lastly, we have Nimue. If anyone is going to be on my side, it's her. She drowned a few men in lakes back in the fifteenth century. If anyone will understand my need for revenge, she will. She still wears clothing that would be better suited for a Renaissance fair. Her dirty blonde hair reaches her butt with two long braids in the front.

All three of the witches take their respective places in front of me. In complete synchronization, they all cross their left leg over their right and look down on me.

Hadiza speaks first. "Blair Bellamy, it's been quite some time. I was hoping you would heed our warning."

Nimue speaks next. "She's always been a firecracker, this one. Could you expect any less?"

"Endangering one of her own? Hurting someone in her own Coven, it's just abysmal," Elizabeth shrieks.

"Tell us, why did you kidnap and poison your fellow witch? In the process, also almost exposing us to a mere mortal?" Hadiza asks.

"It's like these young witches don't remember Valais, Trier, Pendle, or Salem. I'll tell you, I do. Watching some of my sisters' flesh burn at the stake. Look at you," Elizabeth spits. "Not even loyal to your own kind, not recognizing what your ancestors sacrificed so you could live freely now. I say we execute."

I glare at Elizabeth, the old coot. I remember the history of those trials, how witches didn't fight back, how they let mostly mortals die at the stake for them. They killed very few actual witches during any of the most famous trials. Seems the witches quite like rewriting history.

"Now, now, Elizabeth, let her speak," Nimue says.

I clear my throat, looking at Nimue as I speak. "There are two reasons why I kidnapped Clover and everything else that followed. The first started with her, my fellow witch sister, as you so kindly put, Elizabeth. Slept with my boyfriend." I watch as Nimue grimaces at the mention of a boyfriend. "If that wasn't enough, my entire coven tried to sacrifice me to be the vessel for a demon. That also doesn't seem sisterly, does it, Elizabeth?"

"And how are you to be believed? Is there anyone who can account for this?"

"Yes, my cousin, Stevie."

"Stevie Sutton?" Hadiza asks.

"Yes."

"Summon her, August," she tells the man in the corner. We sit and wait, all the witches glaring down at me.

It takes about twenty minutes, it's then I realize August portaled here. The council has a demon on payroll?

Stevie's wide eyes look around the room and stick to me, on my knees on the floor. Her expression reads one of 'I told you so', and 'you dumb bitch'.

"Stevie Sutton?" Hadiza asks.

"Yes, high priestess."

"Your cousin states that your coven tried to sacrifice her, is this correct?"

"Yes, ma'am."

"For what cause?"

"Josie thought the coven would be more powerful if Blair was out of the picture."

The three witches furrow their brows. Hadiza leans over to whisper to Nimue and then Elizabeth.

"Why would the coven believe they would be stronger without Blair?"

"They have been pulling from her power for some time," Stevie says, trying to be brief, but also give them enough information that they don't snap at her.

"And why would a coven be pulling power from another witch, and not the Earth? You're telling us this has been going on for years and we've never been told?" Elizabeth asks.

"Yes, that's what we're saying."

"How do you excuse the mortals for almost finding out about our kind?" Elizabeth asks.

"Honestly, that's more Clover's fault than mine. If she didn't barge in there, he would have been none the wiser."

"We do not interfere with humans!" Hadiza says loudly. When did witches become so scared? We could easily take on anything that mankind tried to do against us. But they've always been so reclusive, so passive, so unlike me.

"Something is different about this witch," Nimue says.

"She's not like us," Hadiza agrees, nodding her head.

"We've never had to give a third strike. We must make an example of her."

"Even if what she did was out of self-defense?" Stevie says.

Hadiza snaps her head over to her, her braids flying to the left of her face. "August, take her home." Stevie goes to open her mouth, but I watch as the demon portals her and takes her away.

"Demons can be useful, but not completely trusted," Hadiza says, clearly reading my confusion over August being here.

"Now what to do with you," Elizabeth says, even when she's being villainous, she doesn't smile.

"I need my magic, I need protection right now," I plead.

"You should have thought of that before you dismissed the council's rules," Elizabeth says.

"You don't understand. Someone is coming after me. If I don't have my magic, I have nothing."

"Not our problem. Magic has a price. Did you think you could use magic to solve all of your problems and there would be no consequences? You knew the rules, you have been warned. If we go lenient with you, who knows what other witches might do?"

"It's been far too long since we've had a sentencing, sisters," Elizabeth says.

"I won't let you take my magic," I say. My shackles around my wrists are tight. Too tight. I go to cast a spell and nothing works.

"Ah, quite the tool, those shackles. Like I said, demons can be very useful indeed," Hadiza says. I look at Nimue. She won't rescue me, even if she thinks the punishment is too harsh.

The three witches all stand out of their chairs at an eerily similar pace before they descend on me. Each of them placing a hand on my shoulder.

"I think a month is fair," Nimue finally says.

"So it shall be, sister," Elizabeth says.

The magic hits me harshly, and I feel like I'm having a heart attack. Like all of my magic is being crumpled up into a paper ball and thrown hard against my chest. Like it's locked inside of my body, feral and begging to get out with no escape.

"Now your magic will feel like Clover did," Hadiza says. "August, be a dear and drop her off."

"Sure thing," he says. With the chains still shackled to my wrists, he portals me to the entrance of my driveway.

"Nothing personal," he says as he unlocks my shackles. I tenderly rub my wrists. I feel so defeated and plain. It's painful to have your magic dormant inside of your own body. What kind of spell can even do that?

With my pride and hopes in tatters, I walk the long drive, the gravel crunching under my feet. When I get to my yellow door, I touch my hand against the wood. I can still feel my wards. At least I will be safe here. I guess I will need to hide out here until further notice. If I didn't have the safety of that, I don't know what I would do.

"Blair, no," I hear Stevie say, expecting her to be upset about the hearing. But that's not what happens.

I watch as Clover holds a very similar knife, the one that I saw Paige hold against Stevie's throat at the sex club.

"Clover?"

"Guess again," she says.

I gulp. "Mara?"

"You really should adjust your wards after you let a kidnapping victim go," she says.

"Clearly, I should have just killed Clover."

"That would have worked, too. This is a convenient meat suit, but it's already wearing thin, she's a weak one. I promise if you make it easy, I won't hurt your dear cousin. I'll try to make it painless for you. It's not your fault."

"What's not my fault?"

"That you were the one he cared about."

"What are you talking about, Dax?"

"Wrong Daddy." The knife gets closer to Stevie's throat, and I have no idea what to do.

"Let Stevie go," I ask.

"You'll let me in?" She pushes the blade down, a rivulet of blood dripping down the column of Stevie's throat.

"I'll let you in," I say.

"Blair, no!"

It happens so quick, but in slow motion at the same time. I watch as the inky, smoky, blackness pulls from Clover's mouth as it shoves itself through my own lips. The sensation is painful and completely foreign.

Mara shoves herself into every crevice of my being. It's like we're sharing the same body with two minds, but she's completely in control. I can't move my limbs, I can't blink, I can't speak. I'm just a passenger in my own body. The worst part is there's no escaping.

CHAPTER TWENTY-NINE

DAX

Distraught is really the only way I can describe how I'm feeling. Blair's betrayal stings, but the more I think about it the less it surprises me. I don't doubt her feelings for me, but the lengths she went to hide what she did is concerning. It's obvious her initial intention was to hurt Ryan, my son. The person I can't forget about in this equation. I wonder when it changed for her. When I wasn't meant for revenge anymore. Her reaction in the shower wasn't about me having a son, it's that she already knew and was trying, in her own way, to make things right. I didn't want to let her go, I shouldn't have let her go. She needs to be safe right now with Mara on the loose. I can only hope that she was smart enough to go straight home and not do anything stupid.

Then there's the fact that I'm sitting in front of my son, about to tell him everything that I am, about how I feel about him, and now I need to add a conversation about Blair into the mix. I'm going to need copious amounts of whiskey to get through this.

Everything started to make sense as Ryan dropped off that Clover witch to her house. He was seeing Blair, cheated on her with Clover and that's why we are all in the position we are now. I hate to admit that there is a bubbling jealousy inside of me that he saw my witch, but I push it deep down. There are other concerns at the moment.

"So? You wanted to talk?" Ryan says, sliding a tumbler across his bar top.

"It's time for me to explain to you what I am and why I am the way I am."

His brow furrows, and he takes a sip of his glass, appraising me. "I didn't know there was a special term for an abandoning asshole."

"I'm a demon," I say.

He barks out a laugh. "I really thought this night couldn't get any crazier, but here you go. Yeah, okay, you're a demon. Get the fuck out of my house."

It hurts, and it's unpleasant. But I transform slightly into my true self. It's more of a mid-transformation since I can't leave this form. He watches as black horns descend from my head, my eyes blacken, and my shape enlarges. His eyes widen in fear, and he nearly pours out his whiskey. As quickly as I make the transformation, I easily go back to my standard form. Lucifer's rules on exposing ourselves to humans isn't as strict as other supernaturals. He understands there's a time and place. When making deals, when it's absolutely necessary. He likes the edge of fear of humans, knowing there are demons among them, just not enough to cause hysteria with the other supernaturals in this dimension.

"Holy Hell," Ryan says.

"Indeed, so, like I was saying, I'm a demon."

"Does that mean I'm a demon?" Ryan asks, I almost laugh as I watch him rake a hand through his hair, expecting to find horns.

"No, and that's what I wanted to talk about."

"Okay?"

"I've stayed away because of what I am and the fact you are human. The idea of getting to know you has always seemed so inconceivable to me. That my life span is nearly endless, and yours is so short."

He downs the rest of his whiskey. "You're saying you stayed away because you didn't want to watch me die?"

"Precisely," I reply, happy that he's getting the gist of it.

"Did my mom know what you are?"

I grimace, not wanting to throw the woman under the bus. "It's complicated."

He sighs, pouring himself another glass. "This is a lot to take in. This whole night is a lot to take in."

"I can understand that." I pull out my phone, hoping that Blair texted me. No luck.

"What about Blair? She's human," Ryan says. I give him a look that shows he's being naïve. "You know what? That tracks. There was always something off about her."

"There's nothing wrong with her," I say defensively.

"You really like her?"

"I do," I reply.

"More than you like me."

"No, it's so completely different. It's probably selfish to ask you to be okay with it, but I'm going to ask."

"And if I say no?" Ryan asks.

"I don't think I can stay away from her. It goes beyond feelings and attraction."

"It's some demon thing?" he asks, grimacing.

"Something like that. I'd understand if you want nothing to do with me, Ryan. I know I deserve it, and I know me being with Blair just confuses things further. But I want you to know that I do care about you. As much as I have the capacity to. I would like to spend more time with you, but if that isn't something you want, I would understand. There's no rule book on how to be a parent as a demon. I've done a shit job so far, but I'd like to change that."

"I really need time to process all of this," Ryan says, clearly directing me to leave his house.

"Thank you for hearing me out," I tell him, and he nods his head, not saying anything else as he leads me through his front door. He shuts it gently, and I let out the breath that I was holding. It wasn't easy, but it felt like the weight I had been carrying around with me for so long has finally been lifted off my chest.

Now I need to go find Blair and have a very different conversation with my cunning little witch.

MARA

Damn, this vessel feels perfect. It's finally my perfect match. My happiness is short-lived as I watch the red head try to escape the house. It seems my vessel's magic is dormant. No matter, mine is not. I quickly chase the redhead, grabbing her by the hair and dragging her to the basement. We nearly trip over the body of the vessel I just left. I tried to be gentle in the way I left her, but I was just too excited. Plus Blair didn't really care for her, so I took care of the problem for her.

"Blair, what the fuck did you do?"

I don't answer her, seeing as I'm not Blair and the idiot was there witnessing the whole thing.

"I could still kill you, you know?" I tell her. Really, I don't enjoy killing, well, most of the time. I've tried to leave my vessels intact. While I knew that Josie would die, eventually,

I figured she deserved it. She was going to sacrifice her own daughter for crying out loud. Then there were, of course, a few unfortunate souls along the way who were trying to stop me, so they had to go. But overall, the process of killing is messy and unwarranted in most cases. Look how I kept the blonde male demon alive. While he was mostly a science experiment, I didn't really want him to die. He is quite funny, and I have hopes that we can be friends now that I'm in a form that can hold my power.

I wouldn't have wanted to have a male vessel permanently anyway. I did it twice, and it was fun to have a penis for a few weeks, but after that, I could go without. Being a woman is so much more enjoyable. The softness of the female figure is so much more profound and captivating. It probably has something to do with having had a female human form for so many years before I couldn't be contained in it any longer. Let's not forget about our capacity for multiple orgasms.

I've spent so much time trying to figure out why Blair was blessed and I wasn't. Am I not lovable enough? Did he not care about me because I wasn't half a witch? Can I even trust that the information Beelzebub gave me is accurate?

Never the matter, now I'm Blair, and I will be loved.

I throw the witch into the room in the basement. She doesn't try and do anything to hurt my vessel, so I'm gracious with not restraining her.

"Don't try anything," I say, holding the dark object near her face. I board up the door as best as I can, easily moving multiple heavy items to use as a barricade. I've done some research on witches, but I'm not completely sure of all of their abilities. Hopefully, the witch takes my warning seriously and stays put, at least until I get out of town.

I walk up the stairs until I find what I assume is Blair's bedroom. A snake hisses wildly at me, shaking frantically.

"Shut up, or I'll crush you with my bare hands," I tell him. It stops its hissing and coils away into a corner of its enclosure.

I grab her purse, looking at her credit cards and pull out her phone. "What were your passwords, Blair?"

Fortunately, I don't need them as all of her apps are thumb print based. "You can't beat technology."

I'm not going to let you keep my body, you crazy bitch.

"Oh, you're strong. None of my other vessels could speak to me. It's like having a built-in best friend. Where do you think demons would really hate to go?" I say as I pull up her banking information, happily surprised by the funds. "I appreciate you being such a saver. Now we can really splurge for the best location. Demons probably aren't a fan of the cold I'd imagine with Hell and all?"

Once my magic is back, I'm going to push you out.

"You mean my magic? You just need to sit back and enjoy the ride, Blair."

Dax will come looking for me.

"Oh, I hope he does. He looks like a lot of fun. Maybe I could take him for a spin before we set sail for our new life. Perhaps Svalbard? That seems like a very anti-demon place. Maybe there are vampires there in the dark months. I've been wanting to try a vampire."

I can feel Blair's grimace. "Not Svalbard? How about Iceland?"

A knock on the door breaks my concentration, and I put the phone on the table to see who it is. "Oh, maybe it's your hot demon."

If you hurt him.

"What are you going to do, Blair? Give me the silent treatment?"

I walk down the stairs, enjoying how this body feels. I'm happy Blair has taken such good care of this vessel for me. That was so sweet of her. We really are going to be the best of friends. Once she gets over this little fit she's having.

I open the wooden door to see the demon from the sex club. Dax, she called him. He is quite rugged and handsome. I can see the appeal.

"Can I come in?" he asks. His look is hopeful and pleading.

"Of course," I say, holding out an arm and leading him to the soft couch.

"You look better than I thought you would," he says.

"I'm tough, I can handle it," I say, trying to figure out the context of the conversation.

"I told Ryan everything. Including the fact I want to be with you. But we need to talk about why you felt like you needed to lie to me, and how you could for so long." He places a hand on my thigh, and it feels nice. Really nice. Hopefully, this leads to more.

"I'm sorry, Dax. I was being immature."

Dax raises an eyebrow at me and nods his head. "If we're going to move on from here, I need honesty from you, little witch."

I smile, nodding my head, and Dax looks bewildered in front of me. "Blair, why are you smiling and have a tear rolling down your cheek at the same time?"

I wipe the intrusive tear off my cheek. "Allergies," I reply, standing up. "Let me just go get a napkin."

"Blair?"

I don't immediately answer and groan as I turn around. Dax is holding the dark object I specifically told Beelzebub to get for me. That incompetent, worthless rodent.

"Blair?" he repeats.

"Blair can't come to the phone right now," I reply. "She's going to be my best friend, though. So unless you plan on stabbing me with that blade and hurting your precious little witch, I suggest that you back off and let me leave here peacefully. I promise to take good care of her," I say, rubbing my hands against my new body.

"You're coming with me," he says, taking a step forward.

"I'm not coming with you unless you've changed your mind and would like to go back to having fun. I can be more like Blair if that's what you need, I promise."

"Fuck, let Blair go!" he says.

"No, she's mine, and she's perfect. My new best friend is going to be really mad if I hurt you. So I think you should leave."

"Blair, babe, can you hear me?"

"I told you she's not home!"

Dax! Stab her!

"Blair, how can you say such a thing?"

"What is she saying to you?" he asks me.

"None of your business."

Dax! Portal her to Hell.

"Blair, you're really not being a good friend right now," I tell her.

"Blair, tell me. Come back to me," Dax pleads.

The words fall out of my mouth, Blair pushing heavily against my mental walls. "*Stab her.*"

Dax looks pained as he raises his arm, the blade shiny in his hand. But he doesn't stab me in the heart, the only place that would send me to Hell. He stabs me in a blowing spot in the gut. Knocking the wind out of me. I pant heavily as a pop noise around me makes my ears ring. He grabs my arm roughly as he portals me to Hell.

CHAPTER THIRTY

DAX

Never in my wildest fucking dreams would I have ever imagined portaling directly to Lucifer's private quarters. I'd been here one time, for when he made my body corporeal, that's the only reason I'm able to visualize taking us here.

His room is lavish and dark, black satin sheets cover a four poster California king sized bed. The walls have lavish filigree wallpaper in black velvet. Half of the room is glamoured to the point that I can't make out what else is in the room. The fireplace crackles and garners my attention and there's where I see Lucifer sitting on a large wingback chair, with a just as shocked Lilith on his lap.

The wound on Blair's stomach is deep and blood is covering my shaking hands. As we forcibly land on the deep, rich burgundy carpet. My gaze travels between her body and where Lilith's blonde ponytail is released from Lucifer's hand and she startles off of his lap, pulling her shirt up to cover her breasts. My focus is too set on Blair to worry about Lucifer fucking his assistant.

I can only hope that I can beg him to let me heal Blair once he ejects Mara from her body. I would do anything, give anything to make sure she's okay. That I can fix what I did. I know that I wouldn't have been able to get the upper hand if I didn't wound Mara, but it doesn't make me feel any better. I hurt Blair, when I told her I never would.

"What is this?" Lucifer stands and strides towards where I'm crouched on the floor cradling Blair's body. "Why have you brought my daughter to Hell, Daxaddon?"

"Mara is your daughter?"

His brows furrow, and he gets down on his knees. He strokes Blair's face affectionately. "They both are," he says. "Lilith, love. Fetch Milcom for me."

"Yes, sir," she says. Putting more clothes on before she portals out of the room.

"You have to save her," I say.

"I will save them both," he says, looking up at me, confused. "How do you know my daughter?" he asks.

Of all the women I could have found, of course, it was the boss's daughter. "We're involved romantically. I care for her very much," I say. He looks me up and down before he stands and grabs a blade from the dresser. I'd be lying if I didn't think he was going to destroy my soul right here and now.

He surprises me by cutting his wrist slightly and dripping a few drops of blood onto Blair's wound. It doesn't take long for it to close up, and I imagine it will heal from the inside. I test the skin, touching it lightly with my thumb as I watch the skin graft itself.

"Who stabbed her?" he asks, his tone menacing.

"I did," I say.

"You did *what*?" He is nearly shouting now, still crouched next to Blair's body.

"She told me to. She wanted Mara out of her."

He clicks his tongue. "The situation with Mara is unfortunate. We will need to coax her out gently so she doesn't injure Blair."

"How do you plan on doing that?"

"Worry not of my plans, Daxaddon. I have half the mind to rip your soul apart and set your corporeal body on fire in front of all of Hell to witness."

I shut my mouth. Not wanting to upset him more than I already have. As I watch the way he looks at Blair, I see some resemblance. The dark hair, the brown eyes. If it were any other circumstance, I would ask him if his eyes change color too. It's clear he loves Blair in his own way. I never met Blair's mother, but it seems she gets her lack of patience for people from her father as well.

"Milcom, my lord," Lilith says, bringing the large demon into the opulent bedroom.

"You've asked for me, my lord," Milcom says, and he audibly swallows.

"Yes, well. Once my daughters wake up, we can discuss. Lilith, love. Will you get me some smelling salts?"

"Yes, sir," Lilith replies, and I don't miss the slight twitch of Lucifer's mouth. Lilith's small hand clutches the vial before handing it to her lord.

"Thank you, love. You are dismissed." The petite female demon pouts, her bottom lip sticking out as she looks at the most powerful entity in Hell. "Now darling, what have I said about pouting? I'll see you momentarily."

"Yes, sir," she says with sass, and Lucifer's hand clenches. I wouldn't doubt that Lilith's ass is going to be paying for that later.

My hand cups the back of Blair's head as it rests on my thigh. Lucifer brings the salt to her nose, and she quickly gulps a large inhale of air before sitting up and looking around.

"Are you going to destroy me now?" Mara asks, looking at Lucifer's eyes.

"Do you know who I am?" he asks.

"The father who didn't love me enough to protect me," Mara says, shuffling away on her bottom, no longer in my arms and taking a defensive pose. It's hard to correlate the fact that the person who is scared and shaking isn't my witch. The person I want to comfort is deep down in there, I know she is. But Blair isn't the one who is present right now.

All I want to do is shake this demon out of my girl and get out of here. This family reunion isn't something I signed up for and frankly, I need to conceptualize that I'm falling for the king of Hell's daughter.

"Sweet girl, no. I would never want to destroy either of my daughters. I want you both to be happy and whole." I've never heard Lucifer sound and look so... human.

"But, why? Why did you visit Blair and give her magic to stay whole and you never visited me?"

"Milcom, would you like to answer that?" Lucifer says, spinning to look at the large demon, who looks terrified. It's nearly comical, if the stakes weren't so high right now I would likely be enjoying Milcom's tongue lashing. Lucifer's eyes are flaming red, and my question from earlier is answered when it comes to that particular trait.

"My lord, I've apologized. It was a mistake. I didn't know."

"Your mistake has caused both of my daughters harm. How can I let that slide, Milcom?"

"Please, my lord. I'll do anything."

"Yes, yes, you will." The dagger I stabbed Mara with is still beside me, until Lucifer conjures it into his hand, holding it against Milcom's neck. "The perfect sacrifice I need to create my darling Mara a body of her own."

"No, please. I'm sorry."

Lucifer tsks. "This is going to sting a bit." Lucifer slashes his throat. "Daxaddon, be a dear and hand me that basin." Immediately I'm on my feet handing him the crystal basin from the table. He holds it under his throat, collecting Milcom's blood. I still have no idea what he plans to do. Mara and I watch in fascination as Milcom's soul slips from his lips and his corporeal body crumbles to the floor. "I'll deal with your soul later," Lucifer says. Who knows if Milcom understands? He won't be able to possess anyone in Hell, just another lost soul with no purpose roaming the fiery pits. He can run, try and hide in this dimension, but it would be a waste of time. Lucifer will find him and completely destroy his soul for his betrayal.

"Mara, darling. Please leave Blair's body. I promise to give you a nice, new, shiny one of your own."

"How can I trust you?" she says.

"I'm many things, Mara. A liar isn't one of them. You are my daughter and I plan to make things right with you. I didn't know you lived. I sent Milcom to Earth to see if any of my children held my gift. He came back and reported that you were completely human, with no magical ability. Lilith found Blair and told me about her. So every year on her birthday, I made sure her body was stable enough to handle the demon part of her nature."

"Why doesn't Blair know who you are?" she asks.

"Is she telling you that?" he asks her.

"Yes," Mara replies.

"I thought it would be easier for her to live her life as a witch. As hard as I tried, and thought that creating demons on earth was the motivation, it's become transparent that I have more feelings than I considered."

"You love her?" she asks.

"I love both of you, and I would like to make things right," he says.

"How... how are you going to give me a corporeal body? What will it look like?" she asks.

"I need your soul to collect the blood in the basin, and I'll be able to create your body. I read the soul to see what body would best suit you."

"And Blair?" she asks.

"As long as you leave Blair's body gently, she should be fine. She was born, not created in this way, so you need to be careful."

"I really never wanted to hurt her." She sniffles.

"I know, darling. Please let me make things right."

"Okay," Mara replies. We both watch the most gentle de-possession we've ever watched taking place. Mara slips out of Blair's body like a slow tendril of cigarette smoke. I'm behind her in a flash as I hold her limp body once Mara completely ejects herself.

Blair is breathing, and I keep my fingers on her pulse. Lucifer looks at me, and I nod while he handles Mara's transformation. While I've had my own transformation, it's another thing to watch it.

The blood levitates, each blood cell acting as a puzzle piece as it floats in the air and circles Mara's soul. It starts as a clump of blood, but it slowly shifts into a human female. Lucifer's eyes are closed as he concentrates on creating her form. She takes her shape, taller and leaner than Blair. Her hair forms, the same color as her father and sister, but longer and straight. Her naked form is on display as she collapses to the floor in her new body. Lucifer quickly grabs a throw blanket and wraps it around her as she shivers. She holds her hand out in front of her face and inspects her new hands.

"I'm a person again," she says, a beaming smile on her face.

"As it should have been. I can't apologize enough, darling. I promise to spend all my energy in making things right with you and your sister."

She nods her head. "I think I owe Blair an apology," she says, and I scoff.

Blair's body shifts in my grip, her eyes blinking quickly as her hand grazes my jaw, her eyes purple as she looks up at me. "Dax?"

"I'm here, babe. You're going to be okay."

"I'm going to fucking kill her," she says. She attempts to get up, but I hold her against me.

"Well, I think parricide needs to be the line. Let's not add sororicide."

"Yes, I think not," Lucifer says to Blair, and she glares at him. I've never seen anyone give him a look like this. Not to mention the slight shiver I see in Lucifer as he watches her.

"Dax and I need a moment. Should we portal home, or is there somewhere for us to lie down here?"

"Of course, I have your rooms ready. Lilith?" he says her name, and she portals into the room, arms crossed over her body. "Love, can you show the girls their room?"

"Now that I'm allowed to be a part of the conversation, I would love to. Please follow me." She gives Lucifer a shitty look, and the man can't catch a break from the women in his life today. I watch as he sits on his bed, hands on his forehead and elbows on his knees. Never would I have imagined the devil himself having so many vulnerabilities.

I take Blair's hand in mine. She flinches at the touch but holds my hand. I stand between her and Mara as Lilith directs Mara to the first room.

"Mara, this is your room. If you need anything, please just let me know," she says.

"You're really pretty and nice. Are you my... um.. step-mother?"

"Heavens no, but we can talk more later," Lilith says, showing Mara her room as Blair and I stand in the hallway. Lucifer's estate screams luxury and affluence. Lilith gives us a tight smile as she directs us a few doors down.

She opens the door, ushering us in. There's a large king sized bed with lavender organza hanging from the pillars. The floor is white tile, and there's a purple chaise in the corner, as well as a bookshelf, filled to the brim with books. There's even a decent amount of plants in the room. Definitely not what you would expect from a bedroom in Hell.

"Thank you," Blair says. Lilith touches her arm.

"Give him time. If anyone can confirm he cares, it's me," she says, giving Blair a small smile before turning on her heel and leaving the room.

Blair looks around, her fingertips sliding over different parts of the room. I go to stand behind her, my hand touching her hip and she flinches again.

"Sorry," she says.

"Blair, what is it?"

She turns to look at me, her eyes watering, and I watch her eyes now bright blue as the tears fall. Her arms wrap around herself, and she sighs. "This has just been the worst day imaginable. First the whole thing with Ryan, then my magic is taken away by the council. I get possessed by my long-lost psycho sister. Then the worst part was watching you stab me." I go to reach out to her, but stop as she shivers. "I know I told you to, I know that. But it doesn't stop me from seeing it."

"Babe, you know I would never, ever hurt you. Ever."

She nods her head, the tears still falling. "I know." She sniffles and wipes the tears. "Then there's conceptualizing that I'm the devil's fucking daughter and that how I felt my whole life could have easily been explained. I've been up there suffering, Dax. He lied to me. He had so many chances to tell me what I was. And apparently I'm a liar just like him."

I look down at her blood-stained clothes. Not knowing how I can make this better for her. I don't think there's much I can say. So I decide to offer comfort. "Would you like to take a bath?" I ask her.

"Will... will you take one with me?" I nod my head. She's shaken and trying to wrap her mind around everything that's happened. I don't touch her as we walk to the en suite. A massive ceramic claw-foot tub is in the middle of the room. My hand grips the faucet as I turn the water on and plug the drain. Blair stands behind me, not undressing.

"May I undress you?" I ask her and she nods her head. Tenderly, I remove her clothes, starting with her top. It clings to her skin tightly from the dried blood. I kiss the spot where I stabbed her. There isn't even a mark there, but I know the spot. A small sigh leaves her lips and her hand pets my head as I get to my knees to remove her shoes, skirt, and panties.

I undress myself quickly and hold out an arm for Blair to step into the warm water. Once she's settled, I place myself behind her. Scared of how she will react, but needing her to know how much I care, I wrap my arms around her middle and rock her back against my body.

She relaxes against my chest, the back of her head resting on my shoulder. Her hands wrap around my forearms as the warm water smooths her muscles.

"I'm sorry," she whispers.

"Me too. I should have been there."

She spins slightly so she can look at me. "You didn't do anything wrong, Dax."

"You're mine to protect, Blair. I shouldn't have let you out of my sight knowing Mara was still out there. It was reckless."

"I hurt you," she said.

"Yes," I say, not knowing how else to respond. She did hurt me. It's not as simple of a thing as saying sorry. I forgive her, but rebuilding the trust that we lost will take time. Not to mention I don't plan on letting her out of my sight ever again.

"Is everything okay with Ryan?" she asks.

"Not sure. I told him everything and told him that I wanted to be better. I also told him I couldn't give you up."

"What did he say?"

"Not much, but I'm hoping he comes around. Watching everything that just happened with Lucifer, your dad, makes me want to try harder."

"I will have a talk with my father, Lucifer, whoever the fuck he is, about this breeding program."

"I think after tonight his mind has already been changed."

"I know, I was there," she says.

"You saw everything?" She nods her head.

"I'm so sorry, babe." I hold her tighter against my chest as she inclines her head and we spend the rest of the bath in companionable silence. She falls asleep against me, soft breaths leaving her lips. I wash her body, removing the blood and grime of the day. My mind works a million miles a minute as I try to think of how I can make this better.

I wrap Blair up in a fluffy towel drying her off and placing her on the bed to rest.

I leave the bedroom and wander down the hallway to find Lilith. She's sitting at a desk, manually looking over different forms.

"Lilith?"

"Hey, Dax. Is there something you need?"

"I need to communicate with Kas or Asmo. Do we have a tele-portal I can use?"

"Of course, follow me."

Her heels click along the wooden floor as she walks me down to a smaller room, a demon in his true form stands before the tele-portal.

"Lilith," he says, lowering his head.

"Dax needs to make a call."

The demon moves to the side, and I place my hand on the communication portal. It's like looking through a wishing well. Seeing what you want in a reflection, the picture isn't clear but it's just clear enough.

I see Asmo's face. He looks like he's in the middle of something exerting.

"Asmo?" I say.

"You really do have shit timing, Dax. What do you want and where did you find a tele-portal?"

"I'm in Hell with Blair—the Mara situation has been resolved. I need you and Kas to find Stevie and make sure she's okay."

"Stevie's in trouble?" I hear Kas say, though I can't see her.

"This witch is a pain in my ass. We'll go check on her," Asmo says.

"Thank you." I watch as his eyes widen over my effort to show gratitude. I nod my head at the demon and leave the room with Lilith.

"Thank you as well, Lilith."

"Of course, you know, I've kind of been waiting for this day. Lucifer visited her on her birthday, always. It was his favorite day of the whole year. But seeing her more often than that was hard on him. So he would send me out to keep tabs on her. Blair has a special place in my heart."

"In mine too," I say.

"Wishing you all the luck in the world explaining that to him," she says.

"Thanks," I say.

She pats me on the back. "He'll come around."

We part ways in the hallway and I re-enter the bedroom. I watch as Blair sleeps and I know what I need to do. I can't help myself, I need to make sure that she's having sound dreams and that today's events aren't haunting her in her sleep.

CHAPTER THIRTY-ONE

BLAIR

I wake with a start, my heart racing and my breathing heavy. Blinking open my eyes, I look to my left and see Dax looking at me with concern as he cups my cheek.

"Were you in my dream?"

"I was," he says. I groan and push my face further into the pillow.

"I want to go home," I say.

"I know, babe, but I think you need to talk to your dad first."

"Are you saying that as my boyfriend or someone who works for him?" I ask sharply.

"As your boyfriend," he replies dryly.

"I don't have much to say to him. He's lied to me my whole life, left me with my terrible mother. Wasn't there for Mara, causing her to go bat shit crazy and possess me. And look what a mess he has made with making demons breed on earth. I feel like I don't know him or want to know him."

Dax gently pushes my hair behind my ear before his large palm cups my cheek again, and he kisses my forehead.

"I'm not going to lie, Blair. The thought of you sticking up to Lucifer both terrifies me and turns me on."

I can't help but to let out a small giggle. "I wonder how fucking the boss's daughter is going to pan out for you," I say.

He groans, dragging his other hand over his face. "Don't remind me."

"At least things make sense now. I still have a lot of questions."

"This is why you need to speak with him, if nothing else, to get answers to your questions."

"Ugh, you're probably right."

Part of me wants Dax to try and touch me, bring back that connection that we have physically. The other part of me is scared shitless to be intimate again. I know I told him to stab me, and if he was in my dream last night, he knows I was just watching that over and over. I can't help fixating on it. I've been through Hell and back—literally—in the past few days, and that's the one event that I just can't scrub from my mind.

"Hey," he says, both hands gently holding my face.

"Hey," I reply in a soft voice.

"I'm not going anywhere. I'm yours, Blair, and you're mine. Nothing is going to change that. I don't care if I have to grovel for the rest of my life or if we have to spend eternity learning to trust each other again. It's worth it. You're worth it."

I nod my head and rest my cheek against his chest. I listen to his even breathing as he strokes my back. Not flinching while he touches me is a step. Deep down in the being of my soul, I know Dax would never hurt me, but my heart and brain have a hard time making sense of what happened.

There's a light tapping of knuckles on the door, and Dax looks to me for confirmation. I nod my head. "Come in," Dax bellows.

It's Lilith. I don't know much about the demon before me, but she seems kind enough. She's not what you would imagine a demon to look like at all. She looks sweet and like a barbie doll. "Sorry to wake you, but we're having breakfast in the formal dining room in a half an hour. We were hoping you would join us."

"We being?" I say.

"Your father, myself, Mara, and the two of you," she says, her voice steady.

"All right," I reply. Lilith smiles and spins on her heel, her long blonde ponytail bouncing behind her. She shuts the door, and I groan against Dax's chest. This breakfast should be awkward at best.

The formal dining room is expansive, it looks like they shortened the dining room table to house six people. My father—the fucking devil—sits at the head of the table. As a child I always saw our resemblance. I knew I was his, not just in looks, but by the way he looked at me affectionately. How could he care so much about me but lie to me and leave me with people who wished me harm?

Mara and Lilith sit across the table. Lilith smiles while Mara looks down as her fork pushes her scrambled egg around the plate.

Dax and I take our seats next to each other. He slides his chair closer to mine so he can place a reassuring hand on my thigh. His thumb rubbing circles, keeping me centered as I look at my father.

"Blair—" my father starts to speak.

"Why lie to me? Why not tell me when I was old enough what I was? Do you know how miserable I was up there? How I didn't fit in. Did you know my mother and her coven tried to sacrifice me to Mara?" I say, looking pointedly at my half-sister.

"I am really sorry about that, Blair. Now that I'm in my corporeal body, some of my thoughts are a little more clear," Mara says.

"Oh, like when you took over my body and were going to fuck my boyfriend and move us to an arctic tundra?"

"Yes, that would be a time when I wasn't thinking clearly. It was confusing for my mind not to have a vessel, and I had Beelzebub in my ear telling me lies."

"His soul has already been destroyed," my father says, taking a sip of orange juice. How extremely domestic.

"Why have children at all?" I say, looking at him.

"I know you don't want to hear this all right now, but I do love you. I would do anything for you and your sister. I thought that by letting you live your life out on earth, I was doing the best thing for you. If people knew I had offspring living in a different dimension, they would see you as my weakness, and I couldn't allow you to become a target."

"Why did you come back for every birthday, then?" I ask. Dax's touch is gentle and keeps me from snapping.

"I needed to make sure your body could hold your demon half. So every birthday I bestowed my favor on you so that you would be safe."

"But not for Mara?"

Mara looks down, and my dad looks legitimately guilty. "I didn't know. I would like for you to stay in Hell with me, Mara. So that we can get to know each other better."

My body tenses and my stomach hurts. He wants her to stay, but not me. Still not wanted. My dad looks over at me. "Blair, I would like you to stay as well. But I would understand if you are not ready for that. Either way, I would like to show you how you can embrace your demon side. I believe there are some things I can do to permanently make your body able to handle both the witch and demon inside of you."

"I don't have my magic right now," I tell him.

"You what?"

"The council," I say.

"Fucking cunts," I hear my dad mutter and my eyebrows rise. "I'd like to show you my eagerness to be a better father by getting your magic back."

My eyes widen, but I nod my head. My father stands from his chair and holds out a hand. Dax squeezes my thigh before he lets go and I stand up. I can understand why most people would find my dad menacing, but I can't help but to feel hope.

My father's hand is held out and I take it. His portal is gentler than Dax's. We land on the cobblestone floor in the center of the room where they took my magic.

All three witches are sitting in their thrones and gasp as they see my father's face.

"Lucifer, what do we owe the pleasure?" Hadiza says.

"It's been brought to my attention that you removed my daughter's magic. I would like it reinstated immediately."

"Daughter?" Elizabeth questions.

"Yes, daughter. As you can see, her demon side sometimes prevails over her witch nature and you cannot hold her liable for that. It is not her fault that her soul differs from yours."

"There are rules," Elizabeth says.

"I believe I am above your rules, and as an extension of myself, so is Blair."

"No, we can't let this stand," Elizabeth says, rising. It's then that she's levitating in the air and right in front of my father's face.

"I wasn't asking, Elizabeth," he says calmly into her face. I watch as the witch swallows, eyes wide as she looks deep into the devil's gaze.

"Okay," Elizabeth says. Hadiza and Nimue walk down from their dais and stand before us. All of their hands touch my arm as they chant. It's like the caged ball of magic is released like a bomb in my chest. My father holds me steady as my magic returns to me.

Nimue looks at my father hungrily and he smirks at her. "Watch your wandering eye, Nimue, I believe you've met Lilith." She immediately looks away and returns to her chair.

"I'd like it to be known that any infractions brought to the council about my daughter will now be brought directly to me. Do we understand?" he asks. The witches look extremely put out. I had never really thought about nepotism before, but currently I'm a huge fan.

My father holds out his hand and I take it. He portals us—not back to the formal dining room but what looks to be his private library.

"Will I be able to portal?" I ask him.

"I don't see why not," he says. He picks a book off the shelf and his palm glides along the front before he opens the text and begins to read. "I think that I can do similarly what I did for Mara, basically making it so that your body is still yours, but corporeal enough to contain the demon inside of you. Once we know it's safe is really when more of your abilities as a demon will become usable."

Another question has been weighing on me. "Why my mom?"

"She was powerful. I thought that reproducing with a strong supernatural ability would increase the odds."

"Why, though?"

"Is it not most creatures' innate desire to reproduce, to continue their legacy?"

"I killed her," I tell him, his brown eyes looking at mine.

"I know, and I destroyed her soul when she got here."

I nod my head. He's a hard man to read, very logical and direct with how he handles situations. Even if I'm still hurt, it's clear that he cares and violence is his way of showing that. I can appreciate that.

"Can you stand here?" He directs me to a space in the library that is open. I watch with wide eyes as he grabs a crystal chalice, cutting his wrist and bleeding into the cup. His blood is dark and thick as it fills the crystal. "This won't hurt," he tells me. I close my eyes as I feel his blood circle around me. I feel the substance leak into my pores. If I thought I felt powerful before, this is nothing. It's like a hit of complete overwhelming strength.

I gasp, opening my eyes. My body is still mine, but more. Like it's been reinforced, I feel impenetrable. My father's eyes are still closed as he concentrates. Looking down at my skin, I look the same, but I feel more like everything that has held me back on earth has been washed away and I'm in my ultimate form. Like I no longer have to pretend. I know what I am and my full potential is ready to be released.

He exhales as he sits down on the chaise behind him. He doesn't look worn, just tired.

"Are you okay?" I ask him. It's the first time I see him smile. It's small, but definitely a smile.

"I'm fine, darling. How do you feel?"

"Whole."

"I'm sorry I didn't do it sooner."

"Better late than never," I say, shrugging.

"I hope that you and Mara find you want to spend time here with me. That's all I want."

"Maybe we can do Sunday dinners or some shit?" I watch as Lucifer laughs. It's rumbling and deep as he clutches his stomach.

"You, darling, are definitely mine. Now, let's go see the others."

I nod my head as he directs me out into the hallway. I take in more of the place than I did last night. It's a beautiful and opulent estate. Clearly Hell, well at least this part of Hell, isn't what most people would assume.

We stride past the room where Dax and I stayed last night. "Whenever you want to visit, that room is there for you. And Daxaddon," he says the last line with a little disdain.

"Do you not like Dax?" I ask him.

"Daxaddon is a fine demon, good at what he does. He is certainly not age appropriate," he says.

"How much older are you than Lilith?" I ask him. He glares at me.

"Fuck, the apple did not fall far," he says, holding open the door to the formal dining room. Dax looks relieved to see me as I come and sit down next to him.

His gaze is assessing as he looks at me head to toe. When his hand touches my thigh I feel his magic more strongly than ever before. He acts as if the touch shocked him and his eyes are cautious as he looks over to my father.

"She's whole now?" he asks.

"Yes, she should be able to access all parts of her power, not as fragile as she once was either."

Dax sighs in relief. His hold on my thigh is even tighter than before.

"I would expect you to help her with her training, Daxaddon," my father says.

"Of course, my lord," Dax replies, bowing his head, and I roll my eyes.

Mara looks at me across the table while she bites her nails. "Blair?"

"Yes?"

"I would like to spend some time with you. Not right now, but maybe after I've been in this body a few days?"

"As long as you don't hurt me or anyone I care about, I think that will be fine."

"Lilith is going to teach me how to portal today!" Mara says to the table, Lilith and my dad smiling at her.

"Are you going to teach me how to do that?" I lean over to Daxaddon.

He leans in and whispers, so only I can hear. "Oh, little witch, I'm going to teach you so many things.

CHAPTER THIRTY-TWO

DAX

"**I** need to make sure that Stevie is okay and I think I would be more comfortable at home," Blair tells her father.

"You are always welcome here, and I hope that you'll want to visit soon," he says. I've never seen Lucifer look so pleading before. The man usually demands, stares, and glares. He doesn't look hopeful or near begging. But the way he's looking at Blair is like if she leaves right now, she will never come back.

"I promise I will come back soon."

"Daxaddon, a word," Lucifer says, looking at Blair and then me. I nod my head as Lucifer stands and I follow him into his library.

"My lord," I say.

"That's right, your lord. I need you to look after Blair. Teach her about her demon side. Make sure that she doesn't get caught up in anything unsavory."

"Of course, my lord," I say, ready to get the fuck out of here. He might have been sweet with Blair, but the look he's giving me right now is malicious.

"And Daxaddon?" he says as I'm leaving the room.

"Yes?" I say, turning around to face him.

"Hurt her and you can consider your soul destroyed." I swallow and nod my head.

"Wouldn't dream of it, my lord," I say. There's a first for everything. Being warned by the devil about his daughter is definitely a first I never intended on experiencing.

Hell has never been my favorite place. I've enjoyed the freedom that Lucifer has given me and I don't plan on fucking that up. Most of all, I never want to see Blair hurt or upset again. I'm not sure what life looks like when we're healed and not actively working against some big bad. But I'm eager to find out.

"Blair, are you ready to go home?" I ask her.

"Yes," she says, scooting out of her chair and holding a hand out to me. No flinching when I touch her skin. Her touch feels different now, like she's less fragile against my touch. "Uh, so I guess I'll be seeing you soon," she says, looking between Lucifer, Lilith, and Mara.

"Perhaps once Daxaddon teaches you to portal," Lucifer says.

"Perhaps," she says. Not wanting to stand in this awkward as fuck family function a second longer, I portal her to her front yard.

She doesn't even look nauseous as she stands straight up on the lawn. "That's what it's supposed to feel like?"

"It will only get easier the more you do it. We can start working on it tomorrow if you'd like."

"I'd like that," she says, giving me a tight smile.

"Do you want me to leave?" I ask her.

"No," she says, biting her nail. "I'm just nervous about seeing Stevie."

"If she's not here, she should be with Kas and Asmo," I reply.

She nods her head, and we walk over to her front door. She exhales as she turns the doorknob. As soon as the door opens, a disturbingly foul smell leaks out, making us both want to heave.

"What the fuck is that?" she says, using her arm to cover her nose. Her eyes watering.

"Clover," I reply.

Her eyes widen as she looks over at me and then shrugs, turning around and walking back toward the driveway, away from the stench.

"To the bungalow?" I ask her. She nods her head, I take her soft hand in mine and portal us into the living room.

Epic mistake.

"Ah!" Blair shrieks as we watch Asmo fuck Stevie from behind while she goes down on Kas. All of them turn to face us.

"Fuck off," Asmo says to me.

"Seems like you lot weren't terribly concerned about what was going on with us. We'll be in my room. Come get me when you're done with... whatever this is." I flail an arm in their direction and place a reassuring hand on Blair's back and direct her to my room.

Blair takes in the surroundings, not looking impressed. "Not what I would have pictured for a demon's bedroom."

"I'm just renting the place."

Blair sits down on the bed. Her fingers tracing the patch-work quilt covering it. "Now that things with Mara are done, what does that mean for you?"

I sit down next to her, putting a palm on her hand. "Well, currently I have a new demon to train and I plan on following her wherever she wants to go."

She looks up at me from under her lashes. "That's really what you want?"

"That's really what I want."

She shrugs her shoulders. "So we could go anywhere?" she asks.

"There are multiple dimensions to explore. I've primarily spent most of my time in Hell and on Earth."

"Don't you have a job to do?"

"Nepotism has its perks," I say, smirking at her.

"Would you miss it? Hunting down demons, putting them in line?"

"No, but I would miss not waking up with you every day, seeing your dreams at night, your soft ass in my hands. Those are things I couldn't live without."

She smiles and leans her head against my shoulder. I still feel like she's holding back from me, but at least she's not flinching. "Do you know someone who can get Clover's body out of my house?"

"Yeah, I know a guy."

"He knows a guy," she says softly. It's not long till our moment is ruined and Stevie opens the door. She smells like sex and looks like she's been completely defiled as she looks at her cousin.

"You're good?" she asks.

Blair scoffs. "Clearly you're doing better than me. Too busy to at least clean up the dead witch in our house."

"Oh, yeah. I hate to say it, but I kind of forgot about her," she says. Leaning against the doorframe and looking at Blair, she asks, "So what happened? How did you get her out of you?"

"You know, the simple case of I'm the devil's daughter and Mara was a unhinged demon spawn looking for a vessel that could hold her. She has her own body now. She still seems bat shit crazy, but I guess I have a sister."

Stevie looks uncomfortable. But Kas comes in and rubs her arm. "So I guess you got all the credit for her capture?" Kas says to Dax.

"No, I got told if I didn't treat Blair right, my soul would get ripped to shreds."

"I really needed Lucifer's favor," I hear Kas say.

"Why do you need Lucifer's favor?" I ask. All of us looking at Kas.

"It's complicated, and it doesn't matter now. I guess it's time I get going."

"Wait, you're leaving?" Stevie asks her.

"It's been fun, sweet witch, but I can't stay here any longer."

Stevie glares at Kas. "Then I'm coming with you."

Kas strokes her face with deep affection. "It's too dangerous."

"Why? Why would you make me like you and then just disappear?"

"I'm a demon, darling," Kas states plainly as she turns around. Stevie sits on the bed with Blair. Clearly, both of them need time together. I kiss the side of Blair's head before leaving the room and following Kas where she's talking to Asmo in the living room.

"A little harsh, even for you, Kas."

"It's what she needs. Would you rather me put her in danger?"

"What danger are you in, Kas?"

"Oh, like we're all best friends now because we worked together on a case. You don't care about me, not really.

There's no reason for you to help me. This is something I need to do on my own."

"I'm coming with you," Asmo says.

Kas kisses Asmo and smiles at him. "There's a reason I put you in the fairy realm those years ago. Now I'm letting you take care of our witch. Be the partner you've always wanted to be," Kas says. Asmo goes to open his mouth, but in an instant Kas has portaled out of the room.

"I have to go after her," Asmo says.

"You really don't know what she's so afraid of?"

"You know Kas, she keeps everything a fucking secret. What a bitch! Making me care about her again to just up and leave me?" He rakes his hand through his shaggy blonde hair. "And she's even made me like the red-head. What am I supposed to do now, Dax?"

"Maybe what Kas told you to? If anyone can probably help, it's Blair, but she has so much to learn first."

"Lucifer actually did it. He procreated in this realm?"

"He did, and I think the breeding program is going to be discontinued."

"He can discontinue it all he wants, but cream pies will always be in season," Asmo jokes, trying to hide how he's feeling. It makes me feel uncomfortable.

"It's all right to be upset, you know?"

"I'm not fucking upset. I'm mad. If she ever pops up again and I become a pussy-whipped dumbass again, you have permission to punch me in the face."

"Noted."

"Sorry about the dead girl in Blair's house. We really forgot."

"It's fine, sending a wendigo out there."

"He'll still eat it if it isn't fresh?"

"As long as he's hungry enough. We should all stay here tonight though," I say.

He nods his head and sits down on the couch next to me.

"You're really fucking the boss' daughter?"

"Yeah, I really am."

Blair comes walking out of my room with a teary-eyed Stevie holding her hand.

"She really just left us?" she says to Asmo.

"Come 'er, red."

She walks over and sits on his lap.

"I thought you two didn't like each other?" Blair says.

"We don't," Stevie says, putting her head against Asmo's chest as she lightly cries and he pets her long hair.

"I don't know about you, but I could use some ice cream," Blair says to me.

"That sounds perfect, little witch."

CHAPTER THIRTY-THREE

BLAIR

"Ugh! It's not working!"

"It's going to take some practice, babe," Dax says. He's been so ridiculously patient with me. It's been two weeks since our brief visit to Hell. We haven't had sex, I can't portal to save my life. Plus, the house still smells like dead Clover. Nothing feels right. I thought knowing what I was would make things better, but everything has been so much harder. It's like I'm stuck in between being a witch and a demon and I'm not very good at either right now.

Not being good at things isn't something I have ever experienced before. I'm always good at things, but lately it seems like I can't stop failing. Since I'm part demon, I'm no longer in the coven, something I thought I wanted, but now I feel alone. I signed over Hex to Stevie who has more time to handle the day to day. I'm just not sure what my passion is anymore.

"Are you visualizing the bedroom?"

"Yes, I'm fucking visualizing the bedroom. We've been over this. I can't do it!"

He arches an eyebrow at me and crosses his arms. "I've been patient with you, Blair. But I think you need an incentive."

I cross my arms and match his energy. "An incentive?"

"Portal to your room and I'll spank you and make you come. Don't portal and I'll just spank you to give you the cathartic release you need in the living room without letting you come."

My cheeks heat, and I know he sees it when he smirks. To be honest, neither option is truly bad, but coming over not coming is huge. I need it. I need his hands on me, putting me in that mindless space that only he can put me in.

"So, little witch, what's it going to be?"

"I'm not just a witch anymore."

"You'll always be my little witch," he says, tucking my hair behind my ear.

"I'll try again."

"Attagirl, show daddy what you can do."

My face is probably the color of a tomato as I clear my mind and picture my bedroom. The soft sheets, my plants, Fez. Then I picture exactly what Dax and I could be doing together in my room. I breathe in and out, clearing my mind of everything except the location I want to be in and what I'm looking forward to.

It's a bit of a static feeling as I feel my body shift from where I'm standing to where I want to go. When I open my eyes, I'm greeted by Dax's beautiful face. Green eyes shining, crinkled at the edges and his dimples on full display as he cups my face.

"Appears, my girl just needs the right motivation."

I shove him hard at the shoulders, forgetting the new-found strength that comes with being a demon. He goes flying against my wall, making a Dax shaped imprint into the drywall.

"Shit, I'm sorry." He stands up from the dusty drywall smirking.

"Your ass is gonna pay for that one, pet. How do you want it?" I tug on my skirt, not knowing what to say exactly. His hand wraps around my neck. I watch as his pupils dilate as he looks over my body. "Do you want me to put this perfect body over my knee and spank you? Bend you over the bed? Maybe I should have you stand in the corner, ass out, just waiting for my hand. That will teach you not to push me. The anticipation of when I'll touch you will have you shaking and wet, wanting me. Won't it, pet?"

"Your lap," I reply.

"Excellent choice," he says. Taking a seat on my bed, he slides back, grabs a pillow, and places it to his left. I go to follow him and he tsks. "Too many clothes, strip."

I do just that, not breaking eye contact with him. I need this so bad and he knows it. Admitting that I've been struggling lately is hard for me, and I know how he can make me feel, what kind of mindset he can put me in, and I crave it. I need him. If these two weeks have proven anything, it's that Dax is the man I need in my life. His patience is astounding, his care for me is otherworldly, and I know what it is, but it's hard to voice it. It's too soon.

My shirt and bra are off. I slide my skirt down and toss it at Dax. He gives me his crooked cocky smile before I slide off my panties and place them in his palm. As he did the first night in my living room, he brings them to his face and sniffs before grabbing my forearm and leading me over his lap. Placing my head on the pillow he placed there for me. I won't lie, the configuration is comfortable.

"Do you remember your safe word?" I nod my head and he swats my ass. "Words, pet."

"Planchette," I say.

"Good girl," he replies, his hands kneading my ass cheeks. Not hard, but it's a warning nonetheless about what's to come.

"I've missed this ass," he says. As his hand leaves my cheek and quickly descends back down on my flesh. I groan and jerk in his lap, my hands moving to protect my ass. I don't remember him hitting me that hard last time. "Ah, ah. I can't have you hurting my sweet little witch's hands."

His shadows that I have become so fond of wrap around my wrists, pinning them to my back. Even if I tried to wiggle out of their grasp, I wouldn't be able to. Another tendril of the smoke caresses my face.

"You know you're my girl, right and I would never hurt you. This is what you want?"

"Yes, daddy," I reply relaxing into his touch. The first slap hurt and shocked me. But I know what it can feel like when he brings me to the edge of intolerable pain and brings me so much pleasure.

Smack.

The slap startles me, but this time I don't try to get out of his lap. I take it, his large hand hitting my left cheek and then right.

I feel my body relax against his. The pain making me wet, and I can't help it when I attempt to rub my thighs together.

His next slap is where my ass meets my thigh and another yelp escapes me.

"Is that good, Blair?" he asks.

"I need you," I say. Part of me wanting him to hit me harder, the other part wanting him to fuck me senseless. I'm nearly at the point of being a limp, carefree doll in his hands as he kneads my tender ass before slapping it again.

"I'll always be here when you need this, Blair. When you need to get out of that beautiful head of yours. You're mine to take care of." *Smack.* "Mine to cherish." *Smack.* "Mine to love." *Smack.*

The sound of the last blow ricochets in the room and it's like bells ringing in my ears. His shadows are gone from my wrists immediately as I sit up and straddle his lap. I wince as my ass touches his jean clad thighs but watch his expression. I don't think I've ever seen Dax be shy before. He looks like he's worried I'm going to run for the hills or not say it back.

"Yours to love?" I ask.

He nods his head, and his hands wrap around my waist. "That timing probably wasn't my most profound. These sessions are just as cathartic for me as they are for you. I do love you, Blair. I meant everything I said."

I wrap my arms around his neck and squeeze him tight. "I love you too, you know."

Since my face is pressed into his neck, I can't see him smile, but I feel it. My heart is pounding in my chest as I pull back from the hug and smash my lips against his. He moans into my mouth as I take control and deepen the kiss even further. I show him with each passing of my tongue how much I want him, how much he means to me.

Needing more, needing him inside of me, I lift my weight off of his lap, bracing my knees on the mattress and snaking my hands between us to unclasp his jeans and unzip the zipper. He helps me by sliding his pants down as I free his cock from the confines of his briefs.

Without our lips parting, I fist his length and push him inside of me. Dax groans in my mouth as I sink down on his cock, taking him fully.

I can't help when a little keening noise leaves me as I grip his shoulders and ride him.

"How could I ever live without this pussy?" he asks and I feel myself clench around him. "Does my little demon have any shadows of her own?"

I concentrate hard, just like I did with the portal, imagining what I can do. I watch as a small tendril expands from me. It's like it comes from me, but I don't know where I start and it begins. The tendril tenderly pushes Dax's hair back before it pushes his face into my breasts. I swear I nearly suffocate him as I bring his face to my chest. His hands grip my ribcage right beneath the curve of my tits.

His tongue reaches out, lavishing my nipple and playing with the piercing. The tendril is like an extension of me as it plays with Dax's hair. I bounce on his cock slowly, grinding my clit against his pelvis.

With Dax's hands wrapped around my waist, I'm shocked at the sensation of his shadows spreading my ass apart, gripping me to move faster. I'm intrigued and I can't help myself when I have a tendril of my own magic wrap around his.

"Fuck," Dax hisses, his mouth popping off of my nipple as he looks up at me. "Come on daddy's cock, little witch."

As soon as the words come out of his mouth, my pace picks up. I'm moving against him, trying to find my pleasure.

"That's it, use me, make a mess on me, pet."

That's the sentence that does me in as I shatter apart on top of him. A combination of his hands and shadows hold me up and continue to impale me on his hard length. He keeps the same pace, thrusting into me. I clench around him and I can't help it as my body quakes from the intensity of my orgasm.

His warm cum fills me as his hands tighten around my waist, his beard rubs against my chest as he holds me. I wrap my arms around him and rest my face against his shoulder.

We're both panting, hearts racing as we hold each other. I look down and realize he's fully clothed while I'm naked, yet again.

I feel so much lighter than I did earlier today. Being intimate with Dax is cathartic. I'm never letting this go.

"You did amazing," he says.

"Riding your dick?"

He chuckles. The rumble in his chest makes me smile. "Always that, but portaling and your shadows. You did so good, babe."

"Thanks," I say, gripping his neck tighter. "I have a good teacher."

"My cock is still inside of you. Don't be giving me any ideas."

I stroke his face, loving the feel of his beard against my fingertips. "I wanted to ask you something."

"Okay."

"Is Halloween in Hell fun?"

He grins. "The most fun."

"Can we go?"

"My girl can have whatever she wants."

CHAPTER THIRTY-FOUR

BLAIR

Before I can officially kick off my first Halloween in Hell, we came to the Hallowsdeep Halloween Festival. I'd be lying if I said that I could miss it. I've been every year since I was small. Stevie and I would always save up our money so that we could buy caramel apples, funnel cakes, and take shots at whoever was in the dunk tank that year. The air is crisp and cool, and the nostalgia of my childhood lines Main Street. Venders, game tables, pumpkin carving stations, and so much food you can imagine.

I convinced Dax to dress up. We're dressed as Gomez and Morticia Addams. It took me threatening to call him daddy in front of my dad—the devil—to convince him to dress the part. But eventually he gave in, and I couldn't be happier. He looks delectable as he kisses up my arm. He refused to shave his beard, but I would have hated to part with that as well. I have extensions in my hair and I feel powerful as he pushes the long hair over my shoulder.

I shift on my feet, being under Dax's full attention does something to me. Not to mention the foreign object inside of me eliciting a slight pressure and tingle deep inside of me. If Dax thinks he is the only one who is capable of surprises in the bedroom, he has another think coming. This will definitely be a Halloween surprise he appreciates.

We're in front of the pumpkin carving contest and I watch as an eight-year-old has a cannibal pumpkin devouring another. Seeds and pumpkin guts everywhere. It makes me smile. "Fuck, I love Halloween."

"When we are together, darling, every night is Halloween."

I gasp. "You watched it?" I ask him. His eyes twinkle with mischief. It's still early in the day but the lights down Main Street make his skin glow. He looks perfect.

"I had to know what part I was playing."

"You play it well," I say, tugging on his suit jacket.

"So, this is the Halloween festival you love so much?"

I shrug my shoulders. "I had some of my best memories here. It was always something Stevie and I looked forward to. And like I said, I like to play pretend."

"I think we need to revisit this teacher thing you brought up."

I shrug off his suggestion as I watch my cousin approach, holding hands with Asmo. Since Kas left, they have gotten closer. I'm glad that my cousin found someone she can depend on, especially since things with Dax and I have gotten so intense.

"How's the remodel at Hex going?" I ask her. I thought I would feel more when it came to giving up the restaurant, but really, it's just a relief. The idea of running it seemed more overwhelming than enjoyable after everything that's happened.

"Great! The new lighting is going in today. I can't imagine what that fight looked like with how bad of shape the restaurant was in."

"How's retirement, old man?" Asmo says to Dax.

"I'm not retired," he says back.

"I thought that's what fucking the boss's daughter got you. A cushy pension and no administrative work."

Dax furrows his brows. "My job right now is to train Blair."

"Right," Asmo says, rolling his eyes, and I watch Dax stiffen.

I had a feeling that this was coming, that Dax doesn't like being cooped up in this small town. I want to talk to him more about it, but he's been so invested in helping me learn how to be a demon I didn't know how to bring it up. Maybe Hell is the right place to have this conversation.

"Caramel apple?" Stevie asks and I nod my head, Dax letting go of my hand as I follow her to the booth. "You're leaving soon, aren't you?"

"Stevie," I sigh. As much as I can tell, Dax doesn't want to be here. I also have had the itch to spread my wings. I'm not sure if it's from being able to embrace what I really am or everything that happened with my coven and mother. Hallowsdeep doesn't have the same tether on me as it used to.

"I'm not mad. I'm just going to miss you. You promise to visit as much as you can?" she says, her big, watery eyes pleading with me.

"I promise. What about you and Asmo?"

"Well, he's a demon and I'm a witch. He has things to do in Hell, and well, I'm here."

"If anyone can get you a hall pass into Hell, it's probably me."

She wraps her arms around me and hugs me tightly. "If anyone is worth going to Hell for, it's you. You're my best friend, Blair."

I hug her even tighter. "This is pathetic. We're not driving off a fucking bridge in a Ford Thunderbird. I'll always come back to town. I think I need to see more of the world. Well, the universe. I guess universes?"

Stevie sniffles and wipes her eyes. "I just wish that I could be with you and Asmo and that Kas never left."

"I know, Stevie." I hug her one more time before I order our caramel apples and we rejoin the guys. Stevie gives Asmo a bite and I do the same for Dax. I can't help but laugh when he gets frustrated with how big of a bite he tries to take.

There's a clearing of a throat behind us, and we turn to see Ryan standing there. "Dad, Blair," he says.

"Hey, Ryan," Dax replies.

"Can I talk to you two for a minute?"

"Sure." Dax takes my hand. Stevie gives me a wincing look over my shoulder as I follow Dax and Ryan through the street. I nearly trip over a pumpkin before picking up the train of my dress and stepping over it.

"I was hoping you would want to speak," Dax says, and I can hear the yearning in his voice. But as I look at Ryan, who is looking at our joined hands, all I can feel is regret. Remorse for how this all went down. I don't feel bad for the things I did to Ryan, necessarily, just the aftermath.

"I think maybe we could be friends, like when you're in town we get lunch friends. I don't think I have the capacity for much else than that. But as far as you two go, it's none of my business. And Blair?"

"Yes?"

"I never apologized for how I treated you, and I hope you're happy with Dax."

"Thank you, and I'm sorry for how everything happened. I care about Dax a lot, and I appreciate you putting aside what I did to give him a chance. He really is someone worth knowing." If only Ryan knew a fraction of who Dax is. Sadly, I don't think that will ever happen. We will watch Ryan age as we stay the same. I can't imagine how Dax has had to come to terms with that.

Dax smiles down at me and squeezes my hand. "So the next time I'm in Hallowsdeep maybe we can check out the renovations that Stevie makes to Hex," Dax says to Ryan.

"That would be nice. I'd enjoy that." Ryan goes to walk away but stops himself by spinning on his heel against the pavement of the road. "I hate to ask, but do either of you know what happened to Clover?"

"No," Dax and I both say at the same time. Ryan nods his head.

"Well, see you around."

"See ya," Dax replies.

As soon as Ryan is out of earshot, I squeeze Dax's hand. "Are you okay with that?"

"Yeah, honestly, it's more than I deserve, and I think it's all that either of us can handle."

I nod my head as we walk back to where Stevie and Asmo are waiting for us. Asmo now has a beer in one hand and a funnel cake in another.

"Are you sure you want to take her to Hell? The food is nowhere near as good."

"Oh, I'm sure."

"I'm going to work on getting Stevie a visitor pass to Hell," I tell Asmo and Dax. They both look at me incredulously.

"The princess of darkness is already looking to place favors, it seems. I like it, mean witch. You're really not so bad."

"You hurt my cousin and I'll make sure my father teaches me how to desecrate a soul."

Asmo holds his full hands up in a surrender motion. "Simmer down, Draco, we wouldn't want your father to hear about this."

I glare at him, and Dax takes my hand. "You ready to go?"

"I'm ready." I give Stevie one more smile, one full of promise. Come Hell or high water, I'm going to find a way to have my cousin for as long as I live. She just doesn't know it yet.

Not familiar enough with Hell, Dax is the one to portal us. He takes us somewhere I haven't been before. Well, really, the only place in Hell I've been has been my dad's house. There are a mismatch of creatures here, not just humans.

"Do most people look like they did when they died?" I whisper over to him.

"Only in Hell. Anywhere else, they would be like that black inky material you saw when Mara left that one host. Or when Lucifer destroyed Milcom's body."

"Wasn't awake for that one," I say.

"Probably for the best."

Dax holds my hand tightly as we make our way through the thralls of people. We're in some sort of parking lot, but there are no cars.

"Where are we?"

"In line to the best event that you can get seats for in Hell."

"Which is?" I ask, squeezing his hand. He swats my ass and I tense. He looks over at me with a raised eyebrow, having no idea about the butt plug I have inside of me and how much that small little smack affected me.

He leans over, his hand pushing my long extensions behind my head. "Patience, pet."

Immediately wet. Well, wetter.

And he knows it as he smirks down at me. His fingers toying with the long strands. It's like a timer goes off around us and as soon as it does, everyone is filing quickly through two double doors. They're black and nondescript. Dax has a firm hold on my waist as we enter the building. From there it's almost like a train station with different hallways you can take. The room is large, but dark and there's no writing anywhere.

Is this a movie theater?

"Ah, this way," Dax says, rushing me down a specific hallway. I nearly trip over myself a few times. Very few people are going down the same hallway as us and I get leery.

"Dax?"

"Yeah, babe?"

"What are we doing?"

"Celebrating Halloween the only way a demon ever should."

"Which means?"

"Which means I'm about to make you come in front of a crowd of demons. They're going to watch as I make you writhe and tremble under my touch, restrained so there's nothing you can do about it. How does that sound, pet?"

My eyes are wide as I look at him. I'm so down. I remember the night at the club and how much I enjoyed being watched. But I'm still a little nervous. "How many people?" I ask.

"We're in one of the smaller rooms, only two dozen."

I nod my head. Only two dozen demons, okay? I can handle that, I think.

"If you're not okay with this, we don't have to."

"No, I want to," I say as he kisses the side of my hair.

"Safe word still counts in Hell," he says.

"Dax, you're up," some woman says. I can't even look at her because I'm too busy staring at Dax.

"Come on babe, it's going to be great." Oh, do I believe him wholeheartedly.

My pussy is on full display to about fifteen demons I've never seen before. I'm sitting in a leather sex swing. My ass perched in a harness and my feet in stirrups. My hands grip the chains on the side, attempting to relax in the position. Dax is grinning, looking seductive as sin as he views me in this position.

It's then he finally sees the pink glittering jewel that's shining against my asshole.

He tsks and lightly tugs at the jewel. "Is this for me, little witch?"

"Was just living up to what you promised me at Inferno," I reply.

Dax pushes the plug in and out of me, slowly. I look into the crowd as they watch on with each shallow thrust.

"Such a good girl, getting this ass ready for me. I think you should be rewarded."

I smile at him as he looks into the crowd. He looks over at the two gentlemen closest to us. They are leaned in close, forearms on their knees, like they are trying to get as close to the show as possible.

"Watch out fellas, you're in the splash zone."

"Dax!"

"Oh, little witch, you're in no position to scold me. Plus, the way your pussy is glistening for me, I know you like it."

Guilty.

"It's Halloween, so I had plans to leave your ass alone tonight and fully focus on your pussy. But it appears you have changed tonight's proceedings." His finger swipes through my wetness, making me shiver. "So lovely tonight. Are you going to be my sweet little witch tonight?"

"Is that what you want?" I ask him, arching an eyebrow.

"I want you so wet your cum is dripping off the floor for all of Hell to see. Then once you're nice and soaked, I'm going to fuck your pussy with this precious plug in. After you come I'm going to take your ass." I shift my weight in the harness, and Dax places a hand on my calf, steadying me. Leaning over to whisper so only I can hear. "Show them what your daddy does to you, pet."

Dax drops to his knees. His shadows widening my thighs and his thumbs spreading my pussy lips as his tongue spears my entrance and rolls around my clit. My back arches with nowhere to go. The chain holding the swing jingles as Dax's shadows move me back and forth, causing me to fuck his face.

His beard causes the roughest friction against me, and I moan as his fingers slide inside of me. I swear I can almost hear how wet I am. I look out into the audience and watch as the on goers touch themselves or watch in fascination. Having the power to turn people on makes me feel more powerful than being a demon or having magic. I feel sexy and desired, but no one desires me more than the man between my legs right now.

With two large fingers fucking in and out of me, Dax's lips sucking roughly on my clit and his shadows wrapped around my thighs, I could stop my impending orgasm if I wanted to. My legs shake in the stirrups as I throw my head back and moan in ecstasy. Dax doesn't stop touching me until my body quivers and I release one hand, pushing at his head. His lips leave mine and I wince as his fingers leave me.

"Mmm, not nearly wet enough. I promised the fine gentlemen a splash zone," he says. Standing and re-inserting his fingers into my sensitive cunt. The pressure of his fingers in tandem is euphoric. It's like a tightness in my belly. His fingers hook upward hitting my g-spot. He's relentless with his hand, the meat of his palm rubbing against my clit as his fingers fuck in and out of me.

"That's it," Dax encourages me. I remove one of my hands from the straps and grab his wrists, hard. He smiles at me deviously and doesn't stop as he adds another finger.

It's like a tidal wave hits my core from the stretch of his fingers, pushing me over the edge. A flood of release leaking out of me and over Dax's hand until I hear the splatter of my orgasm hitting the wooden floor.

Dax shifts me in the swing so I can view the floor. "Good girl, now I think they would like to see your tits bounce while I fuck you from behind."

I look at him wide eyed, catching my breath. He doesn't even wait for confirmation as he contorts me on the swing. He turns me around so that one strap is on my chest, above my breasts. The other is around my belly while he wrapped my legs in the stirrups. My arms dangle in front of me, not knowing what to do with them.

"Don't worry, pet. I'll take care of that for you," Dax coos. The shadows wrap around one hand, pinning it behind my back, before he takes the other. It's like I'm floating in the air, completely at Dax's mercy. He could do anything he wanted to do to me. I can't help it as I bring my own magic out, my shadows interlacing with his around my wrists.

Dax's hands grip my hips roughly as he enters me in one thrust, making me moan. One of his hands slightly tugging at the butt plug making me writhe against the straps. I have nowhere to look except the audience who watches us with rapture. I know my tits are bouncing wildly with each of his thrusts. He doesn't take it slow as he fucks me. The man has expert showmanship, showing these other demons who I belong to and what they will never have.

He slows momentarily as his attention is drawn to the butt plug. The stretch with his length and the plug is intense as my breath struggles to catch up to my pleasure. He pulls the plug out of me and I wince from the loss. He no sooner pushes it back inside.

"This ass is going to be the death of me," he groans, before he repeats removing and inserting the plug. The added pressure with his deep thrusts makes me groan. I watch as a few demons in front of me shift themselves. One of them releases his cock from his pants and strokes himself as he watches. I watch his movements as Dax continues to fuck me, his thrusts so hard all I can hear is our breathing and the smacking of our skin.

"You going to come for daddy?" he asks. I groan, not feeling close. "Your words, Blair."

"Touch my clit," I plead, and I don't have to look at him to know he's grinning. One of his shadows wraps underneath me and plays with my clit as he fucks me ruthlessly. The sensation is unreal. Soft leather wrapped around my body. How Dax is playing with my clit, pussy, and ass. Being restrained and at his will while others watch on. Stimulation overload sends me over the edge, a scream ripping out of me. I clench around Dax's length as he removes the plug. I hear the clank of the metal hitting the floor and gasp as he slowly pushes himself inside of me.

"So good for me, preparing this ass. I don't think it's anywhere near pink enough," he says. I made sure that I was lubed up and ready to go before the event, and I can't wait to feel the reward from my pre-planning. Dax spins the swing, so that the audience can now see where he is inside of my ass. "I think my sweet little demon needs me to redden this ass while I fuck it."

"Fuck," I rasp out, Dax's grip on my cheeks punishing as he stills inside of me. It's clear his shadows are holding the swing steady. He grips my left cheek as he smacks the other. My gasp is loud as the smacks hit my bottom.

"That's it, pet."

Smack

"So fucking perfect."

I can no longer see the audience but I know they are all getting off on this show that he is putting on for them. His spanks are nowhere near as hard as he's done them before, but he is definitely bringing a flush to my cheeks.

He picks up his pace. Rocking in and out of me hard. The thwack of his pelvis against my ass, hitting the tender flesh he just got done smacking. He moans behind me as he stills, filling me up with his release.

Dax holds me in this position for a while, letting the crowd watch as he drips from me. I sigh contentedly, knowing that I should feel humiliated, or ashamed. All I feel is contentment and pride, I can nearly feel the jealousy radiating from the audience over Dax's very public claim over me. He twists the swing so I can now face the audience again.

It takes me a moment to collect my thoughts but when my mind clears and I look out into the crowd, who are lightly clapping before getting out of their seats.

The amount of release is obscene as I look at the floor and Dax's pelvis. His shadows release me as he helps me out of the harness. Helping me stand, his hands wrap around my upper arms as he kisses my forehead.

"Happy Halloween, my love."

"Happy Halloween, daddy." He laughs, picking me up and bringing me back to a more comfortable area.

Best Halloween ever.

CHAPTER THIRTY-FIVE

BLAIR

D ax cradles me in his arms, a soft lilac blanket wrapped around me as we sit on a red velvet couch. I really don't have any idea where we are, but in Dax's arms, I always feel safe.

He pats my hair, and strokes soothing circles down my back. "That was something," he says.

"You liked it?" I ask.

"Liked it? I thought I was going to have a heart attack in front of a crowd of demons with how ridiculously sexy you looked with your ass prepped with that cute butt plug."

My head is pressed against his heart. I hear it pounding. What we did was insanely hot, but now it's time to face reality. I've been holding off on discussions of the future, but it's obvious my abandonment issues are mocking me in the back of my mind.

"So, do you have a place to live in Hell? Or do we go back to my dad's place?"

I pull off his lap so I can read his face. He grimaces. "I do have a place, but if you feel more comfortable in the palace, we can go there as well."

"I'd like to see your house."

"It's a small apartment, nothing like Lucifer's house."

I place my palm against his jaw, and his skin warms mine. The light stubble makes me smile. "Anywhere with you is perfect."

He grins at me, my favorite dimples on display. "Then let's get out of here," he says.

Dax's grip is tight on my waist as he has me stand, his arm wrapping around me as he portals us to his apartment.

Apartments in Hell are, well, Hell. He portals us right next to the window, it's a studio. With a bed, kitchenette, and a room for a bathroom. There appears to be some sort of public railway system right outside the window. The noise outside is what I would imagine New York is like during New Years.

Dax scratches the back of his neck. "I don't really spend much time here." I can sense how uncomfortable he is. I place a reassuring arm on his forearm.

"It's just a place to sleep," I remind him.

"Are you sure you wouldn't rather go to Lucifer's?"

"I still am a witch, you know?" I remind him, raising an eyebrow. "*Silentium*," I whisper, shutting out all the outside noise. Though the apartment isn't the best, at least it's quiet. Dax shyly smiles at me while he goes to the bed. We're both still stark naked from the club. Something I have found is that the man loves to sleep naked. He loves for me to sleep naked too, something about easy access.

I can't deny that I enjoy it when I wake up with him on top of me, knowing that he always wants me. I know it's part of his incubus nature, but it's only for me. Dax doesn't crave anyone else like the way he craves me. Especially with my demon nature fully awakened. It's like he can't get enough.

It's clear that Dax isn't fully comfortable here. He was more comfortable in Hallowsdeep, but still never fully relaxed.

Dax lies down, pulling back the beige suede looking blanket for me to crawl in. His arm was already waiting for me to cuddle. I smile and shift into the bed. It's not very comfortable, but no way am I going to ask to go to the palace at this point.

My face is pressed against his beautiful chest, and my fingertips draw patterns against his muscular frame.

"Dax?"

"Yeah, babe?"

"You don't want to stay in Hallowsdeep, do you?"

"I want to be wherever you want to be."

"Dax, I can tell you don't enjoy staying there."

His body shifts so he can look me in the eye. Probably trying to gauge my emotions from my eye color. I've completely dropped the glamour unless we are around humans.

"Blair, I could spend the rest of my life in that town and be fine. As long as you're with me."

I perch myself up on my elbow to look at him.

"I think I'd like to go on some jobs with you, experience the universes with you."

He smiles. "You would like that?"

"As long as I can see Stevie often, yeah, I would like that."

He nods his head. "About Stevie," he says.

"I don't want to think about it right now," I say, lying back down to cuddle into his chest.

"All right, well, tomorrow we can talk to Lucifer and get our first assignment."

I smile against his skin, and he gently kisses my hair.

The water pressure and temperature in Dax's apartment is shit. I guess people who find themselves in Hell shouldn't be living a life of luxury, but damn. Can't a demon get semi-decent hot water? Both of us shower and dress quickly before I attempt to portal us to my dad's house.

I'm standing next to Dax, our fingers interlaced, as I take a few deep breaths. "Just picture a room in the palace and will us to go there."

I nod my head. Images floating around my mind as I finally land on a room and portal.

Wrong room. Wrong fucking room.

I portaled us to my dad's room, sadly. It seems to have left the biggest impression. Unfortunately, my dad also has Lilith restrained and fully naked against a Saint Andrew's Cross.

"Oh, fuck, sorry!" I say, grabbing Dax's hand and dragging him out of the room. I'm too mortified to even look at my dad's and Lilith's faces.

Dax laughs once my dad's bedroom door is shut. I smack his chest lightly. "Shut the fuck up."

He's nearly hunched over laughing, his hands on his knees. "You know they say kinks are hereditary."

I glare at him and step away.

"Oh, come on, babe, you gotta admit it's funny," he says, following me down the hallway. I'm meaning to ditch him when I walk right into Mara.

"What's so funny?" she asks. She seems different, a little less crazy. But she still has very strong single white female energy.

"I portaled us into dad's room and he was, uh, having a moment with Lilith."

"Oh, don't feel too bad. I've walked in on my fair share. They're like rabbits," she says, and I grimace.

"How are you adapting to Hell?" I ask her, trying to make small talk and not bring up the fact that she possessed me.

"I love it here. I don't think I ever want to leave," she says. I give her a smile, not really knowing where to take the conversation.

"Cool, uh—"

Two footfalls alert me to my dad and Lilith walking down the hallway. No shame at all written on their face. It seems like Hell is very much more open to sexuality than Earth.

"My daughters together. Shall we all do lunch?" my dad asks. I know my cheeks are pink, but I nod my head. I look over at Lilith and she just looks happy and carefree as ever, her long blonde ponytail still in perfect condition as we walk to the formal dining room.

We all take the same place at the table as we did before. A few servants bring food. They're shackled and I wonder what they did to get them this gig. My father might be a lot of things, but it seems he only punishes those who truly deserve it. At least I can hope.

"What brings you to Hell, darling?" my father asks.

You can't tell your dad that you came here for a Halloween sex club performance. "Dax wanted to show me Hell on Halloween," I say.

My dad glares at Dax, but then nods his head. "I see, and the reason why you are here?"

"I would like to go on assignments with Dax."

"Hm, and how is your training going?" He looks over at Dax for that answer. His hand is proudly on my shoulder.

"We're working on perfecting portaling and her strength, but she is doing amazing."

"And you do not wish to stay in Hell, take your rightful place as my heir?" my dad asks. I nearly choke on the club sandwich I'm eating and look over at Mara.

"I think I would be better suited elsewhere," I say.

"Very well, and you, Mara?"

"I would love to stay, if that's okay with you, Blair?" She looks at me guiltily, like she's taking something from me.

"I promise, being with Dax, traveling multiple dimensions. That's what I want."

"Very well, but I have a stipulation," my dad says.

"Okay?"

"I choose your missions, not some handler. That way, I can see you often."

"That works for me," I say. I look at Dax, and he doesn't look as happy about this revelation, but he smiles at his lord.

We finish our meal with gentle conversation. Things are nowhere near as awkward as they were last time. Mara is pretty quiet, and I can't help myself when I give her a casual smile. I might not forget about her possessing me, but I can try to forgive. She smiles back and I watch her relax.

My father dabs the side of his lips with his napkin and slides his chair back. "Very well, Blair and Dax. Shall we go to my study to discuss your first assignment together?"

I beam at him and slide out of my chair, eager to see what our first job will be. Dax takes my hand as we follow my dad to the study.

He opens the door, and we enter, Dax shutting it behind us.

My dad hands Dax a file. "This is the kraken realm. There are a few demons who keep setting shit on fire, killing people. Without a food source, the krakens are becoming volatile. None of these demons are corporeal. You should be able to exorcise them or stab them with that handy dandy knife you have, Dax."

Dax nods his head. "You don't think this is too much?" he asks.

"She's the daughter of the devil, and most of these demons are low tier. Should be in and out." Dax nods his head again.

"After your mission is complete, come back for the next."

Dax hands me the file. "Dax, can you give my dad and me a minute?"

"Sure," he says, squeezing my hand.

"Thank you for trusting me with an actual mission."

My dad hugs me, and it brings me back to all my birthdays. I feel his love for me in his hug.

"Of course. Is there something else, Blair?"

We separate from our hug.

"If a soul were to, I don't know, end up in Hell. And I really wanted this soul to have a corporeal body. Is that something you would do for me?"

My father grins at me. "Better yet, darling. I'll teach you how to do it myself."

"Oh, and can my familiar stay here when Dax and I are on missions?"

"Of course, darling."

I hug him again. The hug is tight and warm. "Thanks, Dad."

"Always, my dearest Blair."

He sits at his desk, and I leave the office, taking Dax's hand in mine. "Everything all right?" he asks.

"It will be," I reply.

"The kraken realm is no joke. You sure you're up for this?"

"Absolutely," I reply. He smiles as he portals us to a dimension and it's the start of an adventure I could have never imagined, even in my wildest dreams. No matter what color gray each day brings or what universe we're in, we will always be at each other's side.

CHAPTER THIRTY-SIX

DAX

Epilogue
A few decades later....

As much as this water dimension makes me itch, I don't mind the view of Blair in a bikini. She doesn't tan; she spells her skin to stay perfectly pale as it is. Her snake basks in the sun next to her—hopefully he can chill in Hell for a while on this next mission. He takes up too much of my witch's time.

The black bathing suit clings to her breasts, giving me an excellent view of her pierced nipples.

"We have to get back to Hell, babe."

"But I don't wanna," she says, turning over on the towel giving me a gratuitous view of her ass. There's still a small bruise on her left cheek. She never heals her bruises after a session. Our play has only gotten more intense over the years. The urge to bend over and bite it, then have my way with her, is strong.

"Sorry, babe, vacation's over. Lucifer has a new job for us. Mara is also throwing some sort of Hell fest." Mara has come to grow on us. She takes her job seriously as princess of Hell. Though Blair is older, it's not a title she wanted, she wants to explore and it might sound conceited, but spend her time with me.

"Ugh, vacation is so much better. What's the point of being immortal if you have a fucking job?" She's not wrong, but she loves the thrill of the hunt just as much as I do. Last week, I had to tone her down a little when she was torturing a demon with fire. My cock gets hard thinking about the blood lust in her eyes from that night. It's almost guaranteed that we're fucking after we do something violent. It's a never-ending cycle that I don't ever want to remove myself from.

This little witch has captured my mind, body, and soul. Where she goes, I go.

"You'll have to bring that up with your father."

She rolls her eyes and lies on her back again.

I crawl on top of her, my elbows bracketing her face as I pepper her with kisses. "Don't you enjoy traveling around the universe with me?" I say, kissing behind her ear. Her body is warm from the sun as it presses up against mine. I love seeing her like this, relaxed, with no cares in the world. These last few years have been hard between Ryan's passing and what Blair did to keep Stevie forever. But time is healing us both. I want more of these moments. Blair, soft with no tension beneath me, just us.

"I couldn't imagine life any other way," she says. Her fingers tangling around the hair at the nape of my neck.

"You know, I never put much weight into soul mates, but I think you're mine," I tell her. Her magic unfurls, her eyes pink as she looks at me. I love that she has fully embraced her demon side. It doesn't hurt knowing your partner's mood by the color of their eyes. It's saved me a lot of trouble. I see red eyes, I run for the hills. Blue eyes, I'm giving her whatever her heart desires. Purple eyes, we're fucking on the spot. Pink eyes continue to be my favorite, and one of her standard settings when we're together. Knowing how much she feels for me is more than a meager demon like myself could have ever hoped for.

"I think so too," she says, kissing the side of my mouth. I'll never get tired of her touch. Her fingers play with the back of my hair, and I contemplate risking a sandy dick to be inside of her right now.

"I'll make you a deal. You get your fine ass up so we can go to Hell. Whatever dimension our mission is in, I'll take you on a shopping spree."

She laughs. I know full well being the daughter of Lucifer and the way she's willing to steal other people's money that she's far more well off than me. But at the end of the day, Blair loves spending my money more than she likes spending her own.

"I do need some more underwear. Someone keeps ripping them."

I gasp. "Who would do such a thing?" Her smile is captivating as she jokes around with me.

"I'm not sure. But my suspicion is he's extremely handsome, a supreme dirty talker who has mischievous shadows."

"He sounds like a lucky fucker to me," I say, nuzzling against her. She laughs as my beard tickles her neck.

"Oh, he certainly is."

"How lucky are we talking?" I rock my hard dick against her stomach.

"Didn't you say we needed to get going?"

I look down at my non-existent watch. "I think there's enough time for one of us to get off."

She rolls her eyes and grabs me by the nape of the neck, pushing my body on top of hers. I do my best to keep my full weight off her, but ever since she's been able to embrace her demon side, she's strong as fuck.

"You're the best revenge I could have ever asked for," she whispers.

"I love you, little witch."

"I love you too," she says, kissing me gently. This happiness feels like a figment of my imagination. While the way we found each other might not be the healthiest story, nor are the elements that pushed us together. I wouldn't trade anything in the universe for the way I get to be wrapped up around this small creature for the rest of my life.

Sometimes revenge can be sweet. And Blair is the sweetest kind I could have ever imagined.

The End.

About the Author

Sarah Blue

Sarah loves reading romance and decided to try her hand at writing it herself. During the day she has a corporate job (hence the lovely pen name). She lives in Maryland with her husband, two sons, and two annoying cats. She's an amateur comedian and a huge crafting enthusiast. Her favorite genres of romance books are reverse harems, sports, mafia and the occasional dark romance.

The Heat Haven Omegaverse

Heat Haven

Omega's Obsession

Protector's Promise

Too Tempting

Heat Haven Holidays

Coming 2023

One Pucked Up Pack

Acknowledgements

Sandra - I don't know how to thank you for all that you do. Without you, I'm not sure I would get these books written. Your feedback always means so much to me and you always help me get better. Thank you for the amazing design on the special edition cover as well.

Sam - What am I without a hype team? Thank you for always supporting this dream and reading my books. Thank you for helping me make sure that this magical world made sense and functioned properly.

Jayne - Thank you for your notes, I always know when a spicy scene is good when you comment on it. I appreciate you so much.

Torri - Daddy, sorry, daddy? Thank you for being the daddy checker in my beta team and making sure Dax is the best daddy he could be.

Stephanie - You are always the best, thank you for reading through my stories and adding a million commas. The readers thank you.

Amber & Leslie - I love you both so much, thank you for being proud of me and supporting me through this writing journey. I couldn't have asked for better best friends.

Printed in Great Britain
by Amazon